Lady Impatience

A Series of Senseless Complications
Book Three

Kate Archer

ARE YOU SIGNED UP FOR DRAGONBLADE'S BLOG?

You'll get the latest news and information on exclusive giveaways, exclusive excerpts, coming releases, sales, free books, cover reveals and more.

Check out our complete list of authors, too!

No spam, no junk. That's a promise!

Sign Up Here

www.dragonbladepublishing.com

Dearest Reader;

Thank you for your support of a small press. At Dragonblade Publishing, we strive to bring you the highest quality Historical Romance from some of the best authors in the business. Without your support, there is no 'us', so we sincerely hope you adore these stories and find some new favorite authors along the way.

Happy Reading!

CEO, Dragonblade Publishing

Additional Dragonblade books by Author Kate Archer

A Series of Senseless Complications
Lady Ferocity (Book 1)
Lady Graceless (Book 2)
Lady Impatience (Book 3)

A Very Fine Muddle
Romance Me, Viscount (Book 1)
Be Daring, Duke (Book 2)
Stand With Me, Earl (Book 3)
Sweep Me Up, Baron (Book 4)
Write for Me, Marquess (Book 5)
Convince Me, Viscount (Book 6)

A Series of Worthy Young Ladies
The Meddler (Book 1)
The Sprinter (Book 2)
The Undaunted (Book 3)
The Champion (Book 4)
The Jilter (Book 5)
The Regal (Book 6)

The Dukes' Pact Series
The Viscount's Sinful Bargain (Book 1)
The Marquess' Daring Wager (Book 2)
The Lord's Desperate Pledge (Book 3)
The Baron's Dangerous Contract (Book 4)
The Peer's Roguish Word (Book 5)
The Earl's Iron Warrant (Book 6)

PROLOGUE

R OLAND NICOLET, THE Duke of Pelham, was beginning to think that unloading his seven daughters might be more work than he'd anticipated.

Despite the dire warnings of his sister, Lady Misery, known in the wider world as Lady Marchfield, he'd really thought it would not be much of a trick to convince a string of unsuspecting fellows to take his daughters off his hands.

As it happened, his first two efforts had ended successfully, but it had been quite the thrilling ride to get to a church. His eldest, Felicity, had managed to set a bad-tempered Bengal tiger on the loose, resulting in her rather mauled suitor. His second, Grace, had accidently set a fire and then flung her suitor off the side of a house—mauled suitor number two.

It had all been entertaining in the extreme, until he began to consider what could be done with a dead suitor. Which was nothing. The last two were lucky to be alive; what if the next one did not survive courting one of his daughters? Did these girls of his not realize that they had to at least keep their gentlemen in the land of the living?

Despite the setbacks, the duke was a rather carefree speci-men, as only the rich and powerful had the luxury of being. Trotting his horse through his vast holdings in the Dales, his thoughts turned toward imagining a future ease in unloading the rest of his offspring. Two of that feminine horde were out of his house already and only five more to go—his dream of an empty house was within reach!

This season, Patience would take her turn in society and he expected quick work of it. Patience did absolutely everything quickly, so the duke presumed some gentleman would find himself standing in front of a vicar with little idea of how he got there. The duke did not intend to tell him.

CHAPTER ONE

A Remote Estate in the Yorkshire Dales, 1804

PATIENCE NICOLET STARED at her father as he read the latest missive from her aunt. Though these letters were unwanted, and the lady had been told so many times, they dependably arrived like homing pigeons.

"Papa," Patience said, "it cannot be true that Lady Marchfield would try to force a butler on us. *Again.*"

Her aunt was determined that the duke must have a butler while he was in Town. The problem was, they did not want a butler. Mrs. Right, their dear friend, protector, and housekeeper, ran the duke's household.

Both of the last of Lady Marchfield's butlers had been driven off with very little trouble.

The first, Mr. Sykes-Wycliff, had experienced a mental collapse after hearing various stories of the duke's habits. He'd been told of the duke knocking on doors late at night only to clobber anybody foolish enough to answer. Then he'd been informed of the annual servants' hunt, in which the staff scattered on the hills and valleys and the duke hunted them down with a fowling piece. That butler had been entirely gullible regarding these stories and his departure had been wildly entertaining.

The second attempt, Mr. Button, had left on account of everybody blaming him for making roguish eyes at Mrs. Right, which he certainly had not. Still, with Mrs. Right fanning herself, pulling her shawl close, and claiming she would lock her bedchamber door at night and prop a chair against it, what was he to do? The idea of Mr. Button as a leering lothario had been preposterous, but with all the staff in on it, Mr. Button could not argue his way out of it. There had been a denouement at dinner and that fellow was out the door too.

Why on earth would Lady Marchfield make a run at installing a third butler?

"My sister glories in being a nuisance to everybody," the duke said, as if he could hear Patience's thoughts. He laid down Lady Marchfield's letter. "She explains that Mr. Grimsby has served as a captain in the army and gone on to butler for a brigadier general and his nine ill-behaved children. Nothing, Lady Misery says, will shock this fine man. He is a stalwart and resolute soldier and will not be frightened by our housekeeper."

The two footmen turned their heads to hide their laughter. Valor, the youngest of the duke's daughters, said, "But he should be frightened of our Mrs. Right, Papa. Should he not?"

"He certainly should be," the duke said. "If my sister thinks a stint in the army will stand up to our housekeeper, he's in for a surprise. Well! I'll not trouble myself over this fellow. I rely on Mrs. Right to send him packing."

"And we are packed too, Papa," Winsome said. "We leave in two days' time."

"So we will," the duke said. "The ponies left three days ago and should be there when we arrive."

Patience nodded in approval. That had been her idea. Riding round the park in a carriage the last two seasons had been dreary and slow. In the Dales, they were accustomed to taking out their fine local-bred horses and galloping like mad across the moors. No horse but a Dales pony was as surefooted and brave in that terrain. Four of the ponies were sent ahead to Town, with only Valor's left behind, as she never rode faster than a walk anyway. Nobody was certain whether Tulip's slow going was on account of Valor, or if Tulip just did not like to hurry.

Patience, Serenity, Winsome, and Verity planned to fly across the park at every opportunity.

"Serenity, are you certain you will not make your debut with Patience?" Winsome asked.

Patience glanced at her sister. It was true that they were twins, but it was also true that they had little in common. Serenity was forever weeping over something or other, and causing no end of delays while she was doing it.

Serenity shook her head. "Patience would make me too nervous, rushing this way and that, and toe-tapping all the time."

"I was the first to be born, by eleven minutes," Patience pointed out. "It's in my nature to avoid dilly-dallying. I intend to go into the season with a practical eye and settle things in good time."

"I find I prefer to examine and appreciate things, rather than rush past them to my destination," Serenity said. "For instance, did anybody see the sunrise this morning? It was entirely magical."

"It was entirely usual, Serenity," Verity said. "It is a very common thing for the sun to rise."

The duke snorted. "I should hope so."

Nelson, their lovely little dog, was surreptitiously making his way round the table for scraps. At least, Patience supposed he *would* be surreptitious if he had four working legs and two working eyes. As it was, he was down one leg and blind in one eye and so banged into things on the regular. Fortunately, the duke was rather fond of him, though he called him an ill-bred cur.

Patience handed Nelson a bit of beef. In his enthusiasm, he took it, lost his balance, and rolled under the table.

"Papa," Winsome said, "shall we travel to the sea on our way to London as we did last year? We might find another ship-wrecked gentleman."

"No, my girl, this year we will be all efficiency. We will make record time to Town."

Patience noticed everybody smiling and nodding at their father, though nobody could be convinced of it. Had it been only her and the duke, they might very well be efficient. However, if there were one thing her sisters excelled at, it was causing a delay.

It drove Patience mad at times. Could they not see the fastest way between two points? Could they not get themselves out of the house and into the carriages in under an hour? Winsome would hide Verity's pelisse and then claim Verity was fibbing that she could not find it, Valor would upend the house looking for Mrs. Wendover, her stuffed rabbit, and Serenity was always off mooning over the glories of nature or crying over a dead bee in the garden.

"Are we to go efficiently because Patience does not like to dally, Papa?" Verity asked.

"Just so, my girl."

MARCUS LANGLEY, EARL of Stanford, regarded his friend and current houseguest. "I have no idea what you are talking about."

Viscount Radler paced the drawing room. "I am trying to explain it to you. Your careful decision-making is all well and good for most things, but not for this."

"I would imagine that this circumstance above all others would require thorough planning."

Marcus had determined he was now at a moment in his life when it was time to choose a wife. He had been giving it careful consideration for three years and felt confident in his conclusion.

"Stanford," Viscount Radler said, "there are times when your analyzing backward and forward is merited. However, how many horses have you lost the chance at because you were still mulling over the purchase? Do you really imagine that the sort of lady you wish to wed will stand round while you think about it for months on end?"

That point did give Marcus pause. Ladies were under such pressure to wed lest they end on the shelf. On the gentleman's side, if a man were firmly decided to wed, he might make quick work of it lest the lady he preferred be snatched up by another. There was an underlying frenzy to it all that nobody ever spoke of outright.

Despite the frenzy, he could not rush headlong into a partnership that would last the rest of his days. He must hope there were those cautious ladies he might encounter who would be pleased at his careful going forward as they preferred it themselves.

"Furthermore," Radler went on, "you entirely ignore the power of the heart! A gentleman is meant to be struck by a lady and begin his pursuit, tearing at his hair if he cannot be successful."

Marcus raised his brows. He had no intention of being struck and tearing at his hair. He had learned well enough to avoid that sort of foolishness.

Of course, Radler did not know the entire story of Marcus' parents' marriage. He knew it had been unhappy, but not what had led to it or precisely how bad it had been. His mother and father had been impetuous and had eloped to Gretna Green, though that scandal had been hushed up.

What had they discovered after the first rush of excitement faded? They did not have a thing in common. She wanted one way and he wanted the other, on nearly every subject. By the time Marcus came on the scene, the household was ice cold, unless it was heated up by screaming matches. He was their only issue, as by then they could not stand the sight of one another.

One evening, when he was six, he had been led in for his nightly interview with his parents. If there was one thing they agreed on, it was they were both sticklers for tradition. They had both done nightly interviews with their mother and father and so they carried on with it, though they could barely stand to be in the same room. Night after night, Marcus was led in and asked a series of questions regarding his behavior. He dutifully answered in between their icy glares at one another, and then was led out again.

That night, he gathered his nerve for what he'd been thinking about for months. In a tone cold enough to match his father's own, he demanded the nursery be moved to the other end of the house. He did not care to be forever woken by their shouting matches. His tutors had explained that shouting was bad form, and he did not wish to hear it.

He'd wondered if his father would throw something at his head over hearing such a pronouncement. However, in their utter embarrassment, they complied. As he looked back on it, he thought it rather surprising that they did not dismiss his tutors either, though he had not thought he might be putting them in danger at the time. He supposed they were too ashamed to act on what must have been their wish. It cannot be comfortable to have one's bad behavior pointed out by a six-year-old.

In later years, he'd been delighted to go away to school and to stay with Lady Monroe, his great aunt, between terms.

He would not create such a household for his own family. The idea that he might inadvertently do so kept him awake at night.

Radler, seeing he was not getting anywhere with his ideas, let out one of his long and disappointed sighs. "So, you will go to Almack's and begin your painfully lengthy examination of the ladies of the season?"

Marcus nodded. "You'll see. It will work out for the best. As for how things will go for you, I cannot fathom."

"I will look about, I will be struck, and I will tear at my hair until I've won her," Radler said proudly.

Marcus finished his brandy and set it down. Having Radler in the house for the season was likely to be exhausting.

PATIENCE HAD DONE everything she could possibly do to drive the season forward. Six months ago, she had convinced her father to bring a modiste from London to the Dales. If Madame LaFray had supposed she would need to design Patience's dresses for the season, she was disabused of that idea upon arrival.

Patience had studied the *Journal des Dames et des Modes*, *The Ladies Monthly Museum*, and *Ackerman's Repository*, and knew precisely what she wished for. She had ordered fabrics and embellishments, slippers, reticules, gloves, stockings, and bonnets. She presented her sketches, with notes at the bottom as to which fabrics and embellishments went with which. As well, she presented various drawings of outerwear, a riding habit, and a list of incidentals she would require that had recently occurred to her.

The madame had got to work in a series of spare rooms, hiring local seamstresses and sending away for anything needed. Haberdashers had been notified to have packages waiting at Grosvenor Square. Every detail had been seen to.

Madame LaFray had been invited to dine with the family at table, as they were not an over-formal household and she was an exceedingly sophisticated and well-bred lady, but she had only done so once.

Apparently, the duke made her too nervous to try it again. So many people just did not understand her father's ways. When the duke had been very liberal with his port and claimed he could not wait to see the last of his daughters out of the house and would never allow them back through the doors again, Madame LaFray had been terrified.

Or perhaps she had been terrified when Patience claimed she would chop down the doors with a hatchet to get back inside for Christmas.

Or perhaps she had been terrified when Winsome threw a roll at the duke's head, just as Grace used to do.

Or perhaps she had been terrified when Valor darkly hinted that if they weren't let back in for Christmas they might get attacked by the murdered women on the moors.

Patience had explained backward and forward that the duke was an inveterate liar and it was all in jest, and the murdered women were only the cries of foxes. But Madame LaFray would not be convinced. She said she preferred the relative calm of the servants' hall.

Despite Madame LaFray's leeriness of the duke, Patience's wardrobe had been done in good time. She'd been packed for weeks. She'd toe-tapped for days until it was time to set off.

And they had finally set off. They'd set off almost on schedule, as Patience had pushed all the clocks back an hour and woken everyone pretending they were already behind time.

The trip itself had held its amusements, particularly when her papa ordered brocabbage pie at all the inns. He explained it was a Yorkshire staple, allowed the innkeeper to run round trying to figure out what it was for a while, appeared aghast when they did not have it, then told them he'd made the whole thing up.

Nelson had been delighted with the trip, hanging his head out the window as the carriages rolled along and sampling the various dinners they had with enthusiasm.

Five days later, they made their way through the London streets on their final leg of the trip to Grosvenor Square. Patience peered out the window as the sights went by. It all looked so different now that she was viewing it through the eyes of a lady poised to join society.

Patience rode in the carriage with Mrs. Right, Valor, and Winsome. She said, "What do you think, Mrs. Right? We are soon to encounter this Mr. Grimsby my aunt has installed in the house. Will you make quick work of him?"

Mrs. Right considered the question. "I cannot know just yet. Each situation needs to be seen for itself. This particular specimen is said to be a soldier, so I may require some new ideas."

"You'll think of something, though," Winsome said.

Mrs. Right nodded. "I've a few notions tucked away."

"He sounds scary," Valor said. "His name is Grim, with just some extra letters on the end of it. For another, he was in the army. I bet he's killed people and how can we be sure he won't keep doing it? He might sneak around with a sword in the night when we're all sleeping and chop us to bits!" She clutched Mrs. Wendover to her, the stuffed rabbit's head lolling.

Mrs. Right patted Valor's hand. "Do not you worry, poppet. You are under my care and always safe."

"That's true so far," Valor admitted.

"He might be a rogue, though," Winsome said. "You've warned us ten ways to Sunday about rogues."

"Aye, he may well be. Well, here we are, so I suppose it's time to find out."

The carriage had rolled to a stop. They all peered out the window and watched the door open.

A tall and rail-thin man in a black suit of clothes so starched they might have walked out of their own accord stood at the door. He had a weathered complexion and a serious expression.

"He does look grim, does he not?" Winsome said.

"He looks terrifying," Valor said, burying her head in her stuffed rabbit. "Poor Thomas! How will he survive being bossed about by Mr. Grimsby?"

"Never you mind it," Mrs. Right said, "Thomas will be quite safe."

Just then Thomas opened their carriage door. Valor whispered, "Have courage, Thomas," as she climbed down to the pavement.

"Your Grace," Mr. Grimsby said to the duke, with a formal and extended bow.

The duke looked over Mr. Grimsby and said, "You're the third—did she tell you that? Mrs. Right runs my household, keep out of her way."

By the look on Mr. Grimsby's face, it seemed as if he *had* heard he was the third and he *had* heard of Mrs. Right. He did not look very frightened though. He looked… grim.

His eyes drifted in Mrs. Right's direction and narrowed. She smiled at him as if there was not a thing wrong.

Patience took that moment to bolt into the house. The competition for rooms would be fierce and she was determined to secure the one that had housed Grace last season, and Felicity the season before. It was the largest, had its own sitting room, and a lovely view of the garden.

MRS. RIGHT THOUGHT she'd sized up Mr. Grimsby pretty well. He was exactly what she'd thought he'd be, once she'd heard he'd been a soldier, and then a butler to a brigadier general.

The problem with fellows like that was that they were used to issuing orders, and having those orders followed. The army, and a brigadier general's household for that matter, were regulated environments where rules were adhered to. Struggles for power did not occur, as everybody simply fell in line.

Therefore, she had briefed the staff on exactly how they would interact with Mr. Grimsby.

The would-be butler had informed Mrs. Right, and the rest of the staff, that they were to gather together in the kitchens during the quiet hour before the preparations for dinner would commence. He'd ordered a tea tray, which she supposed made him feel very liberal. Of course, he frowned at the copious amount of milk Thomas added to his cup, which was *not* very liberal of him. Everybody knew Thomas liked his tea very milky.

Mr. Grimsby sipped his own tea and set it down with deliberation. "First, be aware that Lady Marchfield has been the soul of transparency with me. I know all."

Mr. Grimsby's eyes drifted toward Mrs. Right.

"Very kind of her ladyship, I'm sure," Mrs. Right said.

"I rather think it was," Mr. Grimsby said. "A soldier of any worth likes to know as much as possible about the battlefield he ventures into. I have been apprised of what has gone on so far, including the departures of the two less-than stalwart butlers who have preceded me. I will inform you that your experience with *me* is to be markedly different."

They all stared at Mr. Grimsby, keeping their expressions neutral.

"Markedly," he repeated. As he got no response to repeating himself, he went on. "I expect a strict hierarchy. I am at the top, naturally. Orders flow down from me, to be distributed through regulated channels. I brook no nonsense! *I* am in charge, and my least directive is to be carried out with alacrity and precision."

"No," Mrs. Right said, pleasantly smiling.

Mr. Grimsby's teacup clattered onto his saucer.

Charlie and Thomas both raised their cups to their lips to hide their smirks. Cook folded his arms. The kitchen maid looked wildly back and forth between Mr. Grimsby and Mrs. Right as if she attended a play at the theater.

"Pardon me? No?" Mr. Grimsby said. "What can you mean by such a ludicrous response?"

Mrs. Right smiled indulgently. "Oh dear. The word has thrown you off. Well, I do apologize for that. Here is a handy trick I often use to remember its meaning—no is the opposite of yes."

"Mrs. Right," Mr. Grimsby said darkly, "I warn you to refrain from defying me. I will not tolerate such audacity and impertinence."

Mrs. Right sipped her tea. "What will you plan on doing about it, I wonder?" she asked.

"Do about it?" Mr. Grimsby asked.

Mrs. Right thought it a very reasonable question, though it seemed to make Mr. Grimsby red in the face.

"Do you not think I have the power to dismiss you if necessary?" he sputtered.

"No," Mrs. Right said with a snort of laughter.

Mr. Grimsby threw his napkin on the table. It was apparent that he was not accustomed to being defied.

"I warn you, I will speak directly to the duke, if I am pressed to it," Mr. Grimsby said. "Do not press me to it."

That was too much for everybody. All at table but for Mr.

Grimsby heaved with laughter.

Mr. Grimsby rose with a dignified expression and straightened his cuffs. "I think you will regret this insubordination, Mrs. Right."

He strode from the room. She called after him, "I rarely regret anything, Mr. Grimsby."

"I think we've made a good start on it, Mrs. Right," Charlie said.

"Aye," Thomas said, "he got foiled at every turn."

"*Markedly* so," Mrs. Right said.

"Do you think he'll actually try it on with the duke?" Cook asked. "Mr. Grimsby seems a bit more stalwart than the last two fellows."

Mrs. Right shrugged. "Who knows? Though, I suppose his head will blow off his shoulders when I join the duke for a brandy in the drawing room or I'm invited in to play Fact or Fib. If I know Lady Marchfield, she won't have told him anything about that—reflecting too shameful on the family, she'd think."

They all nodded at the genial prediction of Mr. Grimsby's head blown off his shoulders by way of brandy and Fact or Fib.

"Now remember," Mrs. Right said, "whatever Mr. Grimsby orders you to do, either refuse to do it, or if it's something that really needs doing, do it differently than he asked. If he attempts to dismiss you, just laugh at him and stroll away. As for myself, I believe Mr. Grimsby may find bits of Dales' nettles in his bedding this evening."

They all laughed heartily over that idea and had a very pleasant tea.

CHAPTER TWO

THE DAY BEFORE, Patience had secured her preferred room, despite Winsome attempting to knock her out of the way on the stairs. After seeing her trunks into it as an irrefutable claim, she raced downstairs to examine the invitations that had come in so far.

There had been nothing on the great hall table, nothing in the drawing room, nothing in the library. Patience had almost begun to fear that they were being shunned by society. Lady Marchfield had warned them about that incessantly, though nobody had believed her. Her aunt had claimed that society would not tolerate their behavior, though Patience could not really see what she meant by it.

Finally, in the cozy little sitting room meant for ladies to write their letters, she found them. Along with the invitations, there was a neatly filled out calendar, and an envelope addressed to Patience. She tore it open and two tickets fluttered to the desk.

Patience—

I have done you the service of reviewing your invitations and accepting those that would benefit you. You will notice that your Almack's voucher has arrived (and thank heavens for it) and I have purchased two tickets for the opening ball. Please explain to your ne'er-do-well father that it is essential that you attend the opening ball on Wednesday. Also explain to him that it does not do you credit to have a father drinking from a flask or otherwise making a spectacle of himself at that storied institution.

I do hope you perceive why I have taken these steps. The family cannot afford another misstep like last season.

Your concerned Aunt

Patience guessed the particular misstep her aunt referred to was Grace accepting the invitation to the Earl of Doanellen's dinner, which had been hosted by his crass mistress.

She supposed her papa would not be enthusiastic to know that his sister had gone so far as to arrange their social calendar for the season. Patience did not think she minded though, her aunt had been very efficient and, unlike Grace, Patience was eager to attend Almack's. As the first Wednesday was on the morrow, how else could she have done it?

Even though Patience had not informed him of the contents of Lady Marchfield's letter, the duke *had* been irritated to find the calendar arranged. He called Lady Marchfield a polecat sticking her nose into hen houses that were not her own. As he had called her that so many times in the past, it shocked nobody but Mr. Grimsby. He, apparently, had not imagined anyone would name his benefactress a polecat.

That was not the last of shocks for Mr. Grimsby though. He'd nearly staggered when Mrs. Right sailed past him and into the drawing room to have a glass of brandy with the duke before retiring.

This morning, Patience could not imagine what was wrong with the man. In the breakfast room, he'd stood at the sideboard and she'd noticed him scratching at himself several times. Did he suffer from some sort of malady?

She rather hoped he was not in the house long enough for her to find out.

Now, they were on their way to the park. The ponies from the estate had arrived to the stables in good time and had already had days of rest. They were anxious to get going, and so was

Patience. She was always full of nervous energy and a hard ride would be just the thing to tire her out and give her a sense of calm before her debut at Almack's.

They'd got off in good time, as the one thing her sisters would not delay was getting on their horses. They all agreed it was too cruel to make them stand about and none of them, not even Serenity, wished to put up with Serenity weeping over the cruelty of it.

They followed the carriage carrying their papa, Mrs. Right, and Valor, with two grooms on horseback bringing up the rear.

The carriage went through the gate and slowed. Patience reined in her horse at the window.

"Let us confirm our plan," the duke said.

"I know, Papa," Patience said. "We are to never separate or leave the grooms behind. We will canter south and then we may have a gallop down the King's Road. You will make your way there in the carriage."

"That's right," the duke said.

"Be careful, Patience!" Valor shouted from the other side of the carriage. "Be careful, Verity! Be careful, Winsome! Be careful, Serenity!"

Patience nodded at her, though she was not particularly planning on being careful. She was planning on a glorious ride. One did not require caution atop a surefooted Dales pony—they could be counted on to keep the earth firmly under their hooves. All a rider must do was keep themselves firmly in the saddle.

She turned her head and said to Winsome, Verity, and Serenity, "Let's be off."

They spurred their horses across the greenery, heading south toward the King's Road. Or Rotten Row, as it was called by some.

MARCUS AND RADLER had taken their horses for a much-needed

gallop down Rotten Row. It was still early enough that the road was not congested with people coming to see and be seen, which he found wildly annoying. If one wished to just stroll along, one ought to make their way to the enclosure and not get in the way of those who wished to exercise their horse.

They'd reined in, taking their horses down from a gallop to a canter to a trot, and finally, to a walk and a stop.

"I've heard of no end of ladies who will be making their debut this evening at Almack's," Radler said. "My mother writes me endlessly about them, though heaven knows how she finds it out from Derbyshire."

"Letters," Marcus said. "They all write letters daily—the newspapers could not communicate news so efficiently."

"She seems to know a lot about these young ladies, approving of all but one. What she cannot know, though, is who I will be struck by. I've attempted to explain it to her a hundred times."

"You are always trying to explain that theory to anyone who will listen." Marcus paused. "Wait. You said your mother approved of all but one? Who did she *not* approve of?"

"Ah, that was a bit of nonsense, really. She claims I ought to steer well clear of the Duke of Pelham's latest daughter. She says the duke is as mad as a bat in sunshine and his daughters cause the most shocking scandals."

Marcus nodded. Radler's mother was not half wrong. The eldest daughter had something to do with Lady Albright's tiger escaping its cage and the second daughter was in a housefire at Lady Montague's house. Marcus had heard she'd set it herself, presumably accidently.

"After all, how bad can they be?" Radler asked. "The first wed Stratton, everybody knows he's a brick. The second caught Dashlend. Who ever thought Dashlend *could* be caught?" Very suddenly, Radler squinted and peered over Marcus' shoulder. "What on earth is headed our direction?"

Marcus turned his horse.

He had no idea what he was looking at. He'd never seen such

a thing in his life. Four ladies arrayed in matching dark blue habits rode abreast of one another, mounted on short and muscular black horses, and galloping at a furious pace. Two grooms on like-built horses were on their heels.

They whooshed by him, their skirts billowing out and their laughter ringing in the air.

Marcus watched them disappear into the distance.

"Gad," Radler said, "they are rather marvelous."

"They are rather foolish," Marcus said, despite the fact that the lady who'd held the lead by a nose had looked a lovely creature. "I am surprised they are allowed to create such a spectacle and risk their necks in the process."

"Do you suppose it is some sort of new lady's club? My mother says young ladies are becoming too daring these days, though I do not see it."

Before Marcus could compose an answer, and he really did not know what his opinion was on the subject, a carriage rolled to a stop and a window opened.

A middle-aged and seemingly well-funded individual said, "Have you seen my daughters? Four girls on Dales ponies?"

So that was what they'd just witnessed. Marcus nodded. "Yes, my lord. They passed a few minutes ago."

"Your Grace, if you wish to be precise," the man said. "Duke of Pelham. Who are you?"

Marcus was taken aback. Though why should he be? After everything he'd heard of the duke's family, he should have guessed that a feminine battalion on horseback would belong to him. As well, he would have been clever to notice the coat of arms on the carriage door.

"The Earl of Stanford, Your Grace. This is Viscount Radler."

The duke nodded. A young girl peered out of the carriage with wide eyes. The duke seemed to notice her and said, "My youngest, Lady Valor Nicolet. And this is my housekeeper, Mrs. Right."

He'd brought his housekeeper to the park. Marcus had assumed it was a nanny, and even that was odd. And then to introduce her was even more odd.

"Well! We'd best be off to track down this horde of daughters I've been saddled with," the duke said. He closed the window and rapped on the roof. The carriage set off.

Radler laughed. "He's every bit as eccentric as I'd heard."

Marcus nodded. The duke was entirely eccentric. What did he mean, calling his daughters a horde and claiming he'd been saddled with them? For that matter, what did he mean by allowing them to ride breakneck in the park?

"I'll be interested to be introduced to Lady Patience this evening."

"Is that her name?"

"So says my mother."

Marcus shrugged. He could not say if he were looking forward to such an introduction. What he'd seen so far did not bode well.

On the other hand, she was uncommonly pretty. And then her name, Lady Patience, that *did* bode well.

Perhaps he ought not judge a lady by her father. He certainly had never wished to be judged by his own.

"By the by," Radler said, "Kendrickson wrote to me. Remember him from Eton? He is coming this season. He says we will see him at Almack's."

"I am surprised he can afford the fees," Marcus said. He had felt sorry for Kendrickson at school. The fellow's clothes were at times verging on threadbare and he never had any money at his disposal. Everybody knew his father was a gambler who shot too high and too often.

Radler shrugged. "He's found money from somewhere, I suppose. He's got to, doesn't he? He needs a wife with funds to pull his estate back from the brink."

Marcus nodded. He supposed he ought to be grateful. Whatever else his father had been, he'd at least been a competent steward of his inheritance.

"I bet Kendrickson makes his move pretty quick," Radler said. "He won't be able to linger too long without funds to keep him. I'll wager he sizes up the heftiest dowries and moves fast."

"Wager all you like, I will not take you up on it," Marcus said drily. "It was wagering that got Kendrickson's father into debt in the first place. He might also consider that his actions, whatever they may be, will have lifelong consequences. Seeking speedy relief in the present may result in misery in the future."

"He won't have the luxury of waiting to be struck, as I do," Radler said.

Marcus slowly closed his eyes and opened them again. Radler had spoken so many times about being "struck" that he was beginning to worry over what that might mean for the peace of his household. Marcus was not looking forward to finding his houseguest tearing at his hair over being "struck."

RANDOLPH BURTHERINGTON, THE Earl of Kendrickson knew people said that he was down on his luck. He always thought that a ridiculous phrase, as it implied one was showered with luck to begin with and was just momentarily lacking it.

He'd not had a lot of luck. He was an earl—that was lucky. Very lucky. However, it was a title that did not mean much.

He'd been born on an estate that did not generate a vast amount of funds and he'd been sired by an inveterate gambler. The estate had been mortgaged to the hilt to pay his father's gentlemanly debts.

Now his father was in the ground, leaving his losses behind him. All the wagers he'd lost at White's or at the races were just distant memories for all involved.

Except Randolph and his mother. They remembered them very well. Those bets were the anchors tied to their ankles, attempting to drown them.

He'd come of age understanding what he needed to do. He needed to wed a lady with a sizable dowry to rescue the estate. It was the only way out. If he did not, the estate would go and after the mortgages were paid off there would be little left. Whatever funds they could leave with would disappear quickly and no new money could be generated without land.

All that would be left was a bullet in his head to avoid being a charity case and living off a relative's pounds and pence.

Fortunately, he was an earl in good standing, despite his money troubles. The patronesses at Almack's were sympathetic to his situation, as after all, his situation was hardly unique. Lords had been ruining themselves through gambling since time began. He supposed those ladies would help him along, as nobody wished to encounter a landless lord.

He and his mother had used every tactic available to them to get him to this season. He'd fostered his connections at Eton. In Town, they stayed with an old aunt on Bedford Square. He'd had a tailor tear apart his father's clothes and put them together again with some notion of fashion. His mother had done the same with a seamstress. He would not pay for a club and the Duchess of Devonshire had very kindly paid the fees for their vouchers and tickets to Almack's. That particular duchess was known to be overfond of gambling, so perhaps she had a soft spot for his situation.

His mother had sent letters flying in every direction to announce their relocation to Town, thereby generating invitations from her end. Randolph had written casual letters to his old schoolmates that he would be in Town. He and the dowager countess would be invited here and there and they would make themselves pleasant, generating even more invitations.

He must secure a dowry, and he must be extra charming to do it, since all the world knew what he was after. He must convince a lady that while her dowry was pleasant, it was her he was interested in.

He hardly dared dream he would get so lucky that it would

be true. He had not allowed his hopes to run that high. However, he had determined that if he were to wed only for a dowry, he would repay his lady by lifelong courtesy and generosity.

It might be all he had to offer.

PATIENCE HAD KNOWN for months which dress she would wear to her debut at Almack's. She had sketched it out with Almack's in mind. Felicity and Grace might dilly-dally and change minds over what to wear, but Patience Nicolet did not.

It was a divine dress of white shot silk with a Pomona green sarsenet overlay embroidered with silver thread. The skirt had a hint of the French cut. Patience felt the silhouette suited her, though she would never admit to the wider world that she was at all favoring anything French.

Mrs. Right had done wonders with her hair, which could at times be an overwhelming amount of hair to manage. Unlike Grace's hair, which was a very pretty shade of blond, her own was brown. In the sunlight, it had a particular reddish cast to it. She could never decide if she liked it or not. Sometimes she thought it rather pretty, and other times she found it pedestrian.

The carriage rumbled toward King Street. The duke said, "Here we go again. Another rollicking adventure in getting a daughter out of my house."

Patience tapped his hand with her fan. "Do not be dramatic, Papa. I am not Felicity or Grace, I intend to go into this season with rationality and purpose. I will find the gentleman I prefer and we will move forward with no ridiculous delays."

The duke laughed and said, "You have not the first idea how much I would like to believe that, my girl. We'll see, I suppose."

"Really, you will see. After all, there are not thousands of choices, are there? There is a pool of eligible gentlemen, unmarried and of the right age and station, and I will see which of them I prefer. I am certain to make short work of it."

Patience did not choose to verbalize the one concern she had. She had no doubt she would settle her opinions quickly, as she always did. But what if she decided on a gentleman and he had not decided on her? What then?

She pushed it out of her mind, as there was no use jumping a fence one had not ridden up to yet. A well-trained horse did not worry over what it was meant to do, it just did the right things at the right time, as would she.

The carriage slowed to a stop. They had arrived. It was time. Patience Nicolet was to take her place in society.

"Let's get this circus going," the duke said. "I'm all but certain that Lady Misery will be haunting the hall to be sure you've turned up."

"She disapproves of your flask of brandy, Papa," Patience said as she was helped down from the carriage.

"Does she now? Well, she'll have to pry it from my cold, dead hands. Do not expect a duke to survive on lemonade and tea at this time of night, thank you very much."

Patience giggled as they made their way inside. If only her aunt would let her papa be as he was, she would be much happier for it.

They were introduced to a patroness, the Duchess of Devonshire. She was an imposing-looking matron, but she seemed very kind and good-humored. Especially since the duke claimed he'd never heard of Devonshire. She took it as the jest it was and he promptly invited her to visit them in the Dales. She laughed and said he'd regret that invitation, as she had a habit of turning up and setting a card table for high stakes. Then he informed her he'd brought his flask and fully intended to soothe himself with brandy at some point in the evening.

The duchess had said, "I will look the other way. But Duke, do ensure that the other patronesses are looking the other way too. There are some who do take a great amount of satisfaction in enforcing the rules."

Then, the duchess had taken Patience's card, claiming she would return it filled with promising gentlemen. Naturally, Patience was well aware of the habit of the patronesses—other nights she would hold the card herself and be approached directly. But not for her debut. She must trust the duchess to choose wisely.

As the duke led her forward toward the ballroom, Lady Marchfield caught up to them.

"Thank goodness you are here," she said, kissing Patience on the cheek. "Roland," she said to the duke, eyeing his coat for any evidence of a bulge that might hint of a flask of brandy.

The duke patted his pocket to assist her in discovering its location.

Lady Marchfield pursed her lips in response. "Allow me to lead you forward, Patience."

They went into the ballroom while the duke made various comments behind them. Most of it was along the lines of Lord Marchfield trying to rid himself of his bride. Her papa found it amusing to claim that her uncle was always desperate to get away from his wife. It was not true as far as she knew it, but that did not make it less hilarious.

At the moment though, Patience paid little attention. She was too taken up with the ballroom and the people in it. There were ladies dressed in all manner of silk fineries and gentlemen looking elegant as the result of a skilled tailor. There was a glorious group of three men talking to one another who had instantly caught her eye. Two of them she was certain she'd seen in the park as she and her sisters took their gallop down Rotten Row.

They were all rather handsome and seemed to have much similarity in the looks department. They were all tall and broad-shouldered and well-built gentlemen in their prime. But there was one who stood out. His clothes were exquisite. They were not of the dandy or fop style of dress, but they were tailored to within an inch of their lives. He had very prominent cheekbones, which gave his features a rather chiseled appearance. His hair was the color of her departed mama's sable coat—a rich and deep brown. She wrapped herself in that coat and breathed her mother's perfume sometimes, when she felt misunderstood.

Three similar gentlemen until one took in the details. That one man who stood across the ballroom was divine.

Patience watched as the Duchess of Devonshire approached the group of gentlemen. Goodness, she would solicit them to be on her card. Well done, Duchess!

All three men looked in her direction and she averted her eyes. When they'd turned away she continued her observance. Two of the gentlemen put their names down with alacrity. But the divine one, the one with the sable brown hair… was he hesitating? Why would he hesitate?

Finally, the duchess all but put the card in his hand and he did put his name down. Patience felt vaguely uncomfortable over what she'd witnessed.

Lady Marchfield followed her gaze. "Ah, that is the Earl of Stanford on the right. In the middle is Viscount Radler, and on the left is the Earl of Kendrickson. Have a care with Lord Kendrickson, everybody knows he's here dowry hunting. His estate is on very shaky foundations at the moment."

"But the Earl of Stanford," Patience said, "he seemed to hesitate in putting his name down. Why would he hesitate?"

"Did he? Hmmm," Lady Marchfield said.

"*Hmmm?* Aunt? What does that mean?" Patience asked.

"Well, the earl is a very measured sort of person. At least, that is how he's always struck me."

"Why would that make him hesitate? Do not I pass muster on looks?"

"You look positively enchanting, Patience," Lady Marchfield said.

"Then what is it?" Patience asked. She was really beginning to feel anxious or annoyed or she did not know what.

The duke took that moment to join in the conversation. "What Lady Misery means to say, Patience, is perhaps the earl did not approve of you and your sisters taking a gallop down Rotten Row. He might be a little stiff-lipped. At least I imagine so if Lady Misery here approves of him."

She thought he'd been one of the gentlemen they'd passed by. But why should a gallop require approval? What was wrong with it?

"Galloping? Rotten Row? I had thought it might have been something Lord Stanford had heard about the last two rather ridiculous seasons," Lady Marchfield said. "Roland, why on earth would you allow Patience to create such a spectacle before she has even danced her first?" She held her hand up, lest the duke thought to answer the question. "I have seen them ride—all of them abreast and looking like an invading army. Not exactly the picture of femininity that Patience will wish to convey."

Picture of femininity? Well, really. She thought she did convey that just now, but atop a horse was a different matter.

The duke took out his flask and took a long draught by way of answer.

"You might remember that habits in the remote corners of the Dales do not transfer particularly well to Town," Lady Marchfield said.

"Where's Marchfield, by the by?" the duke asked. "Give you the slip again?"

Before Lady Marchfield could answer that salvo, the Duchess of Devonshire returned. She handed Patience her card. "All filled with eligible gentlemen. Now, I'd best locate Lady Alice. I hope I find her not as serious as I did the last I saw her—all well and good in a young lady, but perhaps not suited for a ball."

The duchess sailed off to locate the serious Lady Alice.

"Lady Alice has every right to be serious," Lady Marchfield said. "She is exceedingly well funded. I have heard she brings twenty thousand. A little seriousness would not go amiss for you, Patience, and your sisters as well."

Patience listened and nodded, but she really was not very interested in Lady Alice's temperament.

She felt very much put on the back foot and she did not like it. She wished she'd not been looking when the duchess had presented her card to those three gentlemen.

Or she wished that one of them had not hesitated. In particular, she wished *that* gentleman had not hesitated.

CHAPTER THREE

MARCUS HAD GONE on horseback to Almack's, as both he and Radler preferred it. Cresswell always displayed no end of silent protest to the idea as his valet was convinced that his hard work would be for naught. His concerns were overblown though, as long as one stepped one's horse carefully round mud and puddles. In any case, Cresswell used enough starch on his clothes that he supposed he might wrestle and still come out of it looking pressed.

They'd found Kendrickson coming out of a carriage that certainly was not his own. He supposed some relation or other was pitching in the means and money for the season.

The patronesses seemed especially interested in Kendrickson. Marcus could guess that his old school acquaintance had made himself a project for them. They seemed primed to help him along to the sort of dowry he'd require to keep himself afloat. It was hardly surprising—there was nothing a patroness liked so well as a project they might take credit for.

They'd since gone into the ballroom to engage in the age-old ritual of putting themselves down on ladies' cards. Radler said, "So this trip to Town, Kendrickson, I suppose you are considering marriage?"

Kendrickson smiled. "No need to put it so delicate," he said. "Everybody on God's green earth knows my circumstances. Even if I could hide it, I do not think that I would. If I can convince a lady to hitch her carriage to my horses, I'd just as soon she know the truth of my situation. In any case, her father will be well apprised of it."

Radler had sighed one of his painful to live in the world sighs. "Dashed awful though. What if you are struck by a lady and she does not have the necessary funds?"

"Struck?" Kendrickson asked.

Marcus raised his hand to stop the conversation in its tracks. "Do not inquire further into it, Kendrickson. I have been up to my ears in conversation regarding Radler's ideas of being struck."

The Duchess of Devonshire interrupted their conversation, which Marcus was rather glad of.

"Gentlemen," the duchess said, "I am filling the card of Lady Patience Nicolet, daughter of the Duke of Pelham. She is just across the ballroom, standing by her father."

"Oh, I say," Kendrickson said, reaching for it.

Radler was next. "Very interested in becoming acquainted with that lady."

He passed the card to Marcus, who hesitated.

"Come now, man," Radler said, "do not tell me you are frightened off of a lady on account of a gallop?"

"Of course not," he said, writing his name down.

What had really given him pause was that the only dance open on Lady Patience's card was the one that led to the supper, such as it was at Almack's. He'd been avoiding writing his name down for that one as he'd been told that a certain Lady Alice Gerhard, daughter of the Earl of Kembleford, would attend. It was said that she was of a serious and thoughtful temperament, and he'd been very interested in making her acquaintance.

Marcus glanced once more in Lady Patience's direction. Yes, that was the same lady he'd seen in the park. He'd only seen her very briefly as she'd flown by on her horse, but that was most certainly her. She was undeniably pretty. Really, he supposed she was the prettiest lady in the ballroom.

Well, he'd told himself that he would not judge a person by

their father, however eccentric the duke might be. He would also not judge on the wild ride he'd witnessed, as he did not know the full circumstance. It might very well have been an aberration.

Or even it were not, it did not necessarily sum up the lady's temperament. That really was the key to all his plans. He must find a lady similar in temperament to his own so that he did not end up in a household like the one he'd been raised in. He would insist on peace and cordiality.

He would proceed carefully, as that was his nature, but he would not proceed prejudicially. There could be no benefit to that.

Radler was busy informing Kendrickson of Lady Patience and her sisters galloping down Rotten Row on Dales ponies.

"That must have been a sight—she sounds fun," Kendrickson said.

"Fun?" Marcus said. "Kendrickson, aside from whatever your requirements are regarding a dowry, I do hope you have formulated other considerations. Fun is not exactly a wise decision-making yardstick."

Radler laughed. "You see how it is, Kendrickson. Stanford came into the world an eighty-year-old man and he'll go out of it just the same."

His two friends laughed heartily over the jest, though Marcus failed to see the hilarity in it. He was not eighty. He was simply careful. Rightfully careful. They'd see that in the end.

MRS. RIGHT FOUND that on the rare occasion that she was faced with a butler, it was well to know their plans. Since these unwanted individuals would not deign to tell her outright of any strategies they'd developed, she'd taken to hiding behind doorways to find them out.

As she had suspected, Mr. Grimsby was up to something. It

seemed his idea was to gain the loyalty of the footmen, thereby turning them against her. It was not a terrible plan, actually. It was doomed to fail, however, as the footmen in question were *her* footmen. For all that, it was well that she knew it.

Just now, Mr. Grimsby said, "Charlie, it would be to your benefit to understand how things are done in properly run houses. After all, what are you to do if you decide to move on? What if you wish to become a butler to some elevated person? At the moment, you do not have the first idea of how it is done. Your staff would never respect you, because you would not understand how things are properly done."

Mrs. Right smiled. Everybody knew that Charlie had not the least interest in staying in service all his life. He saved every pence so he might one day open a tavern in their village. Mrs. Right had long ago convinced the duke to hand out rather significant Christmas bonuses for the sole reason of funding Charlie's ambitions.

"If you were to support my efforts," Mr. Grimsby went on, "I would ensure that you learn how things are properly done, Charlie. It would greatly enhance your chances of moving up in the world. Now, I know you are all fond of Mrs. Right, but that is only because she's had you isolated in Yorkshire. You have not known any better examples. However, she does you a disservice! It is outrageous that a housekeeper is bossing about the foot-men."

Disservice, indeed. No footmen in England were paid as well, had as many days off, and had such light duty. No footmen had a leader who treated them as if they were her own sons.

"You were a soldier, Mr. Grimsby, is that right?" Charlie asked.

"Indeed I was, and very good training for running a house-hold it was too," Mr. Grimsby said.

"Now let me ask you this," Charlie said, "let's say you was serving a general for ever so many years. Then, all sudden-like, a new general sidles up to you and says, forget your general and serve me. What would you do?"

"Such a situation would be unheard of. A soldier does not change commanding officers willy-nilly."

"Just so, Mr. Grimsby. Just so."

Mrs. Right tiptoed away, well satisfied that Mr. Grimsby would get precisely nowhere with her boys.

PATIENCE WAS ENJOYING herself so far, despite the niggling little idea in the back of her mind regarding Lord Stanford's hesitation in putting himself down on her card. Especially since he'd penciled in for the dance before supper. She presumed that had been the only space left and she did not like to think that the gentleman had been forced to take her in and engage in extended conversation.

She had already danced with Lord Radler, one of the three that had caught her eye instantly. He was a rather voluble specimen and she discovered that he was a houseguest of Lord Stanford's. They'd had a lively conversation about Dales ponies and Patience had told him of the sort of wild rides she and her sisters took on the moors.

She'd wished to subtly inquire into Lord Stanford's hesitation in putting his name down on her card, but she did not find an opportunity to work it in.

Just now, she danced with Lord Kendrickson, the second of the three gentlemen who'd caught her eye upon arriving. Though, she could not help but notice her aunt frowning at the edge of the ballroom floor.

"I see Lady Marchfield gives me some dark looks," Lord Kendrickson said. "I suppose she's warned you of my circumstances."

"She said you were in Town on a dowry hunt," Patience said, interested to see how he would answer the charge.

The lord laughed. "I suppose it could be called that. I certainly do require a good dowry and I have never attempted to hide my circumstances. I will say, though, that there are few men in England who do not have to take on such considerations. My case is perhaps just more dire. My father was a gambler and not very skilled at it."

Patience found his directness rather refreshing. She was not naïve to the ways of the world. Women had dowries because estates needed infusions. It was the great English money trade between houses. Awkward, of course, but that was why everybody pretended they did not know it. A lady was not meant to consider whether a gentleman had considered her purse.

"My father says gambling is almost as stupid as putting a gun to one's head, pulling the trigger, and hoping not to get shot," she said.

Lord Kendrickson laughed. "My views exactly, though perhaps I have never expressed it in such colorful terms."

"My papa is a darling, though so many do not see it at first. He shocks people, but it is just him going his own way."

"Money and title allow for going one's own way it seems. I hope you do not think less of me because of the situation I've found myself in."

"I do not, and it does you credit that you do not hide it, Lord Kendrickson."

"Of course, I very much wish that it was not the situation I'm in. It would be rather glorious to have no need for practicalities. But duty, you know. My mother, a dowager now, counts on me, as does everyone who works in my household."

Patience nodded. She very much liked Lord Kendrickson. Not as anything more than a friendship, but she found herself feeling as if she would like to help him where she could.

"Lord Kendrickson, I will give you the only hint I am in possession of. I understand Lady Alice comes with twenty thousand and I suppose that would rescue your sagging fortunes."

"Rather," Lord Kendrickson said.

"I have been told that she is a serious personality," Patience said. "It is always well to understand another's temperament. Perhaps if she sees you as serious too, it will put you in her good books."

The lord sighed. "She is unlikely to favor me, then. I cannot say I am a particularly serious person—I do like to laugh. She'll be going for someone like Stanford."

"Oh? Lord Stanford is particularly serious?" Patience asked.

Lord Kendrickson thought for a moment. "Perhaps that is not the right word. He is not so much serious as... cautious? I'm not even sure that is the right word."

Patience felt herself wishing to toe-tap. What *was* the right word?

"Well, I suppose you will come to your own judgments. I will say that he has always been a good friend. When we were at Eton, he did not shun me on account of my shabby clothes or lack of funds."

"Did others do so?" Patience asked.

"Some did. But Stanford and Radler are both bricks. Stanford even gave me some of his shirts and neckcloths when I was hard-pressed."

So that was what she knew so far. Lord Stanford might be serious or cautious, but those might not be the right words, and he was a brick who did not mind giving away his clothes.

She really would have to come to her own judgment. She could not imagine that judgment would be anything but exceedingly pleasing. She had sharp and quick instincts, and they told her that she and Lord Stanford would get on famously.

Despite any mistaken early hesitations he might have displayed.

MARCUS WAS NOT entirely sure where his thoughts were going.

They were usually so regulated and traveled the paths he directed them to do.

Just now, his eyes kept drifting in the same direction. In the direction of Lady Patience. He kept arguing with himself and attempting to turn his eyes toward Lady Alice, or anybody else, really.

His eyes were entirely defiant.

There was something about Lady Patience that demanded his attention. She was so remarkably pretty—her big expressive eyes, her perfectly proportioned features, her piles of brown hair that glinted shades of auburn in the candlelight. Then those lips, full and yet there was a delicacy to them. Perhaps it was the slightest upward curve at the edges that was striking.

But none of that was quite it. She was so *alive*. That was it.

Everything about her was expressive. Her eyes glinted, her smile flashed. There was a confident ease about her.

He could see very well that every gentleman who'd danced with her had enjoyed the experience. He supposed she would be very popular, perhaps even named the season's diamond.

There was something irritating in that, though it was illogical. He did not like illogic. He did not like to think he could suffer from such a state. It might even be dangerous.

He could not allow anything, or anyone, to upset his carefully laid plans. At such a critical moment in his life, he could not throw over all of his judicious conclusions for some fleeting attraction. Surely that was what it was.

His cautiously laid plans would serve him well in the future, and he must always keep that at the forefront of his thoughts.

But then, it could very well turn out that Lady Patience was suited to him. In fact, he found himself hoping so. He just must guard against allowing his opinions to get ahead of the facts. There was an equal chance she was not suited to him.

Whatever the case might be, he was to begin to discover it in moments. He approached the lady, who stood with her father and her aunt.

"Your Grace, Lady Marchfield, Lady Patience," he said, bowing.

"Stanford, is it?" the duke asked.

"The Earl of Stanford," Lady Marchfield said before he could answer. "I have been acquainted with the earl for a number of years and I find him everything a gentleman should be."

"That is very kind, Lady Marchfield," Marcus said.

"Is it kind, though?" the duke said. "Lady Misery here generally approves of everything glum and uninteresting. That is not you, I hope?"

"Roland!" Lady Marchfield exclaimed.

"I hope not, Your Grace," Marcus said, for lack of any cogent sort of reply to such a statement.

"My father jests," Lady Patience said.

"Do I?" the duke asked.

Lady Patience tapped her father with her fan. "You most certainly do, Papa. Do not tease Lord Stanford."

"All right, my girl," the duke said, seeming to be in all good humor to be reprimanded by his daughter.

"Lady Patience," Marcus said, holding out his arm. She laid her hand gently upon it and he led them to their places.

There was something like nearby lightning in her touch. He felt the hair on his arms stand up as though he'd got too close to a summer storm. He had the ungodly urge to rip off her glove and touch her skin.

What was wrong with him?

He led them to their place for La Boulangere. The Duchess of Devonshire had already called that it would be six couples per circle. As was usually the case, the most senior lord and his lady partner of each circle would act the lead couple. For their own circle, that would be the Marquess of Haddonfield.

Kendrickson and Radler had also made their way into his circle. Marcus was annoyed to note them both surreptitiously smile at Lady Patience. They were not very subtle at it either, as evidenced by their partners' rather irritated expressions. Particularly not Lady Rose, who had been acclaimed as last season's diamond and did not seem enthusiastic to encounter more ladies making their debuts.

The music began and the marquess nodded to signal the grand ronde. As they made their way round the circle, Marcus said, "I see you've met my friends."

It was a stupid thing to say, but his mind was not cooperating with him particularly well this evening.

"Yes," Lady Patience said, "I suppose you would have seen them put their names down on my card. As you were there."

"Yes," he said.

"I just happened to be looking that way at the time," Lady Patience said. "I was not certain you would put yourself down."

Marcus' eyes widened. He supposed she'd seen that he'd hesitated. What on earth should he say about it?

He supposed the truth was all he'd got.

"That was not at all what it may have appeared to be," he said. "It was only my caution, as there is another lady here that I have been encouraged to meet and I had already committed myself to the other dances."

Well. That was not *quite* the truth. Nobody had encouraged him to secure Lady Alice for a dance. He'd encouraged himself upon hearing of her sedate temperament.

He felt a need to fill in the ensuing silence. "I was told the lady is rather serious, and so I thought supper might suit..." He was just rambling now, and so he stopped.

Lady Patience's eyes flashed as they came to the end of the grand ronde. "Oh I see. Lady Alice, was it?"

How on earth would she know it had been Lady Alice?

"Uh, yes," he said. "People have mentioned that she and I should meet." Marcus hoped his face did not look as embarrassed as he in fact was. He'd said *people* had encouraged him to seek out Lady Alice. What people? Were there now to be mysterious *people* who went round whispering proposed introductions? It was absurd.

"Indeed," Lady Patience said. "*People* have very good things to say about Lady Alice."

She smiled sweetly at him as she said it. Was she serious, or was she well aware of the nonexistence of *people* and simply mocking him?

What was this creature? She was at once alluring and uncomfortably confrontational. What other lady would question why he'd hesitated in putting his name down on her card? A usual lady would simply tuck her irritation in her reticule and say no more about it. What other lady would mock his pathetic excuse of blaming *people* for the hesitation? He was leaning toward the opinion that she did mock him, too. A usual lady might smile and nod and pretend the excuse had been swallowed whole, even if it had not been.

Certainly, such a lady as this could not be suited to him. They had just met and she questioned and mocked him—what picture did that paint of the future? Not a comfortable one, he was sure.

And yet, he found himself unwilling to look away.

CHAPTER FOUR

Patience had been determined to discover the reason for Lord Stanford's hesitation in putting his name down on her card. And, she had discovered it. He'd wished to dance with Lady Alice. *People* had recommended it. He'd only put himself down for Patience because he'd not been able to refuse the Duchess of Devonshire.

She would really like to despise him for that. However, she could not do it. He was fascinating to look at, for one. For another, his taking her hand in the dance had set something off in her. Her hands had touched various gentlemen this evening, but she'd not felt this particular feeling she could not put a name to. And for another, there was something of a challenge in him that got her blood up.

She'd been struck by him the moment she'd set eyes on him. Was she to be defeated by this Lady Alice individual? Or the *people* who pushed that lady forward? No, that did not sound very like Patience Nicolet.

La Boulangere had come to an end and Lord Stanford led her into the supper room to two empty chairs. He signaled to a footman and they were brought tea and dry cake.

"This is the extent of the offerings, unless you care for sour lemonade or stale bread," Lord Stanford said.

"My father warned me sufficiently," Patience said. "I ate a whopping big dinner before I came."

This seemed to catch Lord Stanford off guard. He laughed and said, "Most ladies would not admit to ever in their lives eating a whopping big dinner."

"Would they not?" Patience asked. "Well, I suppose I do not know such things as my mother died when I was young and our estate is very remote. We do not have close neighbors with the exception of a few farmers, and they are known for their whopping dinners."

"I am very sorry to hear that you lost your mother young."

Patience nodded. "Though, my papa did a marvelous job of it raising us. Just think, he was more wrecked over losing my mama than anybody and he was left to face seven motherless daughters, one of them an infant."

"Oh, well, I assume he had the help of nurses and a governess," Lord Stanford said.

"Nurses came and went, our housekeeper was, and still is, the steady presence. We only had a governess for a short time, actually. Miss Pynchon was not very suited to us; she did not understand us. For instance, I kept my mother's sable coat in my room and put it on sometimes to smell her perfume. Miss Pynchon was against it and took it from me. My papa raised the roof over it and I got it back."

"I see, so the governess thought you ought not wallow in grief."

"I do not know what she thought, but she did not *feel* very much as far as I could tell. She had no sentimentality. She departed one early morning, leaving behind a note." Patience laughed and said, "It only said one word—goodbye. She scrawled it across a sheet of paper. We still laugh about that."

"Do you?"

"Yes, of course we do. Who leaves their employment with such a note? We think she must have been overwhelmed, at there were so many of us. At least, she often mentioned that she did not understand why there were so many of us. In any case, the duke is an absolute dear of a father. It is just that so many seem not to understand him."

"He strikes one as an interesting personality," the lord said.

"That is a very good word for it," Patience said, pleased. "You see, he does not care a whit for societies' constraints. He tells the truth as he sees it. He is also very funny. He always teases us that he cannot wait to get us all out of the house. Mind you, I don't believe him and if anybody attempts to hurt one of his family, he is a beast about it. I really cannot imagine anybody better."

Lord Stanford seemed to take on a pensive expression. Patience thought perhaps he *could* imagine better.

She said, "Of course, it is only what I know. I suppose your parents were cracking good."

This seemed to strike the lord even harder.

Perhaps they were not cracking good? Or good at all?

"May I enquire into your hobbies, Lady Patience?"

As he had changed the subject of the conversation so abruptly, Patience suspected that his home life as a child had not in fact been cracking good. She should have known not to drift into such personal territory. One never knew what another's situation was. She was determined to turn to more usual topics of conversation.

As the lord had asked about her hobbies, she said, "Well, I love my horse. Her name is Penny and she is a Dales pony. You would have seen her in the park."

"Indeed, I did. Along with some others."

"Yes, those were my sisters—Winsome, Verity, and Serenity. We all have ponies from the same breeder. Penny has given me some lovely rides across the moors. She is very surefooted, as they all are. And then I like to sketch, I sketched out all my dresses for the season well ahead of time. I do like to be organized and prepared and do a thing the most efficient way possible. Quite the challenge with my sisters holding things up all the time."

"They are not as organized?"

Patience laughed. "They are not at all organized. They cannot seem to ever come to a quick decision. They are not decisive."

"But you are decisive?"

"Very. I cannot bear to hem and haw over a thing. Why does anybody do it? It's maddening."

"I suppose another sort of temperament might call it careful consideration?"

Patience shrugged. "I call it not knowing one's own mind. When I consider any matter, my mind instantly informs me of its opinion and I go forward with it. I have begun to feel that not knowing one's own mind must just be a lack of confidence in it."

"Perhaps for more serious and consequential endeavors, slow and careful analysis might convey some benefit," Lord Stanford said.

"I am not so certain that it does, though. It seems like it should, but have you noticed that when people go all round the world on a decision, they almost always circle back to the first idea they had? It's almost as if they so little trust their own mind that they must consider all possible decisions before acknowledging that the first one was right all along."

Considering the lord's expression, Patience wondered if she'd gone too far in expressing her long-held and rather strong opinions on the matter. Lady Marchfield often commented that she did. Lord Stanford appeared positively gobsmacked.

"Do not you fear you may make a mistake if you hurry a decision?" Lord Stanford asked, staring at his untouched plate.

Patience shrugged. "Our housekeeper says that most mistakes will not kill a person, so I do not suppose I ought to spend much time afraid of them."

"Well, my girl," the duke said behind her chair, "you'll never guess—my flask has run dry. How did that happen? Well, I supposed I played a significant part in it. That makes me think the moment has arrived for us to make our way out of this cathedral of stuffiness. Stanford, I invite you to dinner on Tuesday next and I assure you that you will get more than bread and weak tea."

"That is very kind, Your Grace. Allow me to check my calendar."

Patience stared at him. Check his calendar?

"Check away, send me a note on the morrow," the duke said.

Patience rose and curtsied to Lord Stanford, doing her best not to appear too frowny. They made their way out to the carriage and once inside, Patience said, "Check his calendar? It feels… insulting. What if there is something on his calendar? Why would he not drop it to come to us?"

The duke laughed. "Stanford strikes me as a fellow who does not jump into the lake without testing the temperature. He'll want to consider it."

"I do not like it."

"I see, you've made up your mind on him already, have you?"

"No."

Her father folded his arms and smiled. He could always see right through his daughters.

"Well, perhaps I do feel some inclination," she said.

"Give him a minute. I do believe he will accept for dinner. Then we'll subject him to Fact or Fib afterward and we'll see what he's made of. Oh, and I've invited Lord Radler too—he's Stanford's houseguest, didn't seem right to leave him out."

Patience would very much like to see what Lord Stanford was made of. She certainly hoped he was made of stuff that would accept an invitation without unnecessary delay. He'd already hesitated in putting his name down on her card, was he to hesitate long before accepting a dinner invitation? Was he a hesitating sort of person?

She hoped not, as there was something arresting about him. Her decisive mind was telling her that he was of the highest interest, and her mind generally knew which way the wind was blowing.

Further, there was the consideration that *people* had been pushing forward Lady Alice to Lord Stanford. Should she not see with her own eyes if there was anything going on in that direction? Her mind told her there should not be, but she must see it confirmed. Since *people* had raised the question with Lord

Stanford.

"Papa, can I extend an invitation to dine to Lady Alice?"

"Invite anybody you like, but for Lady Misery. And this time round, do not let my sister know that there is to be a dinner at all. The last time she found out was rather harrowing. Hilarious, but harrowing."

"Oh goodness, yes. That was when Mr. Button made his dramatic exit from the house. My aunt says he does well for himself these days."

"Good for him," the duke said. "As to the dinner, Felicity and Grace should be in Town by then—we'll have a regular family party."

Patience nodded. It seemed ages since she'd seen her two married sisters. As for Lady Alice, Patience would call on her and make the invitation. She'd only been briefly introduced to the lady when Lord Radler had taken her to the floor, but that must be sufficient to call.

MARCUS FOUND HIMSELF still in his drawing room in the early morning hours. Radler was already staying with him and had dragged Kendrickson along for brandy. They both said it was desperately needed, as they'd had nothing of the sort at Almack's.

"Well, Kendrickson," Radler said, "you've met several ladies with heavy purses, the only one of note not present this evening was Miss Richards. Her money comes from trade, of course. Though her mother is the daughter of a viscount, so that must weigh in her favor."

"Her money will be as good as anybody else's, I reckon," Kendrickson said. "Though we'll never set eyes on her at Almack's."

"But of those you did meet?" Radler pressed on. "Was there anything hopeful in it?"

Kendrickson downed his brandy and Radler helpfully refilled it. "I liked at least two of the ladies, but I have not the first idea what they thought of me. That will be the trick of it."

"Which two, though?" Radler asked.

Marcus sighed. They were like two old women talking together.

"I would have to say that Lady Alice and Lady Patience both stood out for me."

Marcus set his brandy down. He found he did not like that idea, though he had not the least cause to be against it. He had no claim on either lady. He did not wish to have a claim on any lady so soon in the season.

It was just that Lady Alice had been made out to be someone well suited to him and Lady Patience, well, she was very alive and difficult to turn away from.

"Lady Patience seems to understand my circumstances without fanning herself over it," Kendrickson said.

Yes, Marcus supposed that would be the case. He could not imagine Lady Patience fanning herself over much. She seemed a rather stalwart personality. He did not suppose he'd ever encountered a lady who was not afraid of mistakes because they probably would not kill her.

"And then, Lady Alice. She is more serious than I would generally like. I knew it, and tried to match it as best I could. That is not ideal, but I do like her looks exceedingly. I have a weakness for black hair and blue eyes—you don't see it much."

"I suppose both ladies will attend Lady Jenner's musical evening on the morrow," Radler said. "A lady does not like to be left behind in showing off her musical ability."

"Lady Patience's duke invited me to dinner on Tuesday next," Marcus blurted out, apropos of absolutely nothing.

Both gentlemen turned to him. "Lucky," Kendrickson said.

"Excellent, we are going, then. I supposed we would. The duke invited me as well," Radler said. "I told him I'd have to check with my host. Meaning you."

"I said I'd have to check my calendar and would let him know," Marcus said.

"Are you daft?" Radler said. "The only thing of note on the calendar Tuesday next is Mrs. Henning's rout. It will be the usual stupid crush of uninteresting people."

"Surely you will accept," Kendrickson said, eyeing him as if he had two heads.

"Hmm, well, if it is just the rout…"

He found himself playing for time, though he did not know why. It was only a dinner. Probably a very large dinner, as it was a duke hosting it. The man likely just needed to fill two last seats with gentlemen. He should not read any more into it than that.

"I swear your mental paralysis will be the death of me," Radler said.

"My mind is not paralyzed," Marcus said with some asperity. Although, it did feel a little paralyzed. Perhaps he noticed it more because of everything Lady Patience had said on the subject of decisiveness.

He did not wish to view himself as indecisive. It seemed…weak. Surely there was a sensible balance between careful planning and indecisiveness. Of course there was.

"How long will you take to decide?" Kendrickson said. "He is a duke, he might become offended if you take too long."

"I have not taken long at all. As there is nothing compelling on the calendar for that evening, I have decided. I will accept."

There. He'd said it. Now he supposed he must do it. Even if he'd not come to any firm conclusions regarding the wisdom of it.

Since he had committed himself, he supposed he could allow himself to look forward to seeing Lady Patience again. And perhaps seeing her tomorrow night too.

After all, there was that particular something about her and it was perfectly fine to admire the lady. There was no danger in that whatsoever.

Mrs. Right thought Mr. Grimsby was having a time of it. Her staff were so clever at carrying out her instructions. Mr. Grimsby, as it turned out, had very specific ways of doing things. That was exceedingly helpful to their plans.

He would lay out precise instructions on how to do a thing and Charlie and Thomas would do it another way. In the dining room, Mr. Grimsby wanted chargers and plates down, then the silver, then the glasses. The footmen would go willy-nilly with glasses first, then silver, then plates. They would purposefully forget the chargers and have to upset the whole thing and start again. That particular maneuver was done as slowly as possible until the minutes ticked down and Cook raved for someone to come and get his platters.

Service was to the left and clearing to the right? The footmen served right and cleared left, though they knew perfectly well it was wrong. When Mr. Grimsby passed by them and hissed in their ears to correct it, Charlie and Thomas made a great show of bumping into each other and dripping things on the carpet.

A footman was meant to stand ramrod straight at all times? Thomas had slumped so far over while attending the drawing room that Valor had asked him if he was sick and told him he should go to bed.

And what was Mr. Grimsby to do about all of this? He'd made one tentative foray into the duke's library to air his complaints and had come out of it white as new laundered linen.

Mrs. Right did not know what the duke had said, but she knew that gentleman well enough to know it had been appalling to Mr. Grimsby and another visit was not likely to be tried.

Who else could the butler turn to? She supposed he could go running to Lady Marchfield, just as the last one had. No matter, Mrs. Agnes Right was well prepared to do battle with Lady Misery.

As Mrs. Right made her way to her room to change her fichu, which had got a stain on it somehow, she heard quiet weeping from the direction of the men's quarters. Very much fearing it was either Thomas downhearted over how long it would take to save up for his tavern or Cook having his last nerve snapped by an incompetent grocer, and having no idea of anywhere in the house being off-limits to her, she followed the sound.

She paused in the corridor. The weeping came from Mr. Grimsby's room. Of course, she knew perfectly well it was the room he had been assigned, as it had been purposefully done. It was the hottest in hot weather and coldest in cold weather, had creaky floors, and a window so small it did not deserve the name. Charlie and Thomas called it the little box of hell on earth.

Could this be the moment? Had they broken him and now he would flee the house, proving Lady Marchfield wrong for a third time?

It certainly sounded like it. Though, she had to be certain. And help him along with it if that was needed.

She knocked softly.

The weeping paused. There were sniffles. A clearing of the throat. Then the door opened.

Mr. Grimsby staggered back to see her there. "Mrs. Right! This is the gentlemen's end of the corridor!"

"Aye, don't you think I know that," she said, pushing past him. "Now I suppose all this blubbering is on account of you leaving soon?"

"I only wish I could! This house is a shambles, I have never worked with such degenerates in all my life!"

"Dales people aren't for everybody, I reckon. Best you found it out now before you were trapped all remote-like on the estate with no way to escape."

Mr. Grimsby placed a hand over his heart. "Do you actually imagine that I would travel to Yorkshire with this circus?"

"I hadn't imagined, actually. It is well we have the same views on it though." Mrs. Right paused. "Wait a moment. What did you mean when you said 'I only wish I could.' What's holding you up? If it's pride, I'd say that's a mannish and foolish reason. Get packing, get going, and forget you were ever here."

Mr. Grimsby paced the small and rather dim room, his footsteps creaking the floorboards. "That is just it, I cannot leave! Not this soon. Oh, what am I to do? I feel I am wrecked, I am just a shell of the man I was when I arrived. I cannot bear another minute, but I have no choice! What is to be the end of it?"

"Why aren't you to have a choice, though? Lady Marchfield got the last one a new situation, Mr. Button was his name. I'll wager she'll do the same for you."

"No she certainly will not. If I do not last a month, she washes her hands of me. That is our agreement. After one month, she hands over fifty pounds. My seed money to open my own haberdashery. She does not know of the shop, of course. She believes that if I can last a month, I can last forever."

"Does she, now," Mrs. Right said thoughtfully. This was indeed interesting information. It seemed Mr. Grimsby was planning to cross Lady Marchfield by lasting a month and then making off with her fifty pounds.

Mrs. Right had the inclination to help him do it. Not only would he be out of the house, but Lady Misery would be entirely stymied to be out a pile of pounds. Satisfactory on all counts.

"I believe we can come to some sort of genial agreement, Mr. Grimsby. Your whole problem is that you care how the house is run. What's say you stop caring? Then you can relax and ride out the month. Stay up here all day and read books if you like—I'll even put you in a better room. Take turns in the garden. Do whatever strikes you. Then, collect your money and be off."

Mrs. Right was pleased to see a glimmer of hope in Mr. Grimsby's eye.

"Yes, I could do that, I suppose. Yes, of course I could. What do I care how this house is run? Nobody else does! Should I care if that dinner on Tuesday is a shambles? I was caring very much, but why was I doing it?"

"Now you're catching on to it."

Mr. Grimsby straightened his coat. "Consider me disengaged, Mrs. Right. I believe I will go for a walk in the square and everybody can do what they like about tea. If Thomas attends the drawing room slouched like he's broken in half, that's not my concern. He can fall asleep and fall over on the floor for all I care about it!"

CHAPTER FIVE

PATIENCE HAD BEEN pleased that Lord Stanford's acceptance of the dinner invitation had arrived first thing in the morning. He had not delayed overlong to ponder it, and that seemed like a very good sign.

Now she was free to move on to her second goal—inviting Lady Alice. She must know, she must see with her own eyes, how Lord Stanford reacted to the lady over an intimate and protracted dinner. Patience knew what she expected to see, which was nothing, but she must see it all the same.

As she had no lady's maid, Mrs. Right would step forward as a chaperone on the visit to Lady Alice. It was agreed between them that the housekeeper would pose as lady's maid, thereby being led to the servants' hall. Mrs. Right liked nothing better than to have a look round other people's households. She said you could tell a lot about a family by ascertaining how they treated their people.

Lady Alice lived on Bedford Square, the same square Lady Marchfield kept her house. Mrs. Right suggested they ought to keep an eye out for the lady and direct the coachman to keep driving if she was spotted. Patience thought that was as good a plan as any. She would like to avoid her aunt for the time being, as she did not wish to slip up and mention the dinner on Tuesday next.

As it happened, Lady Marchfield was nowhere in sight. The

carriage rolled to a stop, the groom helped them down, and then he jogged up the four steps to rap on the door knocker as they followed.

After some minutes passed, the door was finally opened by what appeared to be a harried and breathless butler.

Patience stepped forward. "Lady Patience Nicolet to see Lady Alice." As the look on the butler's face showed his surprise, she hurriedly said, "I realize it is not her at home day, but I did feel we became friends at Almack's and I might take the liberty of arriving without warning."

Patience did not know if the butler believed that or not. Patience herself certainly did not. She had only been briefly introduced to Lady Alice. It would be bad form to arrive without invitation and demand to be seen rather than drop off a card.

Nevertheless, she was certain that a personal visit was the best way to extend the invitation to dine, as it was so much more difficult to say no while the inviter was staring at one rather than to write their regrets when nobody was looking. She must just plow ahead as if nothing at all was amiss.

"I see, yes, do come in," the harried butler said. "I will check if Lady Alice is at home."

Patience nodded as if she believed that. Down a distant corridor, she could hear music coming from a pianoforte. Certainly it must be Lady Alice playing.

Patience felt the smallest twinge of regret that neither she nor her sisters had ever become proficient on a musical instrument. None of them had taken to it, they did not seem to have a natural ear, and nobody had pressed them to carry on with it.

She dismissed the feeling, as she did not like to dwell on things that could not be changed with any speed.

"Well, I suppose I ought to wait in the drawing room and my lady's maid could be shown downstairs for a cup of tea."

Patience had the distinct impression that they would have been left to stand in the hall had she not put forward the suggestion. As she *had* suggested it, the butler nodded to a footman to lead Mrs. Right below stairs and he showed Patience into the drawing room.

The door closed and very shortly after Patience heard the music stop. Lady Alice was being told of her arrival.

A minute passed, and Patience heard some noises out in the hall, and then the distinct sound of running up the stairs. No doubt, Lady Alice had hurried up to her bedchamber to change her dress. At least, that was her guess, as that was what she would have done herself.

Tea was brought in, which was rather awkward. Was she to pour for herself while in another lady's house?

She decided to do nothing and was soon rewarded by the presence of the hostess, herself.

Lady Alice was a striking woman, she had the sort of coloring that was almost stark in its beauty. Her hair was jet black and her eyes a dark blue, set off by an almost overly pale complexion. Patience envied her just the smallest bit—her looks made a statement, they demanded to be noticed.

"Lady Patience," she said, "what a pleasant…surprise."

"I know it is a surprise, and perhaps even ill-mannered, but I had a very good reason for coming," Patience said. "By the by, you are very good on the pianoforte. I quite admire it."

Lady Alice blushed deeply as she poured the tea. "I venture I am as proficient as any other lady, meaning I meander along as best I can."

"I can assure you that you are far more proficient than I am," Patience said. "I cannot play a note." She paused, then said, "Though perhaps I should not be advertising that fact."

"I suspect it may be modesty on your part," Lady Alice said. "You did say your visit was of a particular nature?"

"Oh yes," Patience said, nearly forgetting why she'd come. "My father is hosting a dinner on Tuesday next, just a small affair. I wondered if you would come. Your parents might be assured that you would be in a duke's household and quite safe."

"Goodness, that is very kind. But if it is to be a small dinner, I do wonder…"

Lady Alice trailed off, but of course Patience understood her meaning.

"Well, it is just this," she said, "Lord Radler and Lord Stanford will attend. I was particularly thinking Lord Radler might suit you." She paused and heaved a sigh. "Of course, it might be Lord Stanford, as I have been told he is serious or cautious or I am not certain what."

Lady Alice had now turned a very alarming shade of purple. Her pale skin seemed to have no ability to mask the blood rushing to her cheeks. She almost looked feverish.

"Lady Patience," she said, "I cannot be so bold as to claim that anybody would suit me. Why should you say so?"

"Well, a lady must decide for herself who she likes and Lord Stanford has been described as serious and people do say you are serious," Patience said.

"I see?"

Patience nodded. "So of course I must wonder if you would prefer a gentleman very like. Serious, that is."

"I most certainly would not," Lady Alice said.

"Would not?"

Lady Alice shook her head rather violently. She sipped her tea and set it down. She picked up a biscuit, looked at it, and dropped it on the tray. She checked on the level of the cream. She tapped her spoon on her saucer.

"Do tell me what you are thinking," Patience said. "I am afraid I have upset you in some way, which I absolutely did not mean to do. It's just, I was raised very remote in the Dales and sometimes London habits escape me."

Lady Alice suddenly laughed, which was the last thing Patience expected. "Goodness, you are amusing. No, Lady Patience, you have not upset me in the least. You are right, I am rather serious, but that is precisely why I do not wish for an over-serious gentleman."

"Oh. Why not?"

"Because I would end in a rather grim household. You see, in my early years, my mother and father thought I had not a drop of humor in me. My father used to tease me and call me Gloomy Alice. But then, when I was eight years old, a cousin of my father's came to stay. Lord Gumfrey—he is a roaringly funny individual and persisted in attempting to make me laugh, which he finally did. That's when we discovered that while I am dismal at making jokes, I am rather gifted with appreciating other people's wit. Therefore, I must wed a man who can make me laugh."

"Ah, you look for balance, rather than same."

"Just so."

"You will come to dinner, though? I suspect Lord Radler made himself out to be far more serious than he actually is. And then, Lord Kendrickson, he will not be at the dinner, but he is a great friend of Lord Radler and Lord Stanford and he is very jolly. You might find out more about him through his friends."

"Lord Kendrickson is the one everyone talks about as a dowry hunter," Lady Alice said pensively.

Patience shook her head. "Do not hold that against him, though. You ought to speak to him about it, as I did."

"Did you?"

"Indeed I did. He does not hide it and he told me the reasons for it. His father was an inveterate gambler and put the estate in a tight spot. But just think, he is very against gambling and that must be a comfort—he will never allow himself to get into trouble as his father did. As well, I did get the sense that he admired you. I very much approve of him."

Lady Alice was pensive. "Naturally, I would not hold Lord Kendrickson responsible for what his father has done. I danced with him at Almack's and found him very pleasant. Handsome too, if I must admit to it. You got the sense he admired me, you said?"

"Absolutely," Patience said. "Clear as day."

"Perhaps he does not mind that I am not lively with quips and jokes, then."

"I imagine he'd be delighted to entertain you and make you laugh. People who are amusing do like an audience."

"Yes, that is very true," Lady Alice said. "I have noticed that."

"I understand Lord Kendrickson stays on this very square. Have you not encountered him by chance?"

"No, indeed I have not," Lady Alice said.

"You ought to go on strolls round the square. I am sure you would encounter him. Of course, you might also encounter my aunt, Lady Marchfield, as she lives just across the way, but she is not half so fun. Just think, if you were to encounter Lord Kendrickson, you might have a conversation."

"Goodness, Lady Patience, you seem so savvy to the ways of the world."

"I do?" Patience said laughing. "I cannot think that can be the case."

"I am glad you came to see me today," Lady Alice said. "Ever since I have arrived in Town, I have felt rather a lone bird looking for its flock. You are my friend, I think?"

"Of course I am your friend," Patience said.

Lady Alice very prettily blushed. "I will speak to my mama about the dinner your father hosts. I am certain she will approve and my papa leaves such judgments with her to decide."

"Excellent. Oh, by the by, if they say anything about my father being unusual in any way, just explain that he really is not. If one does not know him, he could *seem* mad, but he is as sane as you or I."

With that helpful advice, Patience took her leave of a rather startled Lady Alice.

MARCUS WAS NOT at all fond of musical evenings. Especially not Lady Jenner's annual musical evening. A usual evening might consist of some performers thought to be very good. The problem was not that he did not enjoy the music, it was the endless sitting and listening. If he could read a book he'd be happy to sit all night. As it was, simply staring at the musicians was tiring. He always ended working to keep his eyes open.

Lady Jenner's evening took the torture another step further. They were not to hear from professionals, but rather a slew of young ladies who would demonstrate their musical talent. Such as it was.

Last year, Miss Raynard played the pianoforte for so long that her father finally walked forward and tapped her on the shoulder. Lady Rose's hands shook to such a degree that there had been just as many wrong notes as right.

At the conclusion of each performance, it was necessary to applaud as if one had just heard from a famous proficient. After every hopeful lady had finally gone her turn, compliments of the most overblown sort were handed all round.

Nevertheless, he would attend. For one, Lady Jenner had known him long and would notice his absence. For another, he suspected that Lady Alice would attend to showcase her talent.

From everything he'd heard of the lady, it felt a duty to get to know her. As she had been described—quiet, thoughtful, and measured—she fit the description of precisely what he looked for in a wife. Not at all like Lady Patience, who stared him down and made direct, and probably mocking, comments.

Of course, he could not deny that Lady Patience was lovely to look at. As well, there had been something moving in her description of her family life. There had been an ease and warmth to it. Her father, she said, was the best of men.

It was endlessly intriguing to Marcus that there were people who enjoyed spending time in their family home with doting parents. He could not quite imagine how it would be.

As he and Radler dismounted their horses and handed them over to a groom, Radler said, "Did you bring your looking-for-a-particular-sort-of-wife checklist in your coat pocket?"

"Very funny."

"Say Stanford, in the interest of efficiency, why don't you make up a form of inquiry and then you can hand out a copy to any lady you encounter. Gather all the facts, as it were."

"Still not funny," Marcus said. He was beginning to feel as if he were the only man in London who wished to proceed carefully before committing himself in marriage forevermore.

"I only say," Radler pressed on, "you are looking at this from every angle but the right one. In the end, your heart will not be denied. The heart is never defeated in such matters. The heart rules all."

"Thank you for the sage advice, Mr. Shakespeare," Marcus said drily.

They entered Lady Jenner's great hall and the lady herself beamed at them. She was a tall and broad matron with a fondness for damask. She had such a fondness for that heavy material that at times she appeared a walking pair of curtains. Nobody would hold it against her though, she was a very genial personality.

"Ah," Lady Jenner said, "two of my favorite bachelors have not let me down."

Marcus bowed. "I look forward to the invitation each year, Lady Jenner."

Lady Jenner laughed and smacked his arm with her fan. "Nicely said, and I do not believe a word of it. Now, in compensation for your kind attendance, I believe you will find an excellent claret waiting for you on the sideboard."

Marcus nodded, as indeed it would be one of the highlights of the evening. Lady Jenner always made certain that her audience was well-watered to withstand the performances to come.

They made their way into the music room. It had been set up with narrow rectangular tables each having four chairs lined on one side. This was another of Lady Jenner's clever arrangements. One could take what was wished for from the sideboard and have a place to set it down. And, there was quite a lot someone might wish for—baskets of grapes, rolls, herbed butter, cold meats, pickled vegetables, baked chickens quartered, pastries, cakes, bottles of ale, a tea and coffee service, and dozens of wine bottles all scrupulously labeled with bottle tickets.

"Ah, there is Lady Alice," Radler said. "Grab your list of questions of suitability and let us make our way over."

"I do not have a list," Marcus said. "I merely intend to proceed in a rational and cautious manner. You would do well to do the same."

"I would if I could," Radler said. "But my heart will rule me. I will be as Romeo pining after Juliet. Once I find my Juliet, obviously."

Marcus snorted derisively. "Have a care you don't both end up dead then, Romeo."

And then he saw her, Lady Patience. She looked positively glorious in a dark blue silk dress with an elegant cut, done in a restrained hand. Her only adornment was a string of pearls round her slim neck.

He felt stopped in his tracks as she flashed him a smile. He would have to be careful there. The lady did have an effect on him that he felt was counter to applying rationality and common sense.

PATIENCE HAD CHOSEN her dark blue silk for Lady Jenner's soiree. She thought it suited her very well and it was precisely the sort of thing she liked—not overly fussy and made with a clean and elegant cut. It was a dress that got to the point, rather than meander round in ruffles and bits and bobs.

She did not know if she would encounter Lord Stanford at the party, but if she did, she wished to look well.

Lady Alice had sent over a note in the late afternoon, accepting the offer to come to dine. This caused Patience to think over what Lady Alice had said about her temperament and what she looked for. If only Lord Kendrickson was apprised of the idea that the lady liked to laugh.

Then it came to her. She wrote out an unsigned note and had Charlie change out of his livery to his regular clothes to deliver it.

Lord Kendrickson—

I write this anonymously to give you vital information. Lady Alice appears to have a staid and serious temperament. However, she likes to be amused. Do not put on an always serious face in an effort to impress. Be yourself. Make her laugh and you may get somewhere.

A Friend

Interestingly, Mr. Grimsby did not seem at all alarmed that one of his footmen had changed out of his livery and sauntered out of the house. He only shrugged as if he did not care what happened next. Patience assumed that whatever Mrs. Right was doing to speed him out of the house was well underway.

Lady Alice's note had also mentioned she would attend Lady Jenner and hoped to see Patience there too.

Patience had told her father about it in the carriage. "I find her ever so nice," she said. "She wishes to be my friend and of course I accepted."

"She sounds terrific," the duke said. "A regular paragon of geniality."

Patience laughed. "I see you tease me, Papa. However, I think it's important for a lady to develop and maintain friendships with other ladies."

"I see," the duke said, smiling. "Six sisters were not enough to satisfy the requirement. I ought to have quit producing all these females sooner."

"But then you would not have Valor, and I know you adore her."

"She is a funny little thing."

"Do you think Lord Stanford will fall in love with Lady Alice?" Patience said. The question had nothing to do with their current conversation, but it was the question at the forefront of her mind. Even though Lady Alice wished to be amused and so far Lord Stanford had not shown himself particularly amusing, if he were to prefer her…well what lady could resist him?

"Why should Stanford be taken with your new friend?" the duke asked.

Patience gave a little shrug. "I do not know. It is only that he might prefer a lady like her. Temperament-wise, you see. I feel he is more serious than we are used to. And then, Lady Alice is serious and though she says she is not interested in someone very like her…"

"God save me from a serious man, nothing more tedious."

"Oh Papa, you will not condemn him for it?"

"No, no, I rarely condemn anybody outside of Lady Misery. My advice? If Stanford's a serious sort of fellow, shake it out of him. What's he got to be serious about? He's young, he's rich, he's not got a care in the world. If he's too serious now, what will he be like twenty years from now? Crotchety, that's what."

They had arrived to Lady Jenner's house and the duke had laughed uproariously when the lady made him promise not to set her curtains alight. It seemed absolutely everybody knew he had once set Lady Vanderwake's curtains on fire, though it had been twenty years ago.

A footman led them forward and they entered a room with rows of chairs and narrow tables. Sideboards groaning under a whole array of offerings lined the walls of the room. "Goodness, do you suppose we are to see some sort of play or tableau?" Patience asked. "Oh, but there is a pianoforte, perhaps we are to have a singer. I hope it is not operatic; I do not really care for it."

"It'll be some kind of palaver," the duke said. "At least there is a well-stocked sideboard. And tables along with the chairs—a very sensible idea."

"There is Lady Alice," Patience said. "I will go and see her."

"I will go and see the sideboard," the duke said, making his way there.

Patience hurried to Lady Alice's side.

"Mama," Lady Alice said, "this is my friend, Lady Patience."

Patience curtsied to the matron. "Lady Kembleford," she said.

"Ah, Lady Patience, very good to know you. My daughter has told me of your kind invitation to dine."

Patience nodded. "Thank you for allowing her to come, Lady Kembleford."

The lady nodded. Then, looking over Patience's head, she said, "Gracious, there is Lady Violet, I've not seen her in an age. I must catch up."

With that, she sailed off to reacquaint herself with Lady Violet.

"I am glad you are here," Lady Alice said. "I find myself unaccountably nervous."

Patience thought that was indeed unaccountable. Why should Lady Alice be nervous? They were only attending a small party.

"I suppose it's the idea of so many people staring that makes me uneasy."

Patience glanced around but could not identify the people staring. Who did she think was staring?

"Well, I suppose I make too much of it. I suppose people will spend very little time considering me and will likely be thinking of their own affairs as I play."

Now Patience began to understand Lady Alice. "Oh, I see, Lady Jenner has pressed you into playing the pianoforte." She really did not see how Lady Alice had allowed herself to be pressed into such a thing. Patience herself would not have, even if she *could* play an instrument.

Just then, Patience saw Lord Stanford enter the room with Lord Radler. She smiled at him. He was looking smashing!

"I suppose she's pressed us all, has she not?" Lady Alice asked.

Patience turned toward her. "All? She said nothing to me about it. Only that she was glad I'd agreed to come."

"It was in the invitation, though," Lady Alice said. "It is a musical evening and all the young ladies are expected to play."

"Play?" Patience asked. "Play what?"

Lady Alice looked at her quizzically. "The pianoforte, usually. Though there is a harp tucked in the corner so perhaps that too. I imagine she's got a guitar and a violin somewhere as well."

CHAPTER SIX

PATIENCE STARED AT Lady Alice. They were meant to play music? That's why the chairs were set in rows?

"Are you quite well, Lady Patience?" Lady Alice asked.

"No, not really. You see, my aunt filled out my social calendar and all it said for this one was that it was a soiree. Lady Alice, I cannot play a note!"

Lady Alice was wide-eyed. "Certainly, you exaggerate. When you said so to me when you came to visit, I did assume you were only modest."

"No, not modest," Patience said.

"You do not play anything?" Lady Alice asked.

"Not anything," Patience said.

Lord Stanford was making his way toward her. This was a musical evening. She was meant to play for an audience. What was she to do?

All those scoldings from Miss Pynchon, and the vicar even, were coming to pass. Miss Pynchon had many times said that having musical ability was de rigeur and had argued with Mrs. Right about getting the pianoforte tuned. Patience had thought the idea that she did not play an instrument might be casually mentioned to a husband at some point. She had not thought of a public unmasking.

"Lady Patience," Lord Stanford said.

Then he looked pointedly at Lady Alice. He wished to be

introduced. Of course he did. *People* had told him he must.

"Lord Stanford," she said, as her mind raced on what to do about her current predicament, "may I present Lady Alice Gerhard, daughter of the Earl of Kembleford."

Lady Alice curtsied.

Lord Radler joined them, having made a stop at the sideboard for a glass of wine. "Lady Alice, Lady Patience. I am delighted to be one of the audience to hear your musical stylings."

Musical stylings! She did not have any musical stylings. She did not have any stylings of any sort. Think, think, think, Patience, think faster than you have ever thought before. How to avoid playing?

Was there any possibility that she *could* play?

No, of course not. Their pianoforte in the Dales had not even been tuned in years. Her only lessons had been rudimentary and she recalled very little of them. She'd have better luck playing on some of the ridiculous instruments she'd read about in her father's library.

As they'd only had a governess for a short period, most of Patience's education was self-directed by picking up odd facts and bits of information from whatever books took her fancy. There had been that one book full of pictures of all sorts of instruments nobody played anymore.

Patience paused. If nobody played them, then nobody would own them. Lady Jenner would not own them.

What if she claimed she only played one of those mysterious instruments?

Lord Radler and Lord Stanford were listening as Lady Alice spoke of her favorite musical pieces and which one she would play for the party.

Then it came to her. The crwth. It was an odd stringed in-strument, a little like a lyre and only played in Wales. Even there, not widely these days. Certainly, Lady Jenner would not have even heard of it.

"And you, Lady Patience?" Lord Stanford said. "What did you

plan on playing this evening?"

Patience could see Lady Alice flush for her, as she already knew the terrible truth. With any luck though, Lady Alice would be the only one to ever know it.

"I am afraid I may have to disappoint Lady Jenner," Patience said. "I play the crwth and while I am sure I directed it to be put in the luggage carriage this season, it was somehow missed. It is just now sitting in my father's music room in the Dales."

"The crwth?" Lord Stanford asked.

Patience nodded. Now that she'd picked a direction, she'd best keep going with it. "It is an old Welsh stringed instrument. Unfortunately, they are not widely available."

"And you play the crwth to the exclusion of all else?" Lord Radler asked. "That is very original."

"Indeed," Patience said, for lack of anything more astute to say regarding how or why she played an old Welsh instrument that nobody had ever heard of.

The duke sauntered over to their party and Patience stared meaningfully at him. He would have to go along with the crwth idea or the story would fall apart.

"Stanford, Radler," he said, "and this must be the famed Lady Alice."

Lady Alice curtsied. "Your Grace."

"Your Grace," Lord Radler said, "Lady Patience was just telling us that she plays the crwth and it has been unfortunately left behind at home."

The duke's brows raised just the slightest bit.

"You see, Papa, this is a musical evening where all the young ladies are meant to play," Patience said, looking at him meaning-fully.

"Ah, yes of course," the duke said, instantly perceiving the situation. "And you've left your crwth behind in the Dales."

"Just so."

"Well, a disappointment all round," the duke said. "We'd better let Lady Jenner in on the situation." The duke turned round and saw the lady on the far side of the room. "Lady Jenner," he called, "if you will."

Lady Jenner heard his call and made her way to them forthwith, likely concerned there was some musical question to be settled. Which there was.

"Is there a piece of music you are looking for?" Lady Jenner asked. "I have quite the wide selection."

"No, nothing of that sort. My daughter and I only wished to express our regrets. We'd entirely forgot this was a musical evening. Patience plays the crwth, I'd wonder if you've ever even heard of it, but she's very fond of it. Sadly, it has been left behind at home, I'm afraid. Very careless on our part."

"Very careless," Patience confirmed.

She had expected Lady Jenner to react with some sort of disappointment or resignation. Or perhaps confusion as to how they'd forgot it was a musical evening. Why did she look like the sun had just come out on a cloudy day?

"Lady Patience, you are in luck. The earl owns a crwth, they are so rare these days, are they not? It is in the library in a glass case. Goodness, he shall be very tickled that somebody knows how to play it. Come, come—follow me!"

Patience could feel the blood drain from her face. Why did Lady Jenner own a crwth? Now she would have to play the crwth? She had not the first idea how to even begin—she'd only seen a drawing of it.

She looked toward her father, whose brow was decidedly wrinkled.

"Come now, Lady Patience, let us not tarry," Lady Jenner said, taking her by the arm. "Goodness, this is exciting."

She was led away and the duke followed, though Patience had not the first idea what they were to do now. Should she pretend to faint?

Lady Jenner hustled them down the hall to the library, leaving go of Patience's arm to throw open the doors and hurry to the glass case.

While Lady Jenner's back was turned, the duke tapped Patience on the shoulder. He pointed to the door, and then to her hand.

She thought she understood his meaning.

With no time to lose, the duke shut the door with a thump and then cried, "My dear, are you all right? I have caught your hand in the doorframe."

Patience cried out as if in pain and then scratched at her fingers to make them red.

"Oh dear, Papa, that does hurt!"

Lady Jenner came running back to them. "What's happened?"

Patience held her hand gently, as if every bone in it was broken. "It was just an accident. My papa shut the door and my hand was caught."

"Gracious," Lady Jenner said, peering down at the hand in question. "Oh dear, it is very red. I hope there is not a bone broken."

"Likely not," the duke said, "but I'll have my physician have a look at it on the morrow. For now, I think the most sensible course is to get it wrapped and keep it still."

"Yes, of course, oh dear I feel as if this is my fault, our butler is fond of forever oiling the door hinges so they do not creak, but I really feel it makes the doors rather unpredictable."

"Yes, I believe that is it," the duke said. "It got away from me somehow. Well, no need to blame him, I prefer a well-oiled hinge myself."

Lady Jenner heaved a deep sigh. "As does my lord, so I cannot fault my butler for it. But now you will not have the opportunity to play your beloved crwth."

Patience nodded with what she hoped was a look of deep sadness, though she felt rather giddy. She would not have to pretend to know how to play a crwth. She felt as if she had skated on very thin ice and somehow made it to the other side of the pond without plunging into icy water.

"Well at least have a look at the earl's specimen—there are so few crwths about anymore."

Lady Jenner led them to the glass case and Patience stared down at it. So that was a crwth. Thank the stars above that it would stay under glass, right where it belonged.

MARCUS COULD NOT imagine what had gone on. First, Lady Patience had informed them that she only played the crwth and had inadvertently left her instrument at home. Then Lady Jenner remarkably had that item and they had gone to retrieve it.

He'd been rather looking forward to hearing it, as he never had before. However, when Lady Patience returned, she had a bandaged hand. The duke had managed to slam his daughter's hand in a door and blame it on a well-oiled hinge.

Despite her injury, she was looking rather cheerful.

"Now, Stanford," the duke said, "I will depend on you to manage the patient. As it was my girl's right hand, she will need assistance. Patience? I suppose you will like a glass of Canary?"

Lady Patience nodded, and Marcus was sent off to do the duke's bidding. He was not at all sure how he had been assigned to assist Lady Patience, rather than her own father.

He was not entirely opposed, of course. The lady really was marvelous to look at and then there seemed to be that magnetic quality to her, that aliveness, that he'd noticed.

When he returned with her glass of Canary, Lady Patience was seated with one chair to her right and her father seated to her left.

It was clear enough where he was meant to sit. He felt the slightest twinge over it, as Lady Alice was seated three rows ahead of him. He really had cemented it in his mind that he ought to become better acquainted with the lady, as she was so advertised to be the sort of lady that would be suited to him.

He'd been introduced to her, at least. He'd not felt anything in particular upon the introduction. There had not been an immediate attraction, but he supposed that was because he never had gravitated to her sort of coloring. Her black hair and pale skin felt harsh to his eyes and he preferred a softer coloring. Like Lady Patience's coloring.

However, and it was an *important* however, a lady's coloring was not to dictate his direction. He must use rational sense built of verifiable facts. Hair eventually turned to gray but temperament stayed steady throughout one's life.

Marcus set down Lady Patience's glass of wine as Lady Jenner sorted people into seats so she could get the evening going.

Lady Patience lifted her injured hand and then, seeming to remember it *was* injured, laid it back in her lap and used her left hand to take her wine.

"I hope you are not too disappointed that you will not have the opportunity to play the crwth," he said.

"I'm devastated, naturally. Though, one has to put one's chin up in the face of disappointments, does not one?" Lady Patience said.

"Yes, I suppose so."

The duke leaned forward. "All my daughters are very stalwart." He paused. "Except for Valor, but she might grow into it."

"Valor is my youngest sister," Lady Patience said. "We cannot convince her that the foxes roaming the Dales are not women being murdered. She even accused the vicar of somehow being involved in the murders."

The duke chuckled. "Now she thinks the butler who is currently incommoding my household might murder us all in our beds because he's an army man. Well, she'll settle as soon as that fellow is gone."

Marcus was not certain what to make of that statement. Did the duke say he did not care for his current butler and that fellow had plans to leave the duke's service? It was deuced inconvenient to lose a butler. The senior footman would jockey for the position whether he was ready for it or not. Staff always disliked a new man coming in if that was to be the case.

Whatever decision was made, it would throw everybody into an upset that would take months to settle. A household staff was a delicate balance of personalities and hierarchies.

"Our aunt, Lady Marchfield, keeps hiring butlers for my father," Lady Patience said, "but we do not wish for one, so our housekeeper gets rid of them for us."

Marcus was certain he was fairly wide-eyed. They did not want a butler? Their housekeeper was tasked with getting rid of them? How did she get rid of them? Was there violence involved? How many had been got rid of? Where were they now?

"We know how we like our house run, and so does Mrs. Right," the duke said. "We are snug and comfortable just as we are."

Lady Patience patted her father's hand. "That is a very apt description, Papa—we are snug and comfortable. In the Dales, we do things just as we like them."

"That's right—we don't go in for doing what everybody else does just because they do it. We arrange things to our liking and society's opinion be damned."

"You will see when you come to dine, Lord Stanford," Lady Patience said. "All my sisters will be at table. We do not make the younger of my sisters stay away as others might. It would not be fair to them."

The duke laughed. "I suppose Winsome would have some choice words for us if we tried it."

It all sounded exceedingly odd, and yet there was something to consider in it. For all the eccentricity of it, there was a distinct undercurrent of... what? Solidarity? Of close-knit attachment? Of ease? Contentment?

Marcus was not altogether certain. It did prompt him to think far into the future though. Up until now, he'd employed a falcon-like focus on making the right choice of wife. He'd not thought much beyond that.

If he *did* think beyond that, what would his household look like day to day? What would his household feel like? How would children be treated?

Marcus did not have any example to go on, as all he could be sure of was what he did not want. He did not want his parents' household.

It was becoming rather interesting to ascertain how other people lived. How the duke and Lady Patience lived.

If it really was true, then snug and comfortable sounded... well, it sounded snug and comfortable. He'd not really thought of that as a possibility. There had been times when he'd felt snug and comfortable at his club—a cold rainy day, hot coffee, and a newspaper. He'd been very content at those moments. His club had been a haven.

Could that sort of atmosphere be had at home? It seemed almost impossible.

But perhaps it was possible? Perhaps he'd been shooting too low? He'd been seeking to establish a household where there was not constant shouting. His idea of success had been a reserved and polite arrangement.

Could there be more, though?

He was rather looking forward to attending the duke's dinner and having a closer look at snug and comfortable.

Lady Jenner called everyone to attention and the musical evening began. Marcus did not mind it as much as he usually did—he wished for time to think and he *would* think while one lady after the next played.

Lady Alice was the first to display her talent. She played a lively Irish air to great acclaim.

Though, Marcus did find himself a bit startled regarding the enthusiasm with which Lady Patience clapped at the end of it. He hoped she did not do further damage to her injured hand.

CHAPTER SEVEN

KENDRICKSON HAD BEEN flummoxed to receive an anonymous note regarding Lady Alice. At first, he wondered if it were a jest of some sort. Perhaps Radler had sent it. Perhaps the fellow thought it might be amusing to prompt him into trying to make the serious Lady Alice laugh.

But no, Radler understood his circumstances and would not tamper with his chances. The stakes were too high and Radler was not cruel.

Then it occurred to him that it might be from another gentleman interested in Lady Alice. Someone who wished for him to make a mistake and ruin his own chances.

That did not seem quite right either. Then an idea came upon him that seemed as if it must answer.

Lady Patience.

Who else had he had such a frank conversation with? He'd even said he would try to match Lady Alice in seriousness, though it might prove difficult.

Further, he'd seen Lady Patience and her maid go into Lady Alice's house on the square. She might have got the information then.

He'd been watching Lady Alice's house when he could; it was just in view from the drawing room window. He kept hoping he would see her out for a stroll, and then he would stroll too.

It would really be something if the information was correct.

Lady Alice was heartbreakingly pretty; if she were not quite as serious as she initially appeared, that would be smashing. They might really get on, there might really be something there.

If it were true, if she liked to laugh, well, he would make her laugh.

He sat at the drawing room's bow window, note in hand, feeling very buoyed by the idea.

Thank you, Lady Patience.

At least, I think it was you.

PATIENCE HAD GOT ready early as her sisters were to arrive well ahead of the other guests. Grace and Lord Dashlend had come first, along with their very young son. The boy was up on his feet, but not particularly steady. He'd crashed round the drawing room with everybody sprinting to catch him when he seemed near to going headlong into a piece of furniture. He'd slowed down occasionally to point at something in the room and say its name. When Nelson came into the room, he was like a magnet to the boy.

Nelson was both intrigued and wary of the toddler. The boy shouted "dog" and was determined to catch Nelson. Nelson did not seem sure if they were playing a game or if he were in danger.

Young Miles Delatore was adorable but exhausting and finally Mrs. Right came for him and took him below stairs to his nursemaid. They had set up a contained area in the servants' hall that was surrounded by pillows and blankets so if he fell, which he would, there would be no harm done.

They heard him shouting "bisk" all the way down the hall, which was apparently meant to mean biscuit, as he was obsessed with that item.

Felicity arrived next, with Mr. Stratton in tow, and what a shock that had been. She was decidedly pregnant, as big as a house really.

Patience had not seen Grace when she was with child and so the sight of one of her sisters in such an expanded condition had really taken her aback. It did not look very comfortable.

Now, the three eldest sisters sat at the back of the drawing room having a confidential conversation. Serenity, Verity, Winsome, and Valor had been sent off to check that arrangements were proceeding in the dining room. One never knew these days, as Mr. Grimsby had seemed to give up any notion of supervising things.

"Why did you not write that you expected a child, Felicity?" Grace asked.

"I wished to surprise everybody."

"I am definitely surprised," Patience said, laughing.

"Poor Percy was very against us coming to Town in my condition," Felicity said, "but I told him I would fret terribly if I was not on hand to lend my support to my sister. He does not like me to fret."

"But can you attend parties and routs and things?" Patience asked. She'd never seen a lady so large out and about, except a farmer's wife, as they seemed indefatigable.

"Only where I am known well and it is a small affair. Percy absolutely put his foot down about that. He says he does not mind shocking a little but does not care to shock the whole world. Other ladies might try it and pretend they do not notice the wide-eyed staring, but he convinced me I would not like it."

"From the looks of you," Grace said, "you will be having this baby while you are in Town."

"I expect so," Felicity said. "Now, enough about my situation. We've come to support our sister for her coming out season."

"How do you get on, Patience?" Grace asked.

"I think I will know more after tonight. You know how I am—decisive. I do not dilly-dally around."

"So you have made up your mind?" Felicity asked.

Patience nodded. "The instant I saw him. Lord Stanford, he

comes tonight with his friend, Lord Radler. Lord Stanford is positively glorious, wait until you see him."

Grace grasped Patience's hand. "Do you suppose he might speak to Papa as early as tonight?"

And here was the sticking point. She might not wish to admit the sticking point to an outsider, but her sisters must know all.

"Well… no. You see, I have made up my mind, but things seem a little up in the air on his side."

"Oh, I see," Felicity said, "he's not said anything to you yet."

"Nothing at all, really. I do get the idea that he finds me attractive; he looks at me when he thinks I won't notice."

"Very good sign," Felicity said.

"But there is this idea going round about him. That he's cautious, or careful, or something like that. And I have seen some signs of it. I fear he may not be a gentleman who will declare himself quickly."

"But Patience," Grace said, "would you really be happy with someone who… took their time on things. As you… do not."

Patience was well aware of what Grace meant to say. Further, it was a matter she had given some thought to.

"I think I would. You see, Lady Alice, you will meet her tonight, she is looking for someone not as serious as she is. Well, she is not over-serious, she just seems so because she does not joke and jest. She is not skilled at witty repartee. She wishes for someone who is skilled in that direction—to balance her out. Might I not do the same?"

"That is a very good notion, actually," Felicity said. "After all, if you were to wed a toe tapper, and you know you are one, the two of you would be rushing headlong through life."

"That is just how I view it," Patience said. She was gratified that Felicity saw her reasoning. She was not unaware of her impatient proclivities and that they might be modified. At least a little bit.

Just then, they heard the distinct sound of carriage wheels on the street.

Patience and Grace leapt up from the sofa in their cozy corner. Felicity attempted the same, but halfway up she lost momentum and crashed back down. Her sisters took hold of either arm and hauled her and her enormous middle to her feet.

Charlie had answered the door, as Mr. Grimsby could not be bothered. He led Lord Stanford and Lord Radler into the drawing room.

The duke made the introductions all round, though it seemed their guests were both known to Patience's brothers-in-law. She was pleased to see that they all appeared to approve of one another.

She could not help but notice that Lord Stanford looked exceedingly surprised at Felicity's current condition. Nor that Felicity's husband, Mr. Stratton, wore a somewhat apologetic look for it.

Lady Alice arrived not long after, and the duke once more made the rounds of introductions.

"Well I suppose we need not wander round the drawing room incessantly, eh, Grimsby?" the duke said. "Can we go through?"

Mr. Grimsby shrugged and said, "Sure."

Patience could not quite fathom Mr. Grimsby's current state of mind. It was no matter though, the dinner was set to begin. She had carefully arranged the seating with no nod to tradition whatsoever. She would be on one side of Lord Stanford and Lady Alice would be on the other side. She must confirm her ideas that there was nothing between those two people. And that there was something between herself and the lord.

MARCUS HAD EXPECTED he would meet with some sort of eccentricity in the duke's household from what he'd heard from Lady Patience and what he'd seen of the duke himself.

He'd not quite imagined a lady on the verge of delivering a child though. He'd never encountered a well-born lady in such a condition and it was alarming to say the least. He was well aware it was becoming the fashion to go anywhere and everywhere regardless of how expanded the lady might be, and he'd had a glancing and distant view of some examples at the opera or the theater, but he'd not seen it up close. He at once comprehended how so many women died in childbirth—it seemed impossible that it could be done without a mortal injury.

As if that were not surprising enough, the butler was downright careless. He'd already heard from the duke that the butler was not wanted and was to be driven out by the housekeeper. Well, if this was the sort of butler they employed, it was not a wonder that they did not want one. The man looked positively bored.

They had repaired to the dining room and noted pretty handdrawn place cards in front of each setting that seemed to flout any ideas of rank. People were placed willy-nilly, husbands and wives sat next to each other, and the youngest, who really should not be there at all, was seated at the duke's right.

As for himself, he found Lady Patience on one side and Lady Alice on the other and so he could not be entirely opposed to the unorthodox seating plan.

Radler was on Lady Alice's other side with Lady Winsome on his other side. Marcus did not know what to make of the younger daughters at table, but fortunately that would be Radler's problem and not his own.

The duke dinged one of his forks against his wine glass. "We'd best get things straight before we begin," he said. "We only host small dinners for a reason. We are cozy enough that we will all talk together, so throw out the window any idea of turning to this seatmate and then that, like it's a ritual dance. Also, my youngest daughter has something to say before we commence."

The youngest, Lady Valor, rose from her chair with a look of nervous determination.

What on earth could she say? Why was she to say anything? She should be above stairs in the nursery.

"I wished to bid you welcome," Lady Valor said.

Marcus nodded toward her. If that was it, well he supposed it was prettily enough done.

"Because—"

And there was more.

"Someday all my sisters will be married and I will be left here alone and will be my father's hostess. I, myself, will never get married because… well, the man will sleep in the same room with you and it's scary. Do they watch you sleep? We think Mr. Stratton watches Felicity sleep and now look what's happened to her! She looks very bad!"

With that very alarming statement, Lady Valor curtsied and sat down.

"Well now," the duke said, "I did not know Valor would say precisely that, but here we are."

The footmen snorted as they came round to fill the wine glasses. The lackadaisical butler leaned on the sideboard watching the proceedings. Marcus picked up his glass and took a rather ungentlemanly swig.

At least the wine was very good.

"Never mind how this happened to me," Lady Felicity said, "you must just be assured, Valor, that Percy and I are exceedingly happy over it."

Mr. Stratton had turned red at the insinuation that he had something to do with Lady Felicity's current condition. Lady Valor only shook her head with a decided look of pity.

Behind him, Marcus heard the dining room doors creak open. He glanced over his shoulder to see a mangy-looking cur who was missing a leg and had one eye clouded over make its way into the room. Had it got in from the street?

None of the family seemed at all taken aback to see such a sight, that sight disappearing under the table.

"That is Nelson," Lady Patience said for his enlightenment. "We found him on the road last year."

Marcus was not at all surprised to hear the dog was found on the road. Where else would it have been found? What it was currently doing under the dining room table was another question.

"You see what it is to have seven daughters, Stanford," the duke said. "You end up with a three-legged and half-blind dog."

"As soon as I saw him," Lady Serenity said, "I wept and knew he must come with us. He was hanging about an inn, living on scraps. *Scraps*, you understand!"

"Scraps!" Lady Verity repeated. "A very usual case, but we would not stand for it."

"Scraps," Lady Winsome said in a dark tone.

"Now he chases Mrs. Wendover and sometimes I have to rescue her out of a closet," Lady Valor said.

Good God, who was Mrs. Wendover? Was she an elderly relative? If she was, they ought not allow the dog to chase her. If she ended in a closet, she did not sound up to the task of outrunning a three-legged and half-blind dog.

"Mrs. Wendover likes Nelson, and also she doesn't like Nelson, depending on where she ends up," Lady Valor said.

He was beginning to feel very sorry for Mrs. Wendover.

"Mrs. Wendover is Valor's stuffed rabbit," Lady Patience said, by way of explanation.

That at least made more sense. Though, he must be cognizant of the idea that his mind had leapt to the notion of an elderly relative running from the dog. He thought it indicated his impressions of what might be possible in this household.

Just then, Marcus felt something. He surreptitiously glanced down and saw that Nelson the three-legged dog had settled himself on top of his boot. Apparently, the dog knew the soup course would bring nothing interesting and took that moment to relax until more promising items arrived to table.

The soup was cleared and the next course arrived. Marcus

would admit the duke maintained a fine table. The platters covered every available surface, to be served à la francaise, which he preferred. There was beginning to be a notion in some elevated households of taking on the habit of serving à la russe, which he did not prefer and did not even think made sense. How is one to know how much to eat of one dish if one did not know what was still coming? A menu being provided gave a hint, but Marcus would prefer to have a look at a dish before deciding. Too many times, something *sounded* inviting, only to arrive swimming in a beige sauce of some sort. He could not abide a beige sauce.

The duke had ordered roasted beef, a large ham, Scottish salmon, quails, duckling, and every conceivable vegetable in season. There were vol-a-vents of mushrooms, a lamb pie, salad, and buttered rolls.

To Marcus' deep surprise, the butler leaning against the sideboard just poured himself a glass of wine and drank it. The footmen appeared to find it very amusing.

Lady Patience cut off a piece of her slice of roasted beef and handed it under the table to the three-legged dog. The dog leapt off his boot, took it, and then began to make his way round the table to see what else might be dropped in his direction.

"I know it is not usual to have one's dog in the dining room and feed it under the table," Lady Patience said.

Marcus nodded, as it certainly was not. A lady had a lap dog in the drawing room and a gentleman had his hunting dogs in their kennels. This dog was neither here nor there.

"But we had to take into consideration Nelson's unique circumstances. He had such a terrible start in life—losing a leg, going blind in one eye, and living on scraps—that we became determined that the rest of his life should be lovely and warm and full of ease. Especially regarding food, as that seems to be his primary interest."

"I see," Marcus said. He could not help but to be a little touched by the sentiment. He supposed most ladies would not countenance a dog that was not pleasant to look at, and this one certainly was not, never mind concern themselves with what that dog ate or what the dog felt about it.

"As you have seen," Lady Patience went on, with a small sigh, "we are not very formal people. It's the Dales in us. I suppose you were raised in a formal household?"

The question took him aback, as he was beginning to notice Lady Patience had a proclivity for doing. Not many ladies, or any, would pose such a personal question to a gentleman newly met.

"Relatively formal, yes," he said.

"I know that is what society expects, but I do not think I should like it," Lady Patience said.

"Formal is overrated," the duke said, joining in on the discussion. "A bunch of people doing things they do not want to do, simply because some mysterious arbiter said they ought to. Just think, how would I know anything about my daughters if I had not had them all at table every night?"

"We sit with him while he drinks his port," Lady Winsome said.

"So he does not get too drunk," Lady Valor added.

"If he is alone with the bottle," Lady Verity said, "he is bored and drinks it all. A very common thing."

"Grace used to throw rolls at his head, which was very funny," Lady Valor said, "because she never hit him!"

All of the daughters laughed heartily over the picture. Marcus did not know what to think of this information. On the one hand, it was very wrong on all counts—the dog, staying on at table, hinting that a duke would ever get drunk, all of it. It was off-putting, even.

On the other hand, there was something that struck him rather deeply about the duke wishing to know his daughters well and the care they all took of a three-legged and exceedingly unattractive dog. He did not know what to make of it. He did not know if it were right or wrong or up or down.

"Also," Lady Winsome said, "if our father does not drink too much port or brandy alone, he can bring the bottle into the drawing room, and we can play Fact or Fib."

Marcus could not imagine what Fact or Fib was, but perhaps that might be for the best considering the expressions on both Stratton's and Dashlend's faces. It was some combination of dread and resignation.

"It is a very amusing game, I assure you," Lady Grace said.

Dashlend muttered something he did not quite hear. The duke laughed uproariously. "He says, don't believe her for a minute! Very good."

"The duke gave me some very good advice when I was first faced with it," Stratton said. "He told me, 'prepare to lose'."

"Will we all be expected to play?" Lady Alice said in barely a whisper.

"Oh yes," Lady Valor said, "it's great fun. Until I get too tired and then I have to go to bed."

"Might I inquire into the nature of the game?" Marcus asked, really preferring to know what lay ahead. "I do not believe I've ever heard of it."

"They invented it," Dashlend said. "That's why nobody has ever heard of it."

"Prepare to drown in blue tickets," Stratton said.

"Two yellow tickets wins, but a blue ticket cancels a yellow," Lady Grace said.

"You are asked a question, you see," Lady Felicity said. "Then the group determines whether it was a fact or a fib."

Marcus began to understand the looks of dread from Stratton and Dashlend.

"The group decides?" Stratton asked. "Do not believe a word of it, Stanford. The sisters decide and it really does not matter whether you tell a fact or a fib."

"Stratton is on to it," the duke said. "That's the reason I bring the port and brandy into the drawing room—you'll need it!"

Marcus felt as if his head was spinning. He had never encountered such a household in his life, nor had he imagined one existed.

On his other side, Lady Alice whispered, "I'm a bit scared."

"I'm sure it's nothing at all," Marcus said quietly. He said it because it seemed the gentlemanly thing to reassure a lady. He was not certain he believed it though.

Was this household one to admire or to run from? He really could not decide. All he could be sure of was that it was nothing at all like the household he'd been raised in.

CHAPTER EIGHT

PATIENCE WAS EXCEEDINGLY buoyed by the dinner. Her family really showed their best sides and Lord Stanford could not help but to be impressed. There were moments where she thought he was positively gobsmacked. Even Nelson had been on his best behavior and had not released the noxious fumes that sometimes overtook him, especially after eating.

Most importantly, she did not detect any particular interest between Lord Stanford and Lady Alice. Lord Radler had spent far more time entertaining that lady than Lord Stanford had.

Sitting so close next to him had been glorious. If she leaned just the littlest bit closer, which she did on several occasions, the air felt warmer, as if there was heat coming from him. His scent was of oakmoss and orange blossom.

She looked forward to getting even closer to him than she had been able to manage at table. In truth, she had taken on the habit of thinking about that circumstance well into the night before she fell asleep.

Everything was falling into place. Now they were to play Fact or Fib and she expected to gather even more information. If she knew her sisters at all, they would press Lord Stanford regarding his inclinations.

The ladies had repaired to the drawing room and, as was her father's usual procedure, the gentleman had not stayed long at table. The duke had ordered the bottles brought in and Patience thought that surely Lord Stanford perceived how comfortable a habit it was.

Serenity and Winsome had dragged chairs from all corners of the drawing room to make a circle round the table. Verity piled the yellow and blue tickets in the center.

"I should go first," Valor said, "because I get tired very suddenly and I never know when it will happen."

"Go on, girl," the duke said.

"Lord Stanford," Valor said.

Patience held her breath. Here was the first question for Lord Stanford.

"Do you think it could be true that foxes can sound like women being murdered?"

Patience let out her breath in a disappointed sigh. The screams on the moors were forever on Valor's mind. She could not be convinced that the sounds were from a fox. She had even once consulted the vicar, who assured her it was a fox. Valor had then accused him of being involved in the murders.

"It is true," Lord Stanford said. "I believe what you have heard is a vixen scream. Unsettling if one is not used to hearing it."

"Fib!" Valor cried, throwing a blue ticket at the lord.

"But it's not—"

Lord Stanford was not given the chance to say what it was not. The duke cut him off. "Never mind it, Stanford. This is why we bring the brandy in. We men are on a sinking ship with no rescue boats in sight."

"Fib!" Valor shouted, handing her father his first blue ticket.

"I'll go," Winsome said. "Lady Alice, have you fallen in love with anybody yet?"

Lady Alice looked to the floor, her cheeks burning as brightly as newly lit kindling. "No," she mumbled.

Patience leapt up. "Fact! Though she probably will fall in love with someone who makes her laugh." She snatched a yellow ticket and handed it to her friend.

"Lord Stanford," Grace said, "what was the first thing you noticed about Patience?"

"Here we go," Mr. Stratton muttered.

Patience hurried to her seat and attempted a look of unconcern. Mr. Stratton was right. Here we did go. What would Lord Stanford say?

"Oh, well, as to that," Lord Stanford said. "I suppose, well, it was probably a sense of liveliness."

Grace, Serenity, and Winsome shouted together. "Fib!"

"It's her hair," Valor said, laughing a little hysterically, like she did when she was overtired. "There's so much of it."

"I see," the lord said quietly.

What did he mean? Her sense of liveliness? As opposed to what? A sense of deadliness? He could have chosen so many other things to notice—her hair, her eyes, her complexion. She did not understand what he meant. Did he not think her pretty?

The game went on, with Lord Radler accused of fibbing when he claimed he was not in love. Then the judgment against him was revised when he explained that he hoped to be in love and his blue ticket was traded out for a yellow ticket. The duke was asked about his sorrow at losing daughters to marriage, as it had become a tradition for him to claim he was delighted and be instantly denounced as a fibber. Valor was eventually sent to bed for accusing them all of fibbing about the foxes, throwing blue tickets at everybody, and then weeping over her outburst.

It all went on amusingly, but for Lord Stanford's answer. Liveliness. What did it mean?

He was so confusing. She knew he looked at her a lot—why would he only come up with liveliness? It was the sort of compliment an older matron might give to an exceedingly plain girl. It was the sort of compliment one made when one was hard-pressed to come up with anything.

The party eventually broke up and there was the usual bustle in the hall as coats were retrieved and carriages called. Felicity leaned over to Patience and said, "I believe he only needs a little prompting."

"Really?" Patience whispered back.

Felicity nodded. "His answer was nonsensical, but I kept a close eye on him. He was often looking at you."

Patience felt a wave of relief upon hearing it. Her instincts could not have been wrong, even though it had seemed for a moment that they might be. He only needed prompting.

She just must figure out how a lady went about prompting, as she did not know the first thing about it. She would ask the duke about it, as she was certain her father would have heard of such a thing.

JUST BEFORE MARCUS' carriage had departed the duke's house a footman had come running out with a fan in his hand. The boy looked up and down the road and audibly sighed.

"Lady Alice left her fan," he said.

"No matter, we can return it on the morrow," Marcus said. "We are to visit a friend on her square, it will be an easy matter to drop it off."

They were to see Kendrickson on the morrow and he, as well as Lady Alice, lived on Bedford Square.

"Thank you, my lord," he said, handing over the fan. The footman paused, then said, "I hope you don't have the wrong idea about that butler in there. He'll be leaving soon. What I mean is, it weren't usual for him to drink wine at the sideboard."

With that, the footman turned and jogged back into the house.

Marcus rapped on the roof and the carriage set off. Radler sat across from Marcus with an amused smile on his face.

"Well, well, well," Radler said.

Marcus looked at him quizzically. "Well, what?"

"Despite your carefully composed ideas of who would suit

you, Lady Alice is out of the running."

"What are you talking about?"

"Come now, Stanford, you did not look once in that lady's direction the entire time we were in the drawing room."

"Nonsense, I am sure I did."

"I am sure you did not. It was all eyes on Lady Patience. As well, if you did have an interest, you would not have agreed to return her fan. Your caution and go slowly flags would have been raised up the mast and flap in a brisk wind. But, having no interest in her, it seemed a small matter."

"I believe you are being both illogical and dramatic. In any case, if I did on occasion look toward Lady Patience, we were in her house."

"Her rather deranged house. You see? That's what's so funny about it. The younger ladies at table, the odd conversation, the three-legged dog under the table, the incompetent butler, Fact or Fib with the youngest of them throwing tickets in our faces over a fox—none of it aligns with your measured ideas."

"They are an unusual household."

"The most unusual, as far as I can tell. Very amusing that you would go for precisely what you thought you did not want."

"Go for? Radler, I would appreciate it if you would keep your wild imaginings to yourself."

Radler shrugged and looked out the window.

Surely, he had looked in Lady Alice's direction as often as Lady Patience's direction. Or perhaps he had not.

The whole evening had been exceedingly odd. And yet, he was drawn to Lady Patience. As for her family, they were entirely eccentric. And yet, there was an underlying something to it. An ease, a confidence in one another as if none of them could step too far wrong in the others' eyes.

Even when Lady Valor had a complete breakdown in civility and thrown the tickets at them, the duke had not been angry. Rather, he'd laughed and said she was overtired. The housekeeper had bustled in and took the young lady to bed with all sorts of soothing words and the promise that Mrs. Wendover, the stuffed rabbit, was already waiting for her.

If his family had been all hard angles and sharp glass, the duke's household was an eccentric feather pillow.

The teasing that went on between them, the daughters all denouncing their father a fibber for claiming he wished to be rid of them… that was a different sort of relationship than he'd ever imagined existed. It was as if they all stood on the solid ground of understanding and could therefore venture into teasing without fear.

Would he be the sort of father who could tease his children, or just laugh when one of them lost all manners from being overtired, or who did not blink when a three-legged dog suddenly turned up?

He did not know. But he was beginning to think he might like to be. He'd been a deeply unhappy child, but the duke's children all marched round as if the world must surely approve of them. There must be something in that.

Should he take the risk of pursuing a lady like Lady Patience? Or rather, should he take the risk of pursuing Lady Patience herself, as he did not suppose there was another like her.

He wanted to. He wanted to since first laying eyes on her. His caution had done its best to steer him away.

"I only say," Radler said, "the heart will rule the head."

Marcus did not answer. Radler might be right, but he was loath to admit that Radler might be right.

In any case, no immediate decisions need be made. If he were to pursue Lady Patience, and he began to think he would, he could still proceed carefully and moderately. There was no need to transform himself into a different person. Despite Radler's opinions, the heart would do well to take a dose of sense from the head.

Kendrickson stared at his two friends. Stanford and Radler had come to see him on Bedford Square to discuss how he might be let into White's without the fees associated with the membership. Stanford was willing to front him the fees, though he was reluctant to agree to it.

However, that was not at all what he wished to talk about this moment. He'd seen from his drawing room window Stanford dismount at Lady Alice's house while Radler rode on to his. Then Radler arrived and explained that Stanford was returning a left behind fan from the evening before.

Stanford had been inside the lady's house for a quarter of an hour.

"First," he said to Stanford after he'd finally arrived, "did it not occur to you to bring the fan here and then I could return it? You know I have an interest there."

"That idea is absurd," Stanford said. "You weren't there last evening. How would you explain how you came into possession of it?"

Kendrickson waved his hands. "Simple enough, I might have said no end of things. I might have said you were planning to walk it over from here, but you twisted your ankle."

"I twisted my ankle?" Stanford said, sounding mortally offended. "I am not an old lady, I do not twist ankles."

"Something could have been devised." Kendrickson narrowed his eyes. "But perhaps you did not wish to devise anything. Perhaps you have an interest in Lady Alice yourself."

"He does not," Radler said. "He's all in for Lady Patience."

"I am not all in, as you so charmingly term it," Stanford said. "Furthermore, I offered to return the fan, which is what I set out to do. I was not planning on going in, but Lady Kembleford heard the door and insisted I come in and then she was having tea with Lady Marchfield, and they are both talkers."

"Ah," Radler said, "Lady Marchfield is Lady Patience's aunt. I hope you made a good impression."

At this, Stanford suddenly looked uncomfortable. "I did not

mean to make any impression, as I did not plan on going in. As I was forced in, I attempted some pleasantries and mentioned the dinner last evening. Lady Marchfield appeared positively irate about it. She did not seem to know anything of it, and I suspect she is furious with the duke for failing to invite her."

"Gad, you put your foot in it," Radler said.

"But you really do not have designs on Lady Alice?" Kendrickson said.

"I do not have *designs* on anybody," Stanford said.

"Yes, he does," Radler said, "Lady Patience. He's just not admitting it yet."

Kendrickson could care less what the state of Stanford's feelings were at the moment, as long as they did not drift toward Lady Alice. Even if she were not well funded he would wish to pursue the lady. However, if that had been the case, he would not pursue her. Not to shield himself from financial ruin, but to shield *her*. He would not for the world injure her. He would also not for the world look upon another lady as he did Lady Alice.

"Has she given you any hint that she might favor you?" Radler asked him.

"I think so, at least I hope so. We both attended Lady Peregrine's scavenger hunt for charity two days ago and I helped her unravel the clues. We got on very well, she finds me amusing, I think."

"I did not realize Lady Alice was very fond of being amused," Radler said.

Kendrickson did not mention the note he'd received that had given him that hint, the note he was certain had been sent by Lady Patience. "Well, I believe she is."

In truth, he was sure she was. Once he'd allowed his natural buoyancy and joking manner to surface, it was as if things between them bloomed. He joked and she laughed and they'd had a very merry time of it.

He was certain things between them would continue to bloom as long as some other fellow did not get in the way. He would see her again on the morrow at Lady Jellerbey's candle-light picnic. So would Radler and Stanford and every other eligible gentleman. They must all just stay out of the way.

IT WAS THE late afternoon and Patience and her father were having a confidential conversation in his library.

"I do not think you should fret over it," the duke said. "He is a cautious man and will take his time."

"How much time though?" Patience asked. "Felicity says he needs prompting. How does one go about prompting?"

Her proclivity for moving things forward had haunted her all day. This evening was Lady Jellerbey's candlelight picnic. Certainly he would be there. But what would he say and do there?

The duke laughed and said, "As to prompting, I have sent my own message on the matter. I sent over a bottle of molasses, unsigned. We'll see if he takes the hint."

"Oh, I see, because he is as slow as molasses," Patience said, laughing despite herself. "I suppose I can tolerate slow, as long as he is slowly moving in my direction. You see, he must be, Papa. I just know it is right. I knew the moment I saw him that it was right. Why doesn't he know it too?"

"He might know it, somewhere in his mind. Acting on it is another thing. Not everybody barrels through life as you do."

Patience nodded at the truth of it.

Mrs. Right came into the library with a tray of small cakes. "These have just been cooled and iced. Cook was certain you would care for them."

"Indeed we would," the duke said.

Before Mrs. Right had even a chance to set them down, they heard a commotion in the hall. "Do not lie to me, young man! I checked the stables first and his carriage is still in it."

Patience stared at the door. It was her aunt and she sounded furious.

The duke sighed. "Lady Misery comes to call and darken a perfectly good day."

The lady herself came sailing through the doors. "Roland, I am insulted down to my shoes."

The duke laughed. "I'm getting very good at it then, as I've not even hurled an insult yet. But do not worry, I am sure I will."

"I was forced to discover that my own brother held a dinner party without bothering to invite me. It was humiliating."

Patience could not imagine how she'd heard of it. She was not meant to hear of it. Patience and her sisters had no wish to outright insult their aunt. It was just that… they did not want her to come to dinner because of all the scolding and frowning.

"You were not forced to discover anything. I had a dinner party, that is all," the duke said.

"Lord Marchfield was just as insulted."

"Was he? Then I suspect he was stuck with your company and irritated that he could not have pawned you off on me. I've told him a thousand times, when you finally give her the slip, do not launch her in my direction!"

"There I was, having tea with Lady Kembleford," Lady Marchfield said, as if the duke had said nothing at all, "when Lord Stanford arrived to bring Lady Alice a fan. Naturally, Lady Kembleford urged him to come in despite Lady Alice being out. There, he mentioned he'd been to dinner at this very house the evening before!"

A fan? Why would Lord Stanford bring Lady Alice a fan?

"It was a very small party," the duke said. "Just my girls, Stanford, Radler, and Lady Alice. I invited Stanford and Radler and Patience invited Lady Alice. Nobody, it seems, invited you!"

Lady Marchfield sighed and turned to Patience. "My dear, this is where you require womanly advice. You have a preference for Lord Stanford. That is right?"

Patience nodded, her thoughts still taken up by the fan.

"Yes, as I thought. Now, it was the most foolish thing in the world to invite Lady Alice, which I could have told you. She is comely and well-funded and you provided them extended time together. Now you see the result of it—Lord Stanford did not waste a moment before calling upon Lady Alice bearing a gift."

"Now listen here, Lady Misery, do not go spreading your gloom and doom to my girls," the duke said. "Be off with you."

Lady Marchfield sniffed. She glanced at Mrs. Right. "I suppose you sing a different tune these days, Mrs. Right. I expect Mr. Grimsby has taken things well in hand."

Mrs. Right nodded gravely. "He's a stern taskmaster," she said.

Lady Marchfield, with a gleam of victory in her eye, said, "As I thought. Patience, stop taking your father's terrible advice. If you need advice, turn to me. Perhaps things are not yet set with Lady Alice. Perhaps there is still time to turn things in your direction. You know my address."

With that, she spun on her heel and marched out of the room. They heard the front doors slam shortly after.

Patience slumped in her chair. "Why would Lord Stanford rush over to Lady Alice's house to give her a fan?"

The duke shrugged. "Who knows? I would not read too much into it. Lady Misery is a master at making mountains from molehills. You will see Stanford this evening and take his measure."

Mrs. Right did not look so sanguine, which Patience was afraid meant she thought the fan was very bad news.

The lady laid her hand on Patience's shoulder. "I certainly hope Lord Stanford is made of better stuff than what this looks like," she said.

Patience could not say. It looked very terrible. Why else would a gentleman buy a fan for a lady?

He'd not bought a fan or flowers or anything for Patience.

What if it were not the first thing he'd bought for Lady Alice? He might have sent flowers. After all, she only discovered the fan by happenstance.

Or perhaps there was a reason for it? Perhaps Lady Alice had made some hint that she needed a new fan and then he'd felt obligated?

And then, Lady Alice wished to be her friend, certainly she would not set her sights on Lord Stanford. But perhaps Patience had not made clear her preferences. Lady Alice might not understand them at all.

Or perhaps Patience was only emulating her aunt and making mountains of molehills. She must keep in mind that nothing was positively known yet, but for the delivery of a fan.

She must keep good thoughts in her mind or she would cry.

CHAPTER NINE

Mrs. Right left the library in a fury. How dare Lord Stanford buy Lady Alice a fan when her girl had her heart set on him?

She'd only seen Lady Alice briefly on two occasions, but Mrs. Right felt the lady was rather quiet and reserved. Why was *she* to be the recipient of a fan? Was it because she was likely to fan herself all her life? Did Lord Stanford prefer that sort of thing?

He must pay for this insult to her girl. *Her* girl, Lady Patience Nicolet, who was everything lovely and wonderful and not simpering round the place like that horrid Lady Alice.

How would he pay, though? She did not know very much about him.

It had been rather easy with Mr. Stratton. She'd changed his grocery order to all cabbages, posed as Mr. Stratton's father and irreparably insulted their wine merchant, and had all his clothes that had been sent out to be laundered subsequently donated to charity. Then the duke had delivered piles and piles of chains to his doorstep to answer Mr. Stratton's ridiculous claim that he would not be chained in matrimony. Valor had written to the gentleman, expressing her hope that her father would use the chains to tie him up and drown him in a lake.

Of course, they had later discovered their mistake about that gentleman, but that was water under the bridge now.

Then there had been Lord Dashlend. That was a simple matter of convincing his hysterical valet that he was being let go. Then the duke had sent a cartful of hateful flowers and plants and Valor had sent an anonymous note hoping something terrible would happen to him.

Of course, they'd later discovered their mistake about that gentleman, but that was just more water under the bridge now.

This situation was far different. Lady Misery had seen with her own two beady eyes that Lord Stanford had brought a fan to Lady Alice!

Her dear Patience must be avenged. How, how, how?

Patience had raved about Lord Stanford's clothes and his perfect tailoring. Perhaps she could do something there. Yes, why not? The gentlemen of this town were so prideful over their clothes. They seemed to have the impression that their clothes communicated something to the world. Mrs. Right was not certain what they communicated, other than to advertise that the wearer had enough money to throw some around at frivolous expenses.

And then she began to get an idea, arising from her long years as a housekeeper.

She walked down the corridor and encountered Mr. Grimsby, who was looking not at all grim these days.

"I heard Lady Marchfield's voice and hid, as I did not want to give myself away if she were to question me," Mr. Grimsby said. "Did she ask about me?"

"Oh, aye, I told her you were a regular taskmaster."

Mr. Grimsby snorted, very much amused by the idea.

"Now, Mr. Grimsby, as you are here, perhaps you would help me with a small matter."

"Indeed, Mrs. Right, what do you require?"

"Only this, we are to go up into the attics and find a case that's been infested with case moths."

"They are damnable creatures. They're hard to get rid of and they'll eat right through your clothes in record time."

"Yes, they will."

"And you suppose we will find evidence of them in the attics? We ought to be careful and get them out of the house as quickly as possible."

"Do not worry over it, they will not stay here. I intend to find a case infested and then somehow get it into Lord Stanford's house so the little devils can eat through all his precious clothes. I'm sure I can locate something—most of the things in the attic have been sitting undisturbed for years."

Mr. Grimsby laughed. "I cannot think why you wish to do so, but I don't care! Let us proceed to the attics."

With that happy agreement, they made their way there.

After moving a mountain of trunks and cases, she found just what she was looking for—the telltale signs of a case moth. An old case the right size to carry a bottle of cologne. She would clean up the outside of the case and use a bit of ink to cover the bare spots on the black velvet liner. Then she would nip one of the duke's bottles of scent as he'd never notice, or if he did he would be amused. That would ensure that the case made its way to the lord's dressing chamber and all his clothes. She would send it anonymously and the fool would imagine he had an admirer.

The only thing Mrs. Right intended on admiring about him was the holes in his coats.

MARCUS WAS AT a loss as to who was sending him these odd items. First, it had been a bottle of molasses. Then, it had been a cologne housed in what looked to be an old case. The cologne was from D.R. Harris and certainly of fine quality but looked to be prior used as it was only half-filled.

Was it the same person? Was there some sort of message in it? What was the point?

Cook had taken charge of the molasses and his valet had taken the cologne to his dressing room. Marcus was loath to discard either of them lest the sender suddenly reveal themselves with some logical explanation.

There was the possibility that these things might be from his elderly great aunt. Lady Monroe was in the habit of pressing her dead husband's things on whoever came through her doors. The last he'd visited her, he'd left with three yellowed neckcloths. Last Christmas, she'd sent him a moldy shaving brush.

However, Lady Monroe always sent a note along with her gifts. Usually a very odd note. The one that had come with the shaving brush had said, "May your face enjoy this as much as Lord Monroe's face did while he was still breathing."

As well, and so far at least, Lady Monroe had never given away such a thing as molasses. Perhaps she was running out of Lord Monroe's things. Or perhaps her mental capacities were slipping more than they already had.

He supposed he should not dwell on it. Lady Jellerbey's eccentric candlelight picnic was this evening. Her rooms would be dimly lit with only candles set on tables and none of the chandeliers lit. It was like a rout, but hard to see where one was going and not as crowded. He understood Lady Jellerbey went on with it each year because her fellow matrons of the *ton* appreciated the low light and felt it was flattering to their complexions.

As a habit, he went as a duty. The lady was falcon-eyed regarding who did or did not turn up, despite the dim light they were meant to stagger around in.

This night, he planned to take a step. A small and cautious step. He would not rush headlong into any matter, never mind one of such import. But step, he would. He would subtly communicate his regard to Lady Patience in some manner. He did not know precisely how, but he imagined it would come to him by way of opportunity.

Then, he would attempt to understand her own inclinations. He thought she looked upon him favorably, and the duke too—else why would that gentleman have invited him to dine?

"What? No more bizarre gifts turning up?" Radler asked,

striding in and looking about the drawing room.

"I hope not. I believe they might be from an old aunt."

Radler laughed. "Before the cologne turned up, when it was just the molasses, well I thought…"

"Thought what?" Marcus asked.

"Well, I thought it might be a hint from the duke that you move about as fast as molasses. It seemed like something he would find amusing."

Marcus stared at his friend. Could that be true? No, certainly not. The duke was eccentric, but he was not positively deranged. Because it would be deranged to do such a thing.

"After all," Radler continued, "he covered Stratton's doorstep in chains when that fellow was overheard to say he would not be chained in matrimony and then he sent a cartful of flowers to Dashlend, which sounds nice, but they were all things like columbine and thistle. You see? Indicating his contempt. I am not even certain what Dashlend did to deserve it."

"Those must be rumors," Marcus said. He remembered hearing something about Stratton finding chains on his doorstep, but not who had put them there. In general, he ignored gossip, so he was not very surprised he might have missed these ridiculous stories.

Even if they were true, the idea of the duke sending him molasses to make some comment on his pace was preposterous. Certainly, both the molasses and the half-filled cologne had come from his rapidly deteriorating great aunt.

Radler shrugged. "No way to be sure, I suppose, unless he gives himself away to you in some manner."

Marcus found himself eager to dismiss the subject. "The carriage has been brought round, which I have promised my valet I would make use of. He says he cannot bear the state of my clothes when I ride my horse. I don't see it, but he's been fretting for weeks about it. Let us be off to stagger round Lady Jellerbey's dim rooms."

Radler sauntered out, calling over his shoulder. "Indeed, Lady

Patience and her deranged father await!"

Marcus chose to ignore the salvo. He did not wish to think of the duke as being anything other than mildly eccentric. He already felt as if he might be taking a risk in pursuing Lady Patience; he did not want to contemplate that it might be an even bigger risk than he had yet imagined.

PATIENCE HAD TAKEN a tip from her two eldest sisters regarding Lady Jellerbey's candlelight picnic and chosen to wear a crème silk dress. Both Felicity and Grace had pointed out that wearing something dark would make her fade into the woodwork because of the lack of light.

Lady Jellerbey was a stout and cheerful matron. She also seemed fond of the duke. She shook her fan at him and said, "May I count on you to avoid leaving one of your party behind this year?"

The duke had laughed uproariously. "That's right, I nearly forgot about that. I left without Lady Marchfield and she had to run after the carriage to catch me!"

Patience laughed despite herself. Of course she knew the story. Whenever Lady Marchfield had insisted on going in the duke's carriage he either left her behind or threatened to drop her off at the Seven Dials, or both. Lady Marchfield had seemed to have given up the habit on account of it.

They went forward into Lady Jellerbey's rooms, Patience squinting to try to make out Lord Stanford. Though every surface seemed to hold burning candles, the overhead chandeliers that would have dispersed far more light were cold and dark.

So far, she did not see him.

Her father leaned over. "Do not fret, I am sure he will turn up. By the by, I sent him a clock to point out that time was passing—tick-tock, tick-tock."

"Oh, Papa," Patience said with a giggle. "Please tell me you did not put your name to it."

"Certainly not. When I mean to clobber a gentleman over the head with a heavy hint, I do it anonymously."

"Lady Patience."

She turned and found Lord Kendrickson. "Papa," she said, "this is Lord Kendrickson."

The lord bowed. "Your Grace."

"Kendrickson," the duke said.

"You remember, Papa," Patience said. "The fellow who needs a whopping dowry to rescue his estate."

Lord Kendrickson looked the smallest bit alarmed to be described so to the duke.

"Ah yes, well, that is the way of England, is it not?" the duke said. "I understand your father was a terrible gambler—bad business, that."

"It *was* a rather bad business, for which I have been left to pay the bill," Lord Kendrickson said.

"Gambling, stupid habit," the duke said. "I suppose those running the hells and profiting off ruining people will *not* meet their maker in the fullness of time, but will end up in actual hell attempting to cheat the devil. Something to look forward to, eh? Good luck to them then, eh? Ah, there is a sideboard that would call out to me if it could speak. I spot a very good claret. Entertain my daughter, Kendrickson."

With that, the duke sauntered off in search of his wine.

Lord Kendrickson was rather slack-jawed as he watched the duke depart.

"I am surprised Lord Stanford is not with you," Patience said, really wondering where the lord could be.

Lord Kendrickson recovered himself from marveling at the duke. "He is delayed. Radler tells me that Stanford thinks one of his horses has gone a bit lame and he is consulting with Lady Jellerbey's stablemaster. Radler did not see the lameness, but Stanford is so cautious—he sensed a slight misstep and was determined to investigate."

Cautious. There was that description of him again. Though, Patience did not understand why Lord Cautious would go round giving another lady a fan.

Patience thought she would take the opportunity while she had it to discover more information about Lady Alice and Lord Stanford if she could.

"Have you seen Lady Alice recently?" she asked, in order to introduce the subject.

"Indeed," Lord Kendrickson said. "We had a very jolly time at a charity scavenger hunt. I took *somebody's* advice and attempted to make her laugh."

"Goodness, *somebody* knew what they were about then," Patience said, getting the idea that Lord Kendrickson was perfectly well aware that it had been her that had sent the anonymous note.

"Naturally, I give my thanks to whoever it was that gave me that advice."

"I am sure that person requires no thanks," Patience said. "As it seems to go well between you, I do hope that Lady Alice does not become distracted by any other gentleman."

Lord Kendrickson looked positively stricken.

"What I mean to say is," Patience went on, "that is, I did understand that Lord Stanford brought a fan to Lady Alice."

She paid close attention to Lord Kendrickson's expression. It was some sort of irritated annoyance.

"So he did," Lord Kendrickson said. "I told him my thoughts on the matter in no uncertain terms."

"I just do not know why he thought to bring Lady Alice a fan. I only wondered…"

"I wondered just the same. Why should *he* bring the fan? It should have been me."

"I wish it *had* been you," Patience said.

"No more than I do."

"Lady Patience!"

Patience turned. It was the very lady they spoke about.

"Lord Kendrickson," Lady Alice said in a different tone. It was one of nervousness, Patience thought.

Lord Kendrickson bowed. "Lady Alice. You are positively glowing in the candlelight."

Lady Alice blushed up to her eyebrows, which Patience took as a good sign. She could not say whether or not the lady was glowing, but the compliment had been well received.

"Lady Alice," Patience said, not being able to contain herself, "I understand from my aunt, Lady Marchfield, that Lord Stanford was so good as to bring you a fan."

"It was very kind of the gentleman to think of it, though I was not at home at the time."

"I suppose it is a very nice fan?"

Lady Alice nodded. "It is quite a favorite."

Lord Kendrickson's expression had darkened, though Patience could see that he worked to cover it. "Lady Alice, I noted when I came in that Lady Jellerbey has included a well-aged hock on her sideboards," the lord said, "which I know you prefer. Might I escort you there for a glass?"

"That is very thoughtful, Lord Kendrickson."

"Excellent. I would not care for you to get lost in the darkness, lest we are forced to launch a search party for Lady Alice."

Lady Alice laughed at the jest and Patience thought Lord Kendrickson was doing a very good job at being lighthearted and amusing. She was not feeling so lighthearted and amusing herself. Lady Alice liked the fan. It had become a favorite.

She did wonder, though, that the lady did not wear it tonight. The fan dangling on her wrist looked very like the one she'd worn to dinner.

"Lady Patience, will you come with us?" Lady Alice asked.

Patience was a bit torn. She'd like to go along and see if she could work in more questions about the fan. On the other hand, she wished for Lord Kendrickson to have as many chances with Lady Alice as possible.

"I will stay where I am, thank you," Patience said. "My Papa is heading back toward me."

Lady Alice and Lord Kendrickson drifted away and the duke returned. "Very good claret, I must remember the name on the bottle ticket."

"She likes the fan, Papa," Patience said. "Lady Alice says it has become a favorite."

"Bah, I do not care what she says about it or why he did it. I have eyes, as I fully explained to both Felicity and Grace when they experienced their own trials. Nobody ever believes me."

Patience stood on tiptoes and kissed his cheek. "I wish more than anything to believe you."

Ahead of her, she spotted Lord Stanford. He noticed her and made his way over. "Your Grace, Lady Patience."

"There you are, wondered where you'd got to," the duke said. "But who knows, perhaps you've been here all along—who can see in this dim light?"

"I have just come in, Your Grace. I thought I detected a limp on one of my carriage horses, but it was only a loose shoe."

"I'm going to find a quiet corner where I can drink my claret without tripping over anybody in this gloom. I suppose you'll want to escort Patience through the rooms to see what might be had on the sideboards."

Lord Stanford looked a bit startled by the question that was not really posed as a question but more of an order. He speedily recovered himself and said, "Of course."

The duke made his way to an oversized chair against a far wall. Lord Stanford held his arm out. Patience laid her hand on it and they proceeded forward.

As she had noticed before, touching him was exhilarating. Her heart told her she was right about him. Her head, though, had been assaulted with too many conflicting pieces of information.

They walked the corridor and entered the music room. Patience glanced round, relieved there was not a crwth in sight. At one of the many sideboards set up in Lady Jellerbey's various rooms, Lord Stanford said, "I think you prefer a Canary, Lady Patience?"

He had remembered what she preferred. That must be a good sign, must it not? She nodded her approval.

Lord Stanford poured her a generous glass of wine. "Do you care for something to eat?" he said.

"I do rather," Patience said. "I ate a bit before I came, but my father told me it has been his experience that, despite the dim light, Lady Jellerbey puts out some very good things."

As she examined the sideboard for what might suit, Lord Stanford said, "He is not mistaken in that opinion. If you are inclined to something sweet, I recommend the crème filled pastry puffs. If savory is your preference, the lamb vol-au-vents are particularly good."

Patience chose the crème puffs, as she would always choose something sweet when given the choice. They made their way to one of the tables that had been set up in every room.

They'd had a pleasant conversation so far, but not an illuminating one. Patience was determined to be illuminated.

"I was wondering, Lord Stanford, what your opinion might be on a particular matter. A friend of mine, a lady friend, received the gift of a fan from a gentleman. She wondered if that was significant. She wondered if he were making a statement of some sort? I said I did not know."

CHAPTER TEN

PATIENCE WATCHED LORD Stanford intently to see how he would answer about a lady receiving a fan.

He seemed to consider the question. "I think in general, the nature of the gift might communicate the intent of the message," he said. "Flowers, of course, send their own meanings. As for other things, a book, or something like it, would not say as much. A fan is perhaps more significant as it is meant to be held in the lady's hands."

"I see, yes, that does sound right," Patience said, putting her attention on her pastry.

"But then, who knows?" Lord Stanford said.

Well, if he did not know, who *would* know?

"I suppose it depends on the particular situation and the parties involved."

"No doubt," she said quietly.

"I wonder," Lord Stanford said, "what might be your impression upon receiving such a thing. Would it be a welcome sort of thing, I wonder?"

Was she meant to speculate on Lady Alice's feelings? Was she meant to put herself in Lady Alice's shoes and say how she would feel about it?

"I suppose it would be entirely dependent on how I viewed the gentleman who sent it," she said.

"Yes, I suppose so. It is just that sometimes it is difficult, for a gentleman, to understand how one is perceived or where one stands."

So he did not know what Lady Alice thought about him. He certainly did seem concerned over it. Was she to discover it for him? Did he imagine she would play some sort of matchmaker?

There was something wrong here. There was something wrong with *him*. How could he not see that Lady Alice was not right for him? How could he not see what was right in front of him? How could he not see that he was right for Patience Nicolet? He was, she could feel it in her bones.

He was misguided in some way. But what way? The only thing she could imagine had steered Lord Stanford toward Lady Alice was her outward and very staid-seeming demeanor. He'd said as much at Almack's. *People* had suggested they meet, though Patience did not believe those *people* even existed. And then he'd hinted that type of lady might be something he looked for.

"Lord Stanford, may I ask a personal question that probably ought not be asked?" Patience said. She knew she should not press so far into the lord's personal life but she knew not what else to do!

He nodded, though he had a distinct look of trepidation.

"When we first met, you did not say it directly, but I got the impression that your childhood home was not… everything it could have been?"

"It was not," he said flatly.

Patience longed to say something, to press him forward, but she knew it would be better to allow the silence to linger.

"My home was chaotic. Very chaotic."

"I see," Patience said. Her own household might be named chaotic. It was a happy chaotic, but perhaps Lord Stanford was put off by it? "I suppose then, that you hope for a future household that is… not chaotic."

"I very much hope for it."

That must be it. Lord Stanford looked toward Lady Alice because the last thing anybody would accuse her or her household of was chaos. He looked for calm, even if the calm did not come with happiness.

It was wrong. She knew in her heart it was wrong.

"My intent is that my children experience quite a different household," Lord Stanford said. "I have made it a requirement to my future plans."

That was it. That was the problem. He was so determined to avoid replicating his own childhood that he'd taken aim but drawn the bowstring too far. He was so worried about it that he overcompensated. He was willing to put aside his own happiness for the sake of his future household, but it was all wrong.

Patience could not imagine what sort of household he'd experienced. Only that it must have been dreadful.

Lord Kendrickson and Lady Alice approached them. "Might we join you?" Lord Kendrickson said. "Lady Alice had a wish to spend time with her particular friend."

Lord Stanford had risen and given his chair to Lady Alice, while the two lords took the other empty chairs.

Lady Alice said, "Lord Stanford, I haven't had a moment to thank you for bringing me the fan."

"It was no trouble at all," Lord Stanford said.

Patience and Lord Kendrickson looked at one another. Lord Kendrickson practically rolled his eyes.

"It was just a fan, after all," Lord Kendrickson said. "Anybody might have brought it."

"Of course," Lord Stanford said.

Of course? What did he mean by it?

"I must admit," Lady Alice said, "that seeking out Lady Patience was not my only reason for wishing for a chair. I'm afraid I begin to feel poorly."

Patience looked more closely at Lady Alice. It was true, she did not look well at the present moment. Her skin had gone more pale than was usual and there were tiny beads of sweat on her forehead.

Lord Kendrickson leapt up from his chair. "You must be

taken home at once. A doctor must be called at once. I will seek out your mother."

Lord Stanford was up on his feet just as fast. "Search the back rooms, Kendrickson. I will search the front and have the carriage called round."

Lord Kendrickson nodded and they were off, leaving Patience alone with Lady Alice. Patience would like to make further inquiries about the fan and about the lady's feelings regarding Lord Stanford, but she could not do so in Lady Alice's current condition. She was beginning to look far too weak to be expected to answer any questions.

"Do drink some of my wine, Lady Alice," Patience said. "It will fortify you."

Lady Alice weakly waved a hand. "Thank you, no, I cannot. I dare not drink anything this moment."

"Oh, I see," Patience said, guessing that whatever illness was coming over the lady, it involved her stomach. A very uncomfortable state of affairs, as Patience knew from prior experience.

Lord Kendrickson hurried back with Lady Kembleford.

"My dear," Lady Alice's mother said, "you are ill?"

"Very, Mama. It came over me suddenly. I wish to be home."

"Of course you do. Come, stand and I will give you my arm."

"I will support you on the other side," Lord Kendrickson said.

They assisted the lady, who gave Patience a weak smile of parting, through the dim light of Lady Jellerbey's candlelight picnic.

Patience sat alone in the gloom, considering all that had transpired. She dearly hoped Lady Alice did not suffer a serious malady. Another part of her, though, could not help but notice how both Lord Kendrickson and Lord Stanford had shot out of their seats to assist her.

That thought did not reflect well on her, she knew. It showed a selfishness of spirit, a lowness of some kind. She ought to be grateful that there had been two gentlemen nearby who were capable of assisting Lady Alice. She would try very hard to be grateful for it.

Patience was alone with her thoughts for some minutes. She was tucked away in a corner that would have been very visible had the chandeliers been lit, but she noted several people pass her by that she was certain had not even seen her.

Then she overheard a conversation. Two ladies spoke of Lady Alice being suddenly taken ill and the rush to remove her from the house.

"Apparently," one lady said, "Lady Kembleford's carriage was swiftly located but her coachman could not be found."

"I am not surprised," the other lady said. "I understand the coachmen often gather somewhere for a game of cards or such. I am certain he was not expecting such an early and abrupt departure."

"Lady Alice is lucky to have two such attentive gentlemen nearby."

"And flattered, I'd imagine. It was very dashing of Lord Stanford to leap onto the box and drive the carriage himself."

"And then Lord Kendrickson leapt on his horse with a torch to lead the way and clear any carts or carriages ahead of them."

"It is comforting to know that chivalry is not dead. I will alert my lord to that fact as perhaps he will wish to become reacquainted with the idea."

Both ladies laughed heartily before strolling out of the room. Patience took a large drink from her glass. She was going to have to work very hard at being grateful that Lady Alice had such competent assistance.

Leaping on the box to drive the carriage, indeed. It seemed a bit too... enthusiastic.

Patience pinched her leg through her skirt to silence the terrible thoughts that had come upon her. She would be grateful for the gentlemen's actions, as she should be.

Or at least she would try very hard to be grateful.

MARCUS SAT ALONE in his drawing room in the early hours of the morning. He'd left Lady Jellerbey's house precipitously and without Radler, but he assumed his houseguest would have been told of the circumstances.

He'd driven Lady Kembleford's carriage to Bedford Square in all haste as Lady Alice did really seem very poorly. Once there, Kendrickson got the address of the family's doctor and was off like a shot, leaving him standing on the pavement holding the flaming torch.

Lady Kembleford had hustled Lady Alice into the house with nary a look behind her. There was nothing for Marcus to do but hand over the carriage to a groom, put the torch out, and walk back to Grosvenor Square.

Upon entering his house, he found another odd package waiting for him. With some trepidation, he opened it to find a clock and a note that said, "Not everybody has all the time in the world—tick-tock, tick-tock."

Marcus was certain it was from Lady Monroe, and he was worried over what she meant by it. First the molasses, then the half-filled cologne bottle in an old case, and now a clock and a cryptic reference to time ticking down. He did wonder if she were coming to the end of her days and knew it to be so. He resolved that he'd better go and see for himself. She was only in Kent—it might be easily done.

He did feel he owed the lady that much at least. He'd spent his time between school terms at her house rather than his own and always appreciated that it had been quiet as a tomb. He never failed to send her a birthday present and he attended her at Christmas, but it seemed she might require more at this moment.

He put the matter aside for the moment, as he wished to reflect on his conversation with Lady Patience. She was just as cryptic as Lady Monroe! She brought up the subject of a fan—her friend had received such a gift—and he'd thought it the perfect opportunity to discover if *she* would like such a gift. After all, it would have been a place to begin, a small step to take to indicate his regard.

A fan was important to a lady, far more important than its utilitarian purpose might suggest. It was a way to communicate things that could not be said. As a gift, it must mean more than other things, like a book, as it was to go on a lady's person.

She would not say if she wished for such a gift. She would only say it depended upon her opinion of the gentleman sender. That was not very helpful at all. What was her opinion of him? He could not be certain.

He *felt* she approved of him, but that was only a feeling. It was a guess, an impression. He would not rest easy until he had some firm facts and he had none of those.

Marcus heard the front doors open and close and Radler came bounding into the drawing room.

"Hello, the rescuing hero!" he said jovially.

"It was nothing."

"Not according to the ladies of the *ton*," Radler said. "The rest of the night was taken up by descriptions of your derring-do in leaping up to the box and driving Lady Alice's team of horses while Kendrickson gallantly led the way on horseback with a burning torch."

"Speed was necessary, I think," Marcus said, really wishing the *ton* did not talk quite so much. "Lady Alice did seem very ill."

"It is a feather in your cap, whether you like it or not. Personally, I would like it very much, but no lady ever seems to require such convenient rescuing when she is in my vicinity."

"Did you encounter Lady Patience?" Marcus asked. He did not want to ask, as he was not interested in any further teasing on the matter from Radler, but he could not help himself.

"Indeed, yes. She did not stay long after your rousing departure and looked rather grave as her father escorted her out. I reckon she was worried about Lady Alice."

"No doubt," Marcus said.

"What's that there?" Radler said, pointing to the latest of Lady Monroe's deliveries. "Did you order a clock?"

"I did not," Marcus said. "I am certain it is from Lady Monroe and I think it means to hint that her time grows short. I will make some arrangements to see her, I think."

"Send off a letter on the morrow and see what she says," Radler advised. "You'll have your answer in a day or two—it would be well to understand the situation, rather than race off there. If the old gal really is fading, you might need to be there for an extended period."

Of course, Radler was right. He would send a letter and gauge the reply. It might well turn out that he would have duties to manage, as he was the executor of her estate. He'd write the housekeeper too. If Lady Monroe was losing her wits, it would be well to gather information from somebody who was not.

"By the by, you are on your own tomorrow evening," Marcus said. "I have an engagement of the family duty variety."

Once a year, Marcus dined with a cousin of his late father's— Lord Jeffries. He did not particularly enjoy the encounter. One, the old man was exceedingly staid and they did not have a lot to talk about. Two, he spoke of his late cousin as if he'd been some sort of saint, which he certainly had not been.

Marcus always found himself biting back his words, as he could not tell the old gentleman what he really thought. It was trying in the extreme to hear his father named dignified and distinguished. Marcus felt a great wish to inquire how dignified and distinguished it was to throw a plate at one's wife. Or shout until the roof shook. Or threaten to cut off the lady's funds and lock her in the attic for good measure.

"Guess what the Duke of Pelham did?" Radler said, suddenly laughing. "Somebody brought up the time that he'd set Lady Vanderwake's curtains afire and he decided it would be amusing to reenact the whole thing. I do believe he was well-oiled with claret. He did such a good job of it that he set Lady Jellerbey's curtains afire."

Marcus stared at Radler.

"Lord Wexner put the fire out fast enough so I suppose the lady's curtains were really more singed than burned. In any case, with the excitement of Lady Alice's departure, I do not suppose anybody will remember it."

Marcus thought that unlikely. He also thought it was more evidence that a connection to the duke's family ought to be avoided. That sort of indecorous behavior was not at all what he'd said he wished for. However, he also knew well enough that he would not avoid Lady Patience and her father. He had pushed his caution to one side and apparently he was not going to let it back in. Not even over curtains set afire for no good reason.

It was a risk. It might turn out precisely as he feared, precisely everything he'd been determined to avoid. He did not think so, though. Something inside him told him it would not.

In any case, Lady Patience Nicolet was worth the risk.

Mrs. Right waited until the library doors were closed and then crept silently down the hall to stop in front of them.

Lady Marchfield had arrived to see Mr. Grimsby. She said it was an interview of a private nature and she did not wish for them to be disturbed. Mrs. Right could well guess why she'd come.

She leaned her ear against the door.

"Well, Mr. Grimsby, I must say I am impressed. You seem to have taken this household in hand and brought some order to it."

"I have been a stern taskmaster, my lady," Mr. Grimsby said.

Mrs. Right slapped a hand over her mouth to stifle a laugh.

"I am a lady of my word, Mr. Grimsby," Lady Marchfield went on. "I promised you a payment of fifty pounds if you were still here at this time and I have brought it."

"Very kind, my lady."

Mrs. Right heard the shuffling of paper and slipped down the hall and around a corner.

Very soon, the door opened. "I will see myself out, Mr. Grimsby—carry on as you have done so far!"

Lady Marchfield strode down the hall and Mrs. Right imagined she felt mighty victorious at that moment. It would not last though.

After the lady departed, Mrs. Right hustled down the corridor and approached Mr. Grimsby. He held a handful of notes.

"You've done it, Mr. Grimsby, you've got the money for your haberdashery."

"I am free!" Mr. Grimsby cried.

"Shall I help you pack?"

"Very kind, Mrs. Right. Very kind, indeed."

THE DUKE'S HOUSE was in an uproar and everyone ran this way and that to find their pelisses, though if they would just stay still, the footmen would bring them. Of course, Mrs. Wendover was a more elusive item, as one never knew where Nelson had deposited that stuffed rabbit.

Mrs. Wendover had eventually been located under a table in the kitchens and the family had piled into the duke's carriages.

They were on their way to Viscount Denderby's house. Felicity had delivered her and Mr. Stratton's baby the previous night.

There had been some talk of perhaps Felicity not wishing for visitors so soon, but then Valor had rightly pointed out that she would not have sent the note if she did not. After all, their sister would know that as soon as they had word they would be on their way.

Felicity and Mr. Stratton were staying at the house without the company of Mr. Stratton's viscount. That was thought well all round, as the gentleman was forever shouting about something.

Now, they were the new parents of a fine-spirited baby girl. At least, they imagined she was in fine spirits, as her cries sounded as bad-tempered as anything that ever emanated from Felicity herself.

As the baby had finally decided to stop her wailing and get some sleep in order to be energized for the next round, the family was let in to see her, one at a time, so they did not disturb.

As Patience waited her turn, she listened to her father and Mr. Stratton talk about daughters. According to the duke, no opinion, feeling, or tragic weeping was to be dismissed out of hand. It was all in the nature of things and to deny its validity would only bring it on ten times stronger and longer. The duke advised Mr. Stratton to trim his sails and prepare himself for a gusty breeze if he wished to keep his daughterly boat afloat.

Mr. Stratton was all smiles and nods. Patience wondered if he even heard the duke's advice. He only kept murmuring, "She is perfect." Every minute or so he gazed lovingly up at the ceiling.

Finally, Valor returned weeping. "She is so pretty, you will just not believe it. She is a little red and wrinkly and her eyes are a little crossed, but Felicity says that will all pass and once she is not red, wrinkly, and cross-eyed, she will be so pretty."

Grace, who had prior experience, nodded knowingly. Patience could only assume young Miles Delatore had also arrived a bit red, wrinkly, and cross-eyed.

"Patience, Felicity says to send you up next," Valor said.

CHAPTER ELEVEN

P ATIENCE LEAPT UP and very quietly but quickly went up the stairs to Felicity's bedchamber. She slipped in and found her eldest sister reposed in her bed, the baby sleeping in a bassinet next to her.

She tiptoed over and peeked in. Valor was right, she would be very pretty once she moved past this somewhat awkward stage of life. Just now her face looked a bit scrunched. However, she was a chubby little thing and Mrs. Right always said that was a good sign in a baby.

"No need to be absolutely silent, Patience," Felicity said. "Miss Isabelle Stratton seems to be a sound sleeper, once she decides to do it."

"Isabelle! That's lovely."

Felicity nodded. "I was determined not to name her after a virtue, as *we've* all been saddled with. She can be any which way she wishes without her name hanging over her head like the Sword of Damocles."

Patience sat on the bed. "I imagine she will appreciate that. Are you well, Felicity?"

Felicity smiled. "Well, tired, happy, and relieved. I am glad the whole thing is over—I was dreading it."

Patience nodded, as she supposed anybody would dread it. "Was it awful?" Patience asked.

"I cannot deny it was, I thought it would never end. It did end though, and I must think it well worth the effort."

Patience sometimes wondered how men could be the stronger sex and yet nature left this most difficult and life-threatening task to women. For all that, though, she wished to have her own children. She just would not think too much about the actual birth. Or the chances of death. It was what took their own mother, after all.

"Percy has been a brick," Felicity said. "He's poked his head in constantly since the baby arrived and I think he drives the nursemaid positively mad."

"Papa has been trying to tell him how to raise daughters and I do not think he's heard a word of it. He just keeps looking up at the ceiling and saying she's perfect."

Felicity laughed. "I'd like to think he speaks about me, but he is entirely besotted with his daughter. Now, how do you get on with Lord Stanford?"

"Oh I do not think I should burden you with my problems at such a time as this."

"Please do," Felicity said. "It will distract me, as I am rather sore and my feelings fly up and down like a swooping bird for no reason whatsoever, though I understand that will pass in a few days. In any case, I would like to take my mind off me for a moment."

Patience nodded and laid out all that had happened since the dinner. When she had finished, she said, "I just do not understand why Lord Stanford has gone off and bought a fan for Lady Alice. And then he was a hero to the rescue when she was taken ill. He practically launched out of his chair like a horse taking a high fence."

"Hmm. Perhaps you will not get answers to that from Lord Stanford. Perhaps you might approach Lady Alice when she is on the mend."

"I already did, she went out of her way to say the fan had become a favorite."

"Well, if you are set on him, I would not give up just yet.

After all, many a slip between the cup and the lip. Things may come to nothing with Lady Alice."

"I hope I am not to be some sort of second choice."

"No, I do not think so. I think perhaps Lord Stanford merely needs to understand his own inclinations."

That was of course what Patience was hoping for. "You did mention you thought Lord Stanford might need prompting. I do not know if it would help or not, but how would one go about it?"

Felicity drummed her fingers on her chin. "I do not know Lord Stanford very well, so it is difficult to say. Has he given you any opportunity to hint of your feelings?"

"I do not think so," Patience said. "He's a little… reserved. I do not think it is his true nature, meaning the one he was born with. I think he is reserved because he was not born into a very pleasant household. In fact, I know his household was unpleasant. He said it was chaotic."

"Oh dear," Felicity said chewing her lower lip. "Goodness, Percy and I have had a few conversations about what our children will experience. They come with their own temperament and then it is shaped by our decisions. Just think, Patience, what my temper would have been if Papa were not so kind."

Patience nodded, as everybody knew the duke had been sympathetic to Felicity's boil-overs, especially when she'd been younger and could not control it as well as she did these days.

"I think Lord Stanford is attracted to me but gravitating to Lady Alice because, to him, she represents a dullness and staidness that feels like what he thinks he wants. But he's wrong and I do not know how to show him he is wrong."

"Perhaps if you cannot show him, you will have to come right out and tell him."

"Tell him? Say it? No, I couldn't! What if he were to look upon me as if I were mad? What if he were disgusted by it? What if he felt bad and worked to let me down gently? Or what if he felt trapped? I should positively die."

"I think you are braver than that."

Patience was silent for a few moments. "Well, I will probably see him this evening at Lord Michael's rout. I will see how I feel about it."

Just then, Miss Isabelle Stratton gave the smallest shudder and began screaming bloody murder. Felicity laughed. "The little lady has awakened and wishes to ensure that all the household is aware of this development."

MARCUS HAD FAIRLY dragged himself to Lord Jeffries' house. As usual, and he really wished it were not the case, the two of them dined alone.

Also as usual, and also he wished it were not the case, Lord Jeffries took the opportunity to wax poetic about Marcus' father.

"He was a fine man, dignified, just as an earl should be," Lord Jeffries said.

Marcus did not reply, as there was no reply suitable. His father and dignity had never been well acquainted.

"Not like some we see running round the place these days. I hear the Duke of Pelham is a disgrace and his daughters, well, what can you expect from people raised by a madman?"

Marcus felt his spine stiffening over the comment. "The daughter that is currently out, Lady Patience Nicolet, I have found to be charming."

Lord Jeffries slurped his soup. "They've got nothing wrong in the looks department, at least not those I've seen over the past few seasons, it's all in the head, my dear boy. They do some strange things."

"I am afraid I must disagree with you, Jeffries. I have got to know the duke and I have been to dine at his house. They are an unconventional family, to be sure. For all that, I admire the familial harmony."

"Familial harmony?" Lord Jeffries said, clearly taken aback.

"Yes, indeed. Did you know they have a three-legged dog who is blind in one eye? His name is Nelson, and I find it very telling that they adopted him off the streets rather than pay for a bit of a puffball to sit on their laps and look pretty."

"A cur off the streets is charming now, is it?" Lord Jeffries said with a short laugh. "Your father would not approve of such goings-on, I'm sure."

Lord Jeffries had finally pushed Marcus to the boiling point. All these years, he'd let the fellow drone on and on about his father. The droning would have to come to an end this very night.

"Lord Jeffries, I fear that while you may have respected my father from afar, based on your description of him I must think you did not in fact know him very intimately."

"Well, now, of course we lived on different sides of the country. I did see him in Town from time to time, though, and there was the occasional letter."

"As I thought. Let me acquaint you with who my father really was. He was a bully and a wife beater and prone to throw temper tantrums and threaten death to anybody who was nearby, including very often, his countess. I presume the only reason those death threats did not extend to me was that I was the heir."

Lord Jeffries, rather predictably, looked shocked to his shoes to hear of his illustrious relative spoken of in such a manner.

Marcus went on. "I was but six years old when I mustered up the courage to demand to be moved to the other side of the house so I would not be woken by his shouting and the sounds of breaking glass. I was delighted to be sent to school, and further delighted to spend my time between terms with Lady Monroe, my grandmother's sister. At one point, I went a full two years without setting eyes on my father, and those were a happy two years. That is the man I knew."

Marcus fell to silence. Perhaps he should not have said any of it, but he felt a weight lift off his shoulders. He would no longer pretend his father had been anything but what he'd been.

Lord Jeffries stared into his soup. "Good God, my boy. I didn't know any of it. I really did not know your father very well. I only made a point of saying nice things as I thought it would comfort you to hear them. That was the whole purpose of these dinners, actually. I thought, see here, Jeffries, the boy has lost his father, he'll wish to hear from someone who knew him. Well, I suppose I got that all wrong!"

Marcus dropped his spoon. It had never once occurred to him that Lord Jeffries thought he was doing a kindness.

Then another idea hit him. It had not occurred to him because he had not been raised in a household where kindnesses had been handed out. There had been no experience, and therefore no reason, to expect it from other quarters.

Lady Monroe had always been kind in her own original way, but he had assumed she was somehow an aberration.

"I find that I wish I had told you all of this sooner," Marcus said.

"As do I," Lord Jeffries said. He raised his glass and said, "Now that I have been informed of my cousin's character, let's hope he's with the devil now!"

Marcus raised his glass too. It seemed dinners with Lord Jeffries were to be much more tolerable going forward.

Perhaps there was a lesson in that. Perhaps he ought to just come out and say what was in his mind in all the areas of his life.

"So you say the duke's daughters *are* right in the head? I've been told it wrong?" Lord Jeffries said.

"They are perfectly right in the head," Marcus assured him. "Even the duke, I think, though one must get to know him to perceive it."

"Well now, I was wrong about your father, so I suppose I could be wrong in this idea too. Do I detect a particular inclination toward this Lady Patience?"

"You do, rather."

"I see. I wish you the best of luck with it, then. By the by, I've got a rather spectacular little house in Wales—if you like it, you could use it on a wedding trip. I'll write you a letter of introduction, so the steward does not throw you out on your ear.

Marcus thought the offer very kind, if not entirely precipitous.

Lord Jeffries raised his glass. "To friendship," he said.

Marcus raised his glass too. Surprisingly, he'd be happy to maintain a friendship with the old fellow. He supposed life was full of surprises.

PATIENCE HAD DRAGGED her father through every room of Lord Michael's house, which had been no easy feat considering it was an exceedingly crowded rout. There had been no sign of Lord Stanford, but they had finally encountered his houseguest, Lord Radler. Certainly he would know where his host had got off to. Perhaps his horse's shoe had come loose again?

After the pleasantries were exchanged, Patience said, "I did not see Lord Stanford anywhere."

"No, he's off to some family duty thing," Lord Radler said.

Family duty thing? She was a little surprised Lord Stanford had not mentioned any sort of family duty thing. Unless, of course, it was some sort of emergency come up suddenly.

"Oh dear," she said, "was someone taken ill?"

"No, I do not think it is anything like that. He just told me I was on my own this evening. So, here I am."

"Deuced crowded nuisance, if you ask me," the duke said. "I had to shout, 'Let me through or I'll set the curtains afire' just to get to a sideboard."

Patience nodded. "Everybody moved for him, as they are not very good at being able to tell when he is joking."

Lord Radler laughed. "They probably thought, why risk it?"

"Yes, yes, very good, why risk it," the duke said, laughing.

"Was I joking? I do not even know myself."

"I suppose you will attend Lady Darlington's masque on the morrow?" Lord Radler said. "It is one of the finest events of the season."

Patience nodded. Indeed, it had been a pleasure to spend time dreaming up and designing a costume. The dressmaker had only delivered it and done the alterations the day before. She would go as Anne of Cleves, the remarkable lady who survived Henry VIII's wrath. Of course, if Patience were to be honest with herself, she'd chosen Anne because of a copy of her portrait in one of her father's books. The lady wore a divine red dress with gold trim that she thought would suit her very well.

"Hah! What do you think I'll go as?" the duke said. "Flaming curtains! I've had a white domino made with red flames painted on the bottom of it in honor of the two times I've set curtains afire. That'll put some starch into people."

Lord Radler laughed rather raucously at that idea and Patience had the distinct impression that he had overindulged himself with wine. When he recovered himself, he said, "And Lady Patience?"

"Anne of Cleves," she said.

"Ah, the one that got away."

"And wore a marvelous dress doing it," Patience said. "What does Lord Stanford propose to appear as, if you know it?"

"Ah yes, he wears a simple domino, but he caps it off with a rather wonderful mask—it covers his whole head and face, you see, so nobody can guess who he is. It is made of black leather with only small openings for eyes and mouth. I've seen him in it, it's ominous looking. I rather fancy it, but he will not give up who made it for him."

Patience did not comment on the idea that now she *would* know who he was. Nobody else would wear such a mask and Lord Radler had given the game away.

She was disappointed that he would not come tonight, but she could not think the whole evening a waste. She had discovered what Lord Stanford would wear. Now she just had to decide if she would take Felicity's advice on what to do about that gentleman.

"Well, my dear," the duke said, "are we ready to push our way out of this place or do I need to shout about setting the curtains afire to get another glass of claret?"

"We may go, Papa. Lord Radler, until tomorrow."

Really, tomorrow felt rather momentous. Patience did not know if she would actually find the courage to express her feelings to Lord Stanford. But if she did, and he returned them, it would be the most important day of her life.

It could also be the worst day of her life. However, the more she thought about it, the more impatient she was to find out.

MARCUS HAD COME home after what had turned out to be a rather jolly evening with Lord Jeffries. Once the gentleman no longer felt compelled to praise Marcus' father to the skies, it turned out they got on rather well.

What had marred the evening were the two letters from Lady Monroe that were waiting for him in the great hall. He picked them up and read them again.

Marcus—

I was surprised to hear from you, as I am surprised to hear from anybody these days. Nobody is interested in hearing from an old woman and I have, unfortunately, crossed that milestone years ago.

You inquire if I am doing poorly. Of course I am doing poorly. I am eighty-three years old, how else should I be doing? I can practically feel my lord and maker reaching out to me. I am certain that very soon he will grab my arm and bury me in the ground.

Naturally, I do not wish to interrupt your parties or your escapades with your friends, whoever they may be as you never write about them, with my paltry concerns about death.

Also, do not ever again write my housekeeper as if I am not capable of answering my own letters. The mind is always the last thing to go, so I can still do it. (Though who knows for how long.)

I hope you are enjoying your youth—it flees surprisingly fast.

Margaret Monroe

Marcus looked at the second letter, which was even more bizarre. It simply said:

Tick-Tock Tick-Tock HURRY UP.

He laid the papers down. It was difficult to know what sort of straits the lady was actually in. She'd been talking about death for the past twenty years.

On the other hand, she *was* eighty-three and the second letter was particularly alarming.

He sighed. He would have to go and find out. It was only to Kent, so he need only be gone for a few days, but go he must.

Radler came into the drawing room, back from Lord Michael's rout. "How was your family thing?"

"Surprisingly not as bad as it usually is," Marcus said. "You look a bit worse for wear."

Radler practically stumbled to a chair. "Indeed. You see, once one manages to push through people to make it to one of Lord Michael's sideboards, one has the urge to stay there and drink one's fill."

"I see that you did make it to a sideboard, then."

Radler nodded. "Several times."

"I must go and see Lady Monroe on the morrow. I really do not know if she is sickly or not."

Radler, now rather slumped, said, "Say, as you will miss the masque, do lend me that wonderful mask of yours."

Marcus shrugged. "I do not mind it," he said. "By the by, did you see Lady Patience at the rout?"

"Oh yes, and her father was in fine form—guess how he got to the sideboards? He yelled that if people did not get out of his way he would set the curtains afire. He really is very funny."

"And Lady Patience?" Marcus asked, ignoring the latest of the duke's shenanigans.

"Ah, guess what she will wear to the masque?"

Marcus suppressed a sigh. Radler was very fond of attempting to make people guess at everything when he was in his cups.

"Anne of Cleves," Radler said. "The one who got away." He laid his forefinger along his nose. "But not because of that. It was because of the dress she wore in her portrait to Henry."

Marcus would be sorry not to see it. He knew perfectly well what the dress looked like, as the portrait was well known—red velvet with gold trimmings. There was no help for it, though. He must travel to see Lady Monroe.

CHAPTER TWELVE

KENDRICKSON FELT AS if he walked on air. Somehow, he had done it. Lady Alice had accepted him and her father had been brought round.

After the lady had been taken ill, he'd done everything in his power to express his affection.

First, he'd ridden hellbent in front of her carriage, lighting the way and clearing the streets. Then he'd dragged her physician from his bed and forced the man onto the back of his horse.

The following day, he began a campaign. He sent books that might be of interest, he sent draughts from his relations' kitchens and medicine cases. He sent flowers picked from the garden that the housekeeper arranged prettily.

He dared to call and was admitted. Lady Alice was in the drawing room, properly dressed but with a blanket thrown over her waist. Lady Kembleford said she was on the mend. He'd spent far longer on the visit than was proper but nobody threw him out.

He called the following day too, making no mistake regarding his interest. Lady Kembleford left them for a moment to see about a tea tray and he had asked.

Lady Alice had accepted him. Then she'd admitted that she'd felt an illness of the stomach variety at the candlelight picnic as she was nervous regarding her own growing inclinations. She explained that she was inclined to such nervous complaints.

They both had the same inclinations!

Of course, the hard part was still to be got over. He was all but penniless and needed her father's approval. It had been hard won.

The earl had questioned him closely about his estate and what his plans were for it. Kendrickson laid out the details, of which he'd spent years developing. He intended to put the estate on firm footing and keep it there through close management.

The earl had inquired into his views on gambling, no doubt very much aware of how that habit had landed his father in penniless territory. Kendrickson had no trouble at all answering that question, as the Duke of Pelham had once phrased it so well. A gambler put a gun to his head and pulled the trigger, hoping not to get shot—a stupid business.

Those answers, taken together with Lady Alice's surprisingly forceful leaning on her father, had got the approval.

Somehow, word was going round the town already, though the banns had not yet been read. He'd already been congratulated on securing such a fine lady. He was not sorry at all that the word was out. It would be next to impossible for the earl to change his mind after his wife and daughter told people about it.

The earl's daughter. Lady Alice. She was the finest of ladies. He'd come to London determined to secure a large dowry and save his estate. He'd never imagined that it could come along with a lady he found himself in love with. And then, a lady with dark hair and piercing blue eyes—it was so rare!

His mother was over the moon about Lady Alice. The dowager had already had a tea with her and Lady Kembleford to speak to his betrothed about the estate and the people in it. Despite Lady Alice's protestations, his mother would move to the dower house, and she would not stick her nose into the new mistress' management of the main house unless she was positively asked. Lady Kembleford was most approving of the attitude. He really thought they should all get on well.

He'd done his duty and the fates had rewarded him for it

tenfold. Finally, the world had turned into a happy place and the future might be looked to with anticipation, rather than dread.

It was very good to be alive.

PATIENCE EXAMINED HERSELF in the glass. Mrs. Right had done wonders for her hair. Patience had not thought Anne of Cleves' hairstyle represented in her portrait was particularly attractive, so she'd decided to give some latitude to that. Her hair was swept back in its usual manner and secured with a diamond clip. She donned a delicate and small lace head covering as a nod to the queen.

There had been no latitude to the gown though, as that was divine. The dressmaker had studied Patience's design and looked at a copy of the portrait and had rendered a very faithful likeness.

The dress was a burgundy red velvet with a gold stitched bodice, gold embroidery round the cuffs and a band down the skirt, and a lovely gold belt round her waist. One of the trimmings round the sleeves was between her shoulder and elbow, creating cap sleeves that then draped down into bell sleeves at her wrists.

"You look like a queen, Patience!" Valor said, running her hand along the velvet.

"I should hope so, I am dressed as a queen," she said.

"Lord Stanford will see his queen and just fall over from it," Serenity said, wiping at her eyes. "He will be so moved!"

Patience did not answer that prediction with another "I should hope so," but she really did hope so.

"He better be bowled over," Winsome said. "He's been dragging his heels."

"Of course he will be," Verity said. "It is a very common thing for a gentleman to drag his heels and then be moved."

"Is it?" Winsome asked, eyes narrowing.

Verity did not deign to answer that particular challenge.

"I think," Valor said, "that he will take some very good advice on the matter."

"From who?" Winsome asked.

"It's a secret," Valor said, hugging Mrs. Wendover.

"What secret?" Patience asked. Valor's secrets could be alarming, and Patience did not know why she should have a secret having anything to do with Lord Stanford.

"Patience, I could tell you if it wasn't a secret, but Mrs. Wendover made me promise it would be a secret."

"Valor, tell me this instant," Patience said sternly, "or I will never allow you to crawl into my bed when you think women are being murdered on the moors."

That idea, very naturally, would overcome anything that Mrs. Wendover could come up with. The stuffed rabbit was not all that helpful when Valor thought she was hearing a murder.

"It's nothing, really," Valor said. "It's only that Papa sent Lord Stanford a clock and a note that said tick-tock tick-tock and that was so funny. So I sent a note that said tick-tock tick-tock HURRY UP! You see, that way he'll be sure of what to do."

"Was it signed?" Patience asked.

"No, just tick-tock tick-tock HURRY UP."

Well, it was not ideal, but it was done so she supposed she would not spend time worrying over it. Though really, somebody ought to hide the writing paper from her youngest sister. Valor was becoming a regular novelist in the sending notes department.

Mrs. Right hurried in, as she had left to see how the duke was getting on with his costume. "My dear, I do hope you are nearing ready. His Grace, the Duke of Curtains Afire has just poured his second glass of brandy."

Patience nodded and they set off in a crowd down the stairs to see their Papa in his costume.

As the duke had promised, he was dressed in a white domino, which might have suggested a clergyman of some sort if it were not for the painted red flames around the bottom of it.

Patience laughed at the sight. "Well, Papa, if people do not perceive that you are curtains afire, they will presume you are a naughty clergyman burning in the devil's lair."

The duke laughed heartily. "Oh, that is very good. I hope Lady Misery makes that mistake. She comes as Elizabeth, the virgin queen, if you can imagine it. If she is a virgin at this late date…" The duke paused and said, "Well, never mind it. I suppose I might chase her round as the devil's tempter if I get bored."

Patience was all but certain her father had stopped himself from making a joke about Lord Marchfield leaving his bride in the same pristine condition as she had arrived. Fortunately, it all went over Valor's head.

"I know what I'll do, Papa," Valor said. "When we go home I'll tell the vicar that you dressed as him going to the devil. He will be so cross!"

"Yes, I imagine he will be," the duke said drily. "Well, my girl? Are we ready to depart?"

Patience nodded, and a footman helped her on with the pelisse. She was ready to depart, though she was still ginning herself up to say something bold to Lord Stanford.

She must find the courage. Anne of Cleves had survived far worse circumstances. She must find Anne's courage. After all, it might have been Anne's head on the chopping block. It was only Patience's heart on the block just now. If things went wrong, it might feel a deadly blow, but she would somehow survive it.

She just needed to know how it would be.

MARCUS HAD SET off in the morning and made good time to Maidstone. Lady Monroe's estate was only a few miles farther on. He'd not bothered with his carriage for such a trip but had simply packed some things in panniers.

He found the lady's estate as it ever was—set back at the end of a long lane of ancient oaks. It was an old as the hills Tudor style that had not changed much beyond necessary repairs since Henry the VIII had been riding through the countryside.

The butler, an aged fellow named Bellows, was surprised to see him. He did not seem as if it were a particularly welcome surprise either.

"Tell me, Bellows, how is Lady Monroe's condition?" he asked.

"Her condition?" Bellows said, as if it was the stupidest question imaginable. "She is eighty-three, my lord."

"As I am well aware. Does she keep to her bed?"

"Her bed? My lord, it is three o'clock in the afternoon!"

Marcus supposed that was meant to be a no.

"She is in the drawing room. That is where she is at three o'clock. Always."

"Excellent, lead me in, Bellows."

Interestingly, Bellows almost seemed as if he would refuse to do it. Then, the fellow nodded sadly. "This way, my lord."

He was led into the drawing room to discover Lady Monroe at piquet with her equally ancient lady's maid. The maid made some effort to jump from her chair, but then gave it up and collapsed back into it.

"Lady Monroe," he said, with a quick bow. "I felt inclined to visit and see how you got on."

"How I get on?" Lady Monroe said, looking him up and down in deep suspicion. "I'm eighty-three, how am I to get on? I'd have to roll the clocks back to have any hope of getting on. I'm just clinging to where I am and am not getting on anywhere."

The lady's maid nodded, as if this were the most obvious point in the world.

"I could not be sure, based on your rather opaque letter."

"I suppose you'll want tea, and a dinner too, and a bed. A lot of trouble but I suppose I'll have to put up with it. Marcie," she said to her maid, "do go and see to it and tell Cook it is not my fault. I didn't invite him."

Bellows hurried forward and gave a hand to Marcie, as Marcus could not see how else she would have got out of her chair on her own. The lady toddled out of the room to give the bad news to Cook.

Marcus took the maid's place and glanced at her cards, which did not look very promising.

"Do me the favor of not drinking me out of house and home, if you please. My wine cellar is getting a bit thin these days."

"I would be happy to remedy that deficiency," Marcus said, making mental note to put in an order with his wine merchant. Lady Monroe preferred a light hock at dinner and a sherry before retiring.

"Alright, alright, if you'll fill my cellar, then drink as much as you like," Lady Monroe said. "Now, why have you come?"

"To see if you were doing poorly."

"You don't need eyes for that—I'm eighty-three! No, it is something else. I've known you since you were a boy. Something else weighs on you. Well, I suppose I could spend hours and hours dragging it out of you, but that is not a wise plan! I'm eighty-three and may fall asleep at any moment."

A maid came in with a tea tray and set it down on the table. After she'd left and closed the door behind her, Marcus said, "Where is your housekeeper? Mrs. Gibbons?"

"Dead," Lady Monroe said. She leaned forward and whispered, "One of the reasons she never replied to your letter. Guess what that woman had the nerve to do? She answered the door to Lord Winderly and dropped dead at his feet. She never did like Winderly."

Marcus could hardly suppose that Mrs. Gibbons chose the moment for her last breath to spite Lord Winderly, but he also supposed there was no point in arguing the subject.

"Out with it, Marcus. I might be eighty-three but my eyes still work. What is on your mind? Your awful father is as dead as I will shortly be, so it cannot be that situation. Hah! If I see him in heaven, which I very much doubt, I will have some choice words for him to consider."

"Really, I am quite well, Lady Monroe," Marcus said. He was always a bit befuddled by the lady. She was odd, and yet oddly perceptive.

"It's a woman, it must be. It's always a woman with men your age."

"As it happens, I am thinking of engaging myself," Marcus said. It was the first time he'd said it aloud and it somehow made it more real, as if it were a set thing. Which, he supposed it was, assuming the lady was agreeable.

"Tell me about her," Lady Monroe said, looking over the biscuits and cakes that her cook had sent up.

"Ah, well, her name is Lady Patience Nicolet, daughter of the Duke of Pelham."

Lady Monroe snorted. "Pelham, you say. What a fellow."

"I see you are acquainted with the gentleman."

"Long ago, when I was not eighty-three and still able to ca-vort round the town."

"I know he can seem unusual, but really he is not as strange as he might seem. I do not think."

"Do not climb on your high horse over it. The duke is great fun. Gracious, when he was a young buck he had the matrons of the town fanning themselves. Not this matron though—I found him exceedingly entertaining. Did you know that he challenged a baron to meet him on a green and then did not bother to turn up? Said he wasn't an early riser, hah! Or that he set Lady Vanderwake's curtains on fire? His sister was forever chasing after him crying, 'Roland!' Very amusing."

Marcus supposed he should have known that Lady Monroe would not be fanning himself over the duke's behavior. "They have a one-eyed, three-legged dog now," he said.

"Of course they do. If there is anything unusual to be done, that duke will do it. Good for you, Marcus, you shan't be bored."

"Well, I have not positively decided…"

"Nonsense, of course you have."

"My only concern is, I think you know the sort of household I was raised in. I really did have the intention of securing a more…staid sort of lady."

"Oh I see, you didn't like the ruckus of your youth and so thought you might turn the family pile of bricks into a tomb, did you?"

"Not a tomb, exactly. More a guarantee of peace."

"There are no guarantees in this life but death and inheritance taxes. Death is my problem and the inheritance tax will be yours."

Marcus was beginning to see that Lady Monroe was right, there really were not any guarantees as to how a thing would turn out. Of course, he supposed it did not matter much, as his mind felt decided.

Marcie came back into the room. "My lady, Cook asks if you want beef or beef or if not that, then beef on account of the late notice."

"Tell that scoundrel that beef will do very well. And tell Bellows to bring up a few bottles of wine, two for us and two for the servants' table—Lord Stanford has promised to fill up my cellar."

Marcie seemed delighted with this news and hobbled out as fast as her old legs could carry her.

"Now that you're here, I suppose you ought to stay for a day or two," Lady Monroe said. "I've got a pile of papers in the library that I cannot make heads or tails of."

Marcus nodded. He would of course wish to rush back to Town, but he would stay and do his duty for Lady Monroe.

"So why'd you think I was dying, causing you to turn up?"

"I did not think you were dying, no, certainly not. It was just…well you did send some original items…"

"What items?"

Marcus began to wonder if Lady Monroe's memory was going. "Well, the old case with the scent, which I presume was Lord Monroe's. But then the bottle of molasses, I really could not divine the meaning of it. And the clock with the note that said 'tick-tock tick-tock' that I thought might be some sort of message. Then the second letter arriving the same day that only said tick-tock tick-tock Hurry Up!"

"I did not send you anything. Ask Bellows, he'll tell you. Oh wait, I see it now, you think I'm losing my wits, do you? They are the last to go and I am holding on tight to them. Sending you molasses, indeed. I never heard of anything more ridiculous."

Marcus was not at all certain if the lady did not send the items, or some of them if not all of them. But if she did not send them, then who did? Or perhaps she had sent them and forgotten.

He would ask Bellows about it and he would gather his own observations over the next few days.

THE MASQUE WAS a swirling kaleidoscope of colors and visions. People had come in every description—milkmaids, bishops, ancient Greeks, pirates, highwaymen, faeries, jesters, all peppered with dashing men in dominos. Lady Darlington had some interesting ideas regarding how a masque was to be hosted. An orchestra played in the background and guests were ushered into her ballroom, but it was not a ball.

Rather, there were booths set up where one could cast their vote for the most original costume, or the most daring, or the most like the person who wore it, with charming prizes for the winner.

An army of liveried footmen circulated with trays of champagne, hock, and claret, and sideboards were set up along the walls with all manner of things that might be picked up and did not require a knife and fork.

Patience was falcon-eyed for who she looked for. All she need do is find the gentleman who wore the distinctive black leather full mask. It should not be too much trouble to do so, as every gentleman in a domino that she had viewed so far wore a half mask.

What was more trouble to do was to take Felicity's advice and say something to Lord Stanford. To expose herself to rejection and ridicule. Perhaps he would even find it unladylike. To soothe those terrors, she was just now working on her third glass of champagne.

The duke glanced at her glass and said, "Steady on, girl."

"I am looking for courage in these bubbles, Papa."

"Well if you have not found it in there by now, I suggest looking in another direction. Spirits will only take you so far in that pursuit."

Patience supposed that was true. She felt a little bit braver having fortified herself, but then just the smallest bit wobbly too.

CHAPTER THIRTEEN

O UT OF THE corner of her eye, Patience saw her aunt sailing toward her in Queen Elizabeth's full regalia, right down to the enormous ruff that appeared to choke her round the neck. She laid a hand on her father's arm and whispered, "Behave, Papa."

"Behave? Not likely, my dear. Not with our virgin queen barreling in our direction."

"Roland, what on earth is the meaning of your costume?" Lady Marchfield asked. She briefly turned to Patience and said, "You look lovely, my dear."

"I could very well ask you the same," the duke said, eyeing his sister. "Unless the virgin queen means to say that her lord has not ever got round to doing his duty. Can't say I'm surprised, though."

"Do not be such an uncouth beast, which is helpful advice that I am confident you will ignore. Now seriously, why have you dressed as some sort of, well, a sort of clergyman in a surplice going up in flames? Do you mean to go so far as to insult the church?"

"I don't, though Valor intends to tell our vicar it was him going to the devil, hah! He will be very put out!"

"He is curtains afire, Aunt," Patience said. "You see, because he's set curtains on fire twice."

"Twice?" Lady Marchfield asked. "He's done it *again?*"

"Well, it was really more of a singe this time," Patience said. "At the candlelight picnic. Lady Jellerbey took it in good humor."

Lady Marchfield's complexion went very white and she began to more resemble the powdered virgin queen. "Mark me, Roland, you will bring these girls to ruin. Mark me."

She turned on her heel and the duke called after her. "Do not talk to me of ruin when your lord could not even get round to it!"

"Papa," Patience said. "You tease my aunt too much, I think."

"I would not tease her at all if she did not stick her nose in," the duke said.

Of course, that was true. If Lady Marchfield would just leave the duke be, they would probably get on much better. As it was, it seemed they would always be oil and water. Patience sometimes wondered if it was because Lady Marchfield had not had any children. She speculated that children could be so exhausting that they wore a person out and beat down all their stiff standards. That's what the duke said, in any case. He claimed he was very civilized before he had children, though Patience was not sure she believed *that* part.

Lord Kendrickson approached with Lady Alice on his arm. "Your Grace, Lady Patience."

Lady Alice curtsied prettily and looked quite recovered from her illness. "Your Grace," she said to the duke. She grasped Patience's hand. "Dear Lady Patience, the flower arrangement you sent to speed me on my recovery really did cheer me. They were lovely."

Before Patience could acknowledge the thanks, Lord Kendrickson blurted out, "Have you heard? We are engaged!"

Patience took the smallest stagger back and her father took her arm to steady her. Gracious, she had hoped there would be a match there, but she had not expected Lord Kendrickson to move quite so fast. Lady Alice appeared bashful and delighted.

"You see," Lord Kendrickson went on, "Lady Alice's stomach complaint at the candlelight picnic was caused by her growing inclination toward me. She is prone to such things."

The duke laughed. "Hah! Best to know about that sort of thing up front, eh?"

This caused Lady Alice, who was charmingly dressed as a housekeeper in a prim dress, white cap, and a dangling set of keys to blush up to her eyebrows.

"The banns have not yet been read," Lady Alice said, "but word has somehow got out, so we are telling everyone we know ourselves."

"Our mothers are getting on famously. Really, it is rather wonderful to be alive these days," Lord Kendrickson said.

"We both feel very blessed," Lady Alice said.

"Come, my love," Lord Kendrickson said. "I see Matley over there—he will like to know our news." They set off, arm and arm, across the ballroom.

"Well now, see that?" the duke said, "Nothing has come of your fears regarding Lord Stanford and Lady Alice. Just as I thought."

Though her father appeared quite sanguine over the situation, there was one dire thought that began to haunt Patience. What if Lord Stanford were disappointed in some way upon hearing of the engagement? How would she know? She had told Felicity she would not be a second choice.

Then, she saw him. He stood alone, wearing the distinctive full black leather mask. It really did look a bit ominous, just as Lord Radler had described.

It was now or never. She could act, or she could simply fold her hands and wait. A proper lady would fold her hands and wait. A lady like Lady Alice would maintain a demure disinterest until words had been spoken to her. She certainly would not dare to speak them herself.

But then, as was very usual, Patience could not live up to her name. She was too impatient to bear it.

She handed her glass to her father. "Wish me luck, Papa."

"What ho? What game is this?" her father asked, taking her glass. She did not answer, but hurried across the ballroom floor before her courage failed her. She would just barrel ahead and not pause to think about it. It would be the only way to do it.

She reached Lord Stanford, grasped his harm, and blurted out, "I think there is something between us. That is, I wish it is so. I cannot wait longer to know. You must say something, whether it is what I wish to hear or not. I must know!"

He turned to her and stared, but he did not speak. He suddenly shook her hand from his arm, turned, and strode from the ballroom.

He left. He said nothing at all and just left her standing there.

Patience sank down, her legs giving way. It was as if her spirit was leaving her body, and she no longer had control of it. She had wished for an answer, and she had got it. He had run from her. Her feelings were not returned in the slightest. It was over, all her hopes were to come to nothing.

Why had she said anything? Why had she not been a proper lady and folded her hands and waited? If she had done so, she would have discovered through slow degrees and a thousand cuts what his opinion was. She would have held on to her dignity though. He would not have known of her feelings. Now, he would always know them. Every time she encountered him, he would know them.

People were turning to stare at her. The orchestra paused its playing. Ladies looked on in alarm. Lord Bakersfield rushed to her side to help her to her feet. They almost felt numb, as if she'd walked long on the moors in the wintertime and they'd got too cold.

Her father pushed through. "Thank you, Bakersfield, I'll take it from here. My daughter was feeling faint earlier, I should have forbidden her to come. Now it's caught up to her. Do me the favor of calling my carriage, would you?"

Bakersfield hurried ahead of them to do the duke's bidding. "There now, girl," her father whispered, "I do not know what has gone on, but keep it all inside until we are safely in the carriage."

Patience nodded and worked to suppress the tears that were

working their way to her eyes. Her father was right, she must work to avoid turning this disaster into a widely known spectacle. She had already lost her pride and dignity to Lord Stanford; it would be well to try to keep that information from the *ton*. If her shame were to get out, what a story it would be!

"Did you hear? The Duke of Pelham's daughter imposed herself on Lord Stanford and then fell on the floor when she was rebuffed. How has that girl been raised? So unladylike. We imagine Stanford is positively mortified to be importuned in such a manner."

They would be cruel words and very well earned.

What an idiot she was! She'd lost her heart, her pride, and her dignity, all in one fell swoop. Her impatience and determination that things go her way, accompanied by three ill-advised glasses of champagne, had driven her right off the road and into an impossible ditch.

The next minutes went by in a blur—both in her mind and her rapidly filling eyes. The duke shooed off any onlookers in the great hall and, such was his reputation, not a single person defied him. Thankfully, the carriage turned up quickly. The duke hustled his daughter inside and rapped on the roof.

As the carriage set off, he said, "All right, cry away. In between sobs, do tell me what Stanford has done."

"He's done nothing but communicate his disdain, Papa," Patience said, wiping her eyes with his handkerchief. "I said that I thought there was something between us and he just stared at me and then ran away. I was all wrong, though I was certain I was right."

"I don't understand this at all," the duke said, rubbing his chin. "All I can think is that it came as a shock. He's a cautious and reserved sort of fellow, perhaps the shock overtook him. I speculate that the next you see him he will sing a different tune. Perhaps he will even call on the morrow to apologize for his beastly behavior and declare himself. Yes, I really would not be surprised if he did so."

Patience wiped her eyes. "Do you really think so, Papa?"

"I do. It would not surprise me if he's collected himself already and returned to the ballroom. It will be well for him to discover you gone—let him spend a tortuous night reflecting on his actions."

Patience found she did find the smallest bit of comfort in imagining Lord Stanford spending a tortuous night. She did not know if her father was right in his assumptions or not, but she must hold on to the hope that he was. If he was not…if Lord Stanford had found her declaration so repulsive or alarming or whatever he had found it…

"Papa, if you are not right, if Lord Stanford really wishes nothing to do with me, well then… I am afraid we must return home. I could not bear to be here. And then next season, I will come back recovered and help Serenity and I promise not to make her nervous with my toe-tapping. After this night, I will work very hard to stop my toe-tapping altogether."

"Let us just see what unfolds," the duke counseled.

"But if you are wrong, we will go home?"

"Why not? If you are right, which I very much doubt you are, then I have been just as mistaken as you have been. The Dales air will do us both good. *If* you are to be disappointed, that is, which I still do not believe you are."

There it was then. If Lord Stanford did not come rushing to her side on the morrow, she would know that his first reaction was his permanent and final reaction—she had been rebuffed.

KENDRICKSON HAD GONE to see Radler while Stanford was away on account of Radler sending him an alarming communication that he must come at once.

Having found happiness so recently that he was always the slightest bit nervous that his happiness could suddenly vanish, he'd rushed there as fast as he could. What had happened? Had he heard something about the match between himself and Lady Alice? Was it all to be snatched away somehow? Perhaps the earl was enraged that they so publicly spoke of it before the banns were even read or he had time to advertise it himself?

The only other thing it could possibly be was that Radler had caused some kind of mischief while Stanford was away. Had he caused a fire or driven a valued servant to turn in their notice?

He was led into the drawing room and had seen no evidence of fire in the great hall. He came upon a very poorly-looking Radler curled up on a sofa and deep under a blanket with a pillow behind his head.

Waiting until the door was shut and they were alone, Kendrickson said, "What has happened?"

"I've ruined everything. At least, I am fairly confident that I have. I am a terrible friend. The worst friend a fellow could have. Nobody should have anything to do with me."

"Ruined what, though?" Kendrickson asked, looking round for anything broken.

"The match! The match between Stanford and Lady Patience. It will never happen now and I have been the author of the disaster."

Kendrickson was so taken aback that he sank down into a chair. "My God, you did not… meddle with the lady?"

"Meddle? No, not in the way you mean."

"You'd better tell me everything," Kendrickson said, not entirely sure he wished to hear what everything was.

Radler took a swig from a brandy bottle that had been apparently lurking under his blanket. He then went on to describe how he'd borrowed Stanford's mask and he'd forgotten he'd told Lady Patience about it. That lady approached him and expressed her very fond feelings for him and he was so shocked that she should declare herself to him and not Stanford that he'd run away. But then, after he'd returned home, he remembered that he'd told Lady Patience that Stanford would wear the mask. She had approached him as if he *were* Stanford. And then, she'd watched him run away. As Stanford. Because that's who she thought he was.

"You've got to tell her!" Kendrickson cried. "You've got to tell her it was you and not Stanford right away!"

"I've thought of that, but then I thought I must tell Stanford first. He may wish to tell her. I've already mucked things up enough, I do not wish to do any further damage. I sent him a letter by messenger today, outlining the… unfortunate mix-up. I'll do as he directs me. I expect he'll return himself, throw me from the house, and then go fix it. As I said, I am a terrible friend."

"No you are not. You did run off when you thought she was relaying feelings for you when you know that Stanford carries a torch. She's a duke's daughter with a hefty dowry, other men might not have been so scrupulous."

"Very kind, I'm sure, but I do not think Stanford will be so charitable. He will think me an absolute idiot."

"Oh, well as to that, he will be right—you *have* been an absolute idiot. But that does not make you a bad friend."

"Very kind again," Radler mumbled.

"You've got to get yourself together and look on the sunny side of things. It's likely to all work out in the end. I am engaged to Lady Alice, after all—you see how things work out well eventually."

Kendrickson did not think that sentiment particularly cheered his friend. But it would probably work out in the end. At least, he hoped so. Radler had been an absolute idiot, but an honorable idiot all the same.

As well, he was probably right to allow Stanford to decide what to do next. And right about Stanford's temper over it. Kendrickson could only imagine his own feelings if anything of the sort had gone on with Lady Alice.

Thank heavens it had not.

Just then, the drawing room doors were thrown open. Stanford's very harried-looking valet stood in the doorway. "Lord Radler, terrible news."

"More terrible news?" Radler said, sinking further under his blanket.

"We have somehow been invaded by case moths! I do not know how it could have happened. They are everywhere—I just now found a hole in one of my lord's coats and then I checked the other ones, and well, the damage is extensive. I will air out his clothes and cover them in cedar shavings, but so much has been ruined already!"

"Case moths," Radler whispered. "I will be relocating out of the house sooner than I had planned."

"As will I," Kendrickson said, leaping to his feet. "I have no extra funds for a new wardrobe and Lady Alice will not like to see me moth-eaten. No, I am sure she would not. Good-day, Radler, I'm sure things will come right."

Kendrickson took a speedy leave of the premises. The bane of every valet's existence was moths. They were crafty creatures and it was never enough to eliminate the ones that could be seen.

He could not imagine what Stanford's feelings would be on discovering that not only had his match with Lady Patience been endangered, but his clothes were fast being devoured by case moths.

THOUGH PATIENCE HAD sworn to herself that she would give up her toe-tapping, she'd so far spent all day in the drawing room, toe-tapping. And with an aching head to boot, due to her overindulgence the evening before. Her father had been convinced that Lord Stanford would show himself, but he had not yet made an appearance.

Her sisters were well aware that something was afoot, but Patience had not wept in front of them, so they were not sure what. Mrs. Right had very kindly taken them all out of the house to the shops to give her some peace.

She'd listened to the carriage wheels that had passed through the square all day long and finally she'd heard wheels roll to a stop in front of the house. She leapt from her chair and ran to the window, pulling the curtain aside.

She dropped it closed. It was her aunt come to call. She could not bear a scolding just now. Patience was certain her aunt had seen her sink to the floor at the masque and had arrived for an explanation.

Well, she would not get one. Nothing would induce Patience to provide a recitation of last night's events to her aunt, only to be told how foolish she'd been. She already knew she'd been foolish.

Charlie led Lady Marchfield into the room. Her aunt said, "Where is Mr. Grimsby? I asked this scoundrel of a footman, but he refuses to say."

"Oh, him. He left to open a haberdashery somewhere or other."

Lady Marchfield's reticule slipped off her wrist and fell to the floor. "What?"

Charlie hurried to retrieve it from the carpet and handed it to her under a severe glare. He then fairly ran from the room and shut the door behind him.

"Come now, Aunt, you know very well that my papa does not wish for a butler. Mr. Grimsby was bound to be gone some way or other."

"This is outrageous. I have done everything in my power to help you girls get settled respectably and at every turn I am defied and insulted. Now look what you've come to! You have no butler in the house, unlike every other decent household in London, and you've gone mooning over a gentleman who apparently takes issue with the lax goings-on in this family."

Patience felt her heart freeze into a hard and cold stone in her chest. What did she know? What had she heard? Was it possible that Lord Stanford had told people what she'd done? She would not have believed it of him. If it were to get out, she imagined it would be someone who had somehow overheard her. "What do you mean, Lord Stanford takes issue with the family?"

"Well he's gone, hasn't he? A gentleman does not decamp in the middle of the season because he is interested in a lady, does he? No, he runs off to get away. I have told you girls a thousand times that your ill-conceived habits would catch up to you and now they have."

"What do you mean? Lord Stanford has left Town?" Patience felt short of breath, as if all the air in the room had gone somewhere else.

"He went off somewhere, Kent, I believe it is said. The point is, he left. Now I hope that serves as some sort of lesson. Really, you all must stop going on as you have. I heard that you fell on the floor in a faint at the masque. I am very glad not to have witnessed it as I suspect the real cause was an overindulgence in champagne. If you decide to take on more sense, I will offer a room for you in my own house and give you instruction on how to proceed appropriately. Until then, I take my leave of this circus."

Lady Marchfield strode to the door, threw it open, practically ran over Charlie, and slammed the front door behind her.

Lord Stanford was gone. Now she knew. There could be no doubt now. He'd found her feelings abhorrent. He was probably in love with Lady Alice and then he'd discovered that lady had engaged herself to Lord Kendrickson. Then, as if that were not painful enough, strange Lady Patience Nicolet had the effrontery to throw herself at him. He must be disgusted with her. So disgusted that he'd packed up and left.

Patience leapt up and ran out into the hall. She shouted up the stairs. "Papa! Papa, we must go home at first light tomorrow! Papa! We really must go!"

The duke made his way to the landing in response to her shouting. "Give him time, Patience, the day is not done yet."

"He's left Town," Patience said. "Do you see? He's left Town to get away from me. There cannot be any firmer answer than that."

Patience burst into tears in the great hall, which was really very aggravating. She never wished for the footmen to see her in such a state. They looked downright terrified.

Her father came down the stairs and walked her to her bedchamber. "I cannot say I understand any of this, but I think you ought to rest. What does Mrs. Right usually do in such situations?" the duke asked.

Patience sniffled. "She closes the curtains and she brings tea with a drop of laudanum and some of the spice biscuits she keeps for such occasions," she said. "And a cold cloth for my forehead. Then she pats my hand and tells me everything will look brighter after I've slept for a while."

"That sounds full of good sense and so that is precisely what I will do," the duke said.

"But we will go home? I could not bear to stay here, pretending all is well. I could not bear for people who saw me sink to the floor at the masque inquire into how I am feeling. We could say I went consumptive and you have taken me home."

"You will sleep and I will get everything moving in the right direction. We will leave at dawn."

The duke strode out of the room and if Patience could be grateful for anything just now, it was that she had a very sympathetic father. She would go home and be surrounded by all the things she was used to. She would sink into the comfort of her sisters' company and all the familiar faces and places. Somehow, she would recover from this disastrous season.

CHAPTER FOURTEEN

MRS. RIGHT WAS well aware that something awful had happened to Patience and it had to do with Lord Stanford. She did not know the details of it until she'd brought the younger girls back from shopping.

Then she, along with her younger charges, were told all by the duke. Stanford was a scoundrel and had skipped Town. They would leave for the Dales in the morning.

Serenity, Winsome, and Verity had hurried above stairs. Mrs. Right sat in the drawing room, while Valor whispered heatedly to Mrs. Wendover.

Valor jumped up. "Mrs. Right, I am going to write a terrible letter to Lord Stanford and tell him exactly what I think." She marched off and Mrs. Right thought she might do just the same. She would leave it unsigned, but that breaker of hearts would be forced to hear a few words from her.

After that, she would begin the arduous process of packing trunks. The duke was quite right in taking her dear Patience home—she would recover her spirits far faster in the Dales than she ever would in this pit of vipers.

Before she could enact such a plan, Winsome hurried into the room. "We are surrounding Patience with sisterly love, but I had to step out a moment to tell you something. Lady Marchfield was here and Patience told her Mr. Grimsby had left to open a haberdashery and her head nearly blew off her shoulders. I thought that might cheer you up."

Mrs. Right smiled, inordinately pleased. "My girls know me so well, I am cheered indeed. I am only sorry I was not here to tell her myself."

Winsome nodded knowingly. "Now I am going to get the blue, knitted blanket from my room and take it to Patience. She really likes it and I stole it out of her room two days ago."

"Very considerate, my dear."

Winsome jogged out of the room. Mrs. Right called, "Charlie, Thomas, alert Cook and the stables that we depart on the morrow. Check with Mr. Reynolds too." She supposed the duke would have already told his valet of it, but it was best to be certain. Mr. Reynolds was a serious sort and liked to be well-organized and not rushed.

She crossed the room and took the writing things from the desk.

Stanford—

That's right, I call you Stanford. I will not even give you the courtesy of calling you a lord. Lords must act lordly to earn the title.

As you have chosen to allow the greatest thing in your life to slip through your hands, I thought I would take this opportunity to point out your idiocy. I will not name the lady, but rest assured she will recover her spirits and return to this town to make a brilliant match as you look on, wallowing in your grave error. It will be too late, sir!

Regards from a disgusted onlooker who looks forward to you drowning in wallowing grief

Also, have a care for your clothes. I understand the moths are terrible this season.

As she folded the letter, she heard Valor in the hall. "Thomas, could you put your regular clothes on and deliver this to Lord Stanford's house?"

"I am not sure I should, Lady Valor, we are leaving on the

morrow and there are heaps to do."

Mrs. Right strode out to the hall. "You may go, Thomas, and take this letter too."

"Did you give him the what-for, Mrs. Right?" Valor asked.

"I most certainly did."

Valor looked pleased to hear it. "I gave him the what-for too. The most awful what-for I've ever wrote in my life." She clapped her hands. "He will be devastated!"

Mrs. Right thought that must really be saying something, considering some of the other letters Valor had authored in other seasons. Lord Stanford would shortly feel the wrath of the Nicolet household.

MARCUS HAD SPENT the past two days in two different activities. One, sorting through the mountain of papers that Lady Monroe had allowed to pile on her desk. There were all sorts of bills from vendors to the house that the housekeeper would have organized for the steward, had that lady been still living. Bellows might have taken over the task, and really should have been doing it from the beginning, but that fellow did not do things he did not like to do. He did not like the steward much and did not like to do anything for the fellow at all. The steward, not being informed of the pile up of bills, had allowed things to fall behind.

When Marcus was not untangling paperwork, Lady Monroe had him captured in the drawing room playing piquet and interrogating him on his life. Most particularly, interrogating him about Lady Patience. Lady Monroe was vastly amused to hear that Lady Patience played the crwth, for one thing.

He occasionally was able to escape to the gardens, usually when Lady Monroe's lady's maid was occupying her with some matter. He'd found the gardens in rather overgrown and shabby shape and resolved to bring in a gardener to straighten it all out.

Apparently, the old gardener had retired and Lady Monroe had got it into her head that nobody could ever take his place, and so nobody had.

The sun was beginning to set, and Marcus had reluctantly just come in from one of these outdoor respites when he found Bellows standing in the hall with a letter for him.

He took it and slipped into the library, as he could hear Lady Monroe and Marcie the maid chattering in the drawing room. The letter was from Radler. Marcus opened it and read through it, eager for news of Lady Patience.

He felt his heart speed up and his blood course through his body in triple time by the time he got to the end of it. He read it again, just to be certain that his first idea of throttling Radler was the correct one.

Stanford—

I have some surprising news. Or distressing news, or minor hiccup news, depending on how sanguine about life you are feeling at the moment.

Remember that wondrous full mask you had made and so generously let me borrow for Lady Darlington's masque? I reckon you do. Well, here is what happened because of that blasted mask.

Lady Patience approached me very abruptly. (She looked smashing, by the way) And she said she was sure there was something between us and she would know what it was, for good or ill, and she hoped for good.

Well, as you can imagine, I could hardly anticipate that Lady Patience would express any feelings for me and did what any right-minded gentleman would do. I said nothing and ran away.

After getting home and recovering myself from the shock, I remembered that I'd told Lady Patience that you would wear the mask. I described exactly what it looked like. Then it became apparent to me that when she approached me, she believed that she approached you. (Bad luck that we are so similar in build!)

> *I thought I might rush to her house to attempt to clear up the confusion but Kendrickson agrees with me that I ought to alert you to this mix-up first, as you may wish to handle it yourself with no further involvement from me. Kendrickson also says that I have not been a terrible friend, as I did run away upon hearing Lady Patience express her mistaken regard.*
>
> *I know you will not wish to encounter me when you return so have taken myself off to a cousin's house in Bedford Square. Also, I probably would have gone anyway. Your valet reports that your dressing room has suddenly been beset with case moths and we all know how they cannot be contained. (The fellow is in a state at the moment, as apparently the moths have been fond of your coats. He suspects they came from that old case that housed the half-filled bottle of scent.)*
>
> *I suppose the good news is that Lady Patience does indeed seem inclined to you. Of course, the bad news is that she believes she apprised you of it and you ran away.*

Let us hope for better days ahead,
Your idiot friend, Radler

Idiot indeed, that was painting it very lightly. What must Lady Patience think?

But then, she'd expressed her regard. Why had he not been there!

As the entire situation settled into his mind, several things began to bubble up that had not been spelled out in the letter. Had he really dragged his heels to such a degree that Lady Patience had been forced to outright question him?

If he was perceived as particularly slow off the mark, had all these clock-related things not come from Lady Monroe? Had they in fact emanated from the duke's household?

But most importantly, he must fix Lady Patience's impression of who she had spoken to at the masque. What must she think of him? What must she feel at this moment? Radler had run away. Not walked, but run. She had been humiliated.

He strode into the drawing room. "Lady Monroe, it has been a pleasure to visit but I find I must return to London at first light to attend to some urgent business."

Lady Monroe nodded. "Finally decided to get off the pot, did you?"

Marcus would hardly dignify that sort of vulgarity with an answer and really thought Lady Monroe spent far too much time in the company of her lady's maid. "I have things to attend to," he said.

"By things, I hope you mean Lady Patience. It's time you stop trying to avoid what you did not like in your youth and go forward securing what you do like."

As usual, Lady Monroe was odd and oddly insightful. "Are you certain you did not send the scent in the old case to me?"

"Entirely certain."

"Well, I only say, it has brought case moths into my house. Perhaps you ought to check round the house and make sure they've not made any inroads here."

"Case moths!" the lady's maid said, laughing. "Gracious, you'll never get rid of them. Stoic little monsters, those."

"I would not tolerate case moths in this house, young man," Lady Monroe said. "I can assure you we guard against that sort of thing here—cedar chests are the way to go. Now, off with you, pack your things, and I will have some of the last good wine brought up from the cellars for dinner. Remember, you promised to fill my wine cellar—don't send cheap stuff."

PATIENCE VERY MUCH appreciated her family's efforts to cheer her up over dinner the evening before. They'd had fricasseed chicken, which everyone knew was Patience's favorite dinner and her father had directed Charlie to be very liberal with the wine pouring.

Grace had heard the news, probably from Serenity, and had joined them. She found herself very disappointed in Lord Stanford and she said Dashlend was positively puzzled by his decampment.

Felicity had sent over a note of encouragement. She did not know what had gone wrong, but it was bound to eventually come right.

Winsome said that, in solidarity with her sister, she would hate Lord Stanford forever. If there was the slightest thing she might do for him in future, she would absolutely refuse.

Serenity claimed that she would not look at him twice next season, else she wept over the hurt done to her sister.

Verity posited that it was very usual for a gentleman to run away, but even though it was usual, she could not like it.

Of all of them, Valor's stance had been the most alarming. She'd bided her time and after everyone expressed their disdain for Lord Stanford and what they intended to do about it, she said, "You are all thinking of the future, but I have already taken steps."

This rather stopped the conversation in its tracks.

"Not another letter, eh, Valor?" the duke asked.

Valor shrugged. "What else can I do, Papa? I'm not allowed to take the carriage out by myself. If I was allowed, I'd take a bucketful of horse leavings and tip it over his head, but I'm not allowed."

"Valor," Patience said with trepidation, "what exactly did you write?"

For some reason, Valor seemed less enthusiastic about revealing what precisely she'd said. "Well, you know, the usual sort of thing one writes in this situation."

The duke laughed. "I bet it was a corker!"

"Valor? Spill it," Patience said.

"All right. First, I did not come up with it on my own. Mrs. Wendover thought of it. Also, I did not have time to write a long letter. Finally, I'd appreciate it if nobody tells the vicar. Also finally, Papa, do not be angry that I cursed."

The duke was wiping his eyes with laughter. "It'll be a corker!"

"Valor?" Patience asked, her toes tapping the floor.

Valor shrugged and said, "I wrote, I hope you die because you are so awful the devil will take you to hell and burn you up forever." She paused, examining her fingernails. "Or something like that."

"Oh Valor, you did not sign your name to it?" Patience said, embarrassed to think that Lord Stanford would realize how devastated she was.

"No, I signed it Mrs. W. because it really was her idea. I just agreed with it," Valor said.

Patience had done everything she possibly could to convince herself that Lord Stanford would not connect that letter to her household. She'd already been shamed enough. She knew Valor meant to help, but her youngest sister could not be allowed to send any more letters out of the house!

Now, they were blessedly on their way home. They had not informed Lady Marchfield of the decampment. She would discover it sooner or later and would write a stern letter of some sort. That was best, as Patience did not wish to be closely questioned by her aunt.

She certainly would not take the lady up on her offer to move to the Marchfield household. Even if Patience could bear to stay in London, she could not bear the constant lectures. She loved her aunt, in her own way, but she loved her more in small doses and great distances.

The departure from Grosvenor Square had been far more organized than it usually was, all her sisters seeming to understand the necessity of it. Winsome did not bother hiding Verity's pelisse. Serenity did not lollygag round the garden, checking for dead bees. Even Valor had taken care not to lose track of Mrs. Wendover, thereby avoiding an extensive search. Nelson had been absolutely stymied in his efforts to get hold of that stuffed rabbit.

Unlike other trips, where Patience might be in a carriage with Verity, Serenity, and Winsome, she rode with her father and Mrs. Right. She got the idea that they wished to keep an eye on her.

"It is all right, Papa," she said, in answer to the question he had not asked. "I've made a fool of myself and given my heart where it was not wanted. It will not be the death of me. I am not some swooning and delicate sort of girl who cannot withstand a tragedy or two."

Mrs. Right patted her hand. "Stanford is a fool, if you ask me. He'll realize it one of these days. He'll wed some dry lady and then wake up to his mistake."

"That will not especially help me, though," Patience pointed out.

"I cannot say I understand what's happened," the duke said. "My instincts are never wrong about these things."

Patience sighed. "There is a first time for everything, I suppose."

"Somehow, the fates have something else in store for you, my dear girl," Mrs. Right said. "Your head was turned by that fellow, but my guess is next season you'll find your true love. You will come to think that rogue has done you a favor."

Patience nodded, though she did not really think that would be the case. She imagined she'd always be pining in some manner over Lord Stanford.

She would marry, of course she would. But it would not be to him. If her future lord wished to attend the season in Town, then she would be forced to see Lord Stanford from time to time. It would be impossible to avoid it and a constant reminder of her heartbreak and shame.

"I know what I'll do to cheer you up," the duke said. "We will be stopping for the night soon, and it is an inn that does not know us. How about I launch the old brocabbage pie gambit? I'll have them all run round trying to figure out what this supposed Yorkshire staple is that the duke is insisting he wants, and then I'll tell them I made the whole thing up. That's always good for amusement."

"You are very kind to think of it, Papa," Patience said. "Though, why do we go to a new place? The one we usually stay in was very comfortable, I thought."

"Oh yes, very comfortable indeed. As it happens, that inn-keeper had a private word with Reynolds the last time we stayed there. Apparently, the man was in tears and begged that we not return. You know how some people are—no stamina for a jest."

"I see," Patience said. She supposed it was the brocabbage pie gambit, or the footman drinking like lords before heaving it all up in the yard, or Valor hiding in linen closets, or Winsome claiming one of the waiters looked shifty, or Verity explaining that shifty waiters were a very usual thing... or perhaps all of that together that had discomposed the innkeeper.

"Your father indulges that innkeeper's temperament on ac-count of his liberality of spirit," Mrs. Right said.

"That's true, I am very liberal, am I not?"

"Very liberal, Papa."

The carriage pulled into the innyard. "Well then," the duke said, "let us proceed inside and send these young fellows on the wild goose chase of their lives in search of brocabbage pie. If a duke cannot act eccentric, who can?"

Patience forced herself to smile. This was to be her life now. Her father would run an innkeeper's staff ragged to distract her from her own foolishness.

Aside from the devastation of a broken heart, she felt like a failure. Felicity and Grace had been successful in their seasons. Not so their younger sister. She'd gone into the season so full of confidence. She was certain she would make quick work of finding her match. Then she had done so. Unfortunately, her match had not agreed with her.

CHAPTER FIFTEEN

MARCUS MADE GOOD time back to London. He'd not expected to see Lady Monroe so early in the morning before his departure, but she had been up and dressed. She'd also gone through Lord Monroe's things, as was her habit, and pressed on him a yellowed neckcloth and tortoiseshell comb.

He did not wish to take those two items, but he knew he'd spend an inordinate amount of time on the drive attempting to refuse them. He thanked Lady Monroe and packed them in his panniers.

Bellows, her lady's maid, and Lady Monroe herself stood on the drive to see him off. He could not say any of them were particularly sorry to see him go. He suspected they'd long fallen into a quiet routine and he'd brought a disruption to it.

After wrenching another assurance from him that he would replenish her wine cellar and would not send cheap stuff, Lady Monroe wished him Godspeed and sent him on his way. Bellows even gave his horse a little push on the rump to get him going.

Marcus was determined to go to his house before rushing off to see Lady Patience. He had a lot to explain, and then a momentous idea to propose, and he would not show up looking travel-worn and shabby. Considering what had happened, he already had a very steep hill to climb. It would be well to look as presentable as possible, or at least appear to have made an effort.

He presumed Radler had exaggerated the problem of moths

getting into his coats. His valet would have seen one small evidence of a moth's existence and raised the roof over it. He would not be surprised to find half his wardrobe hanging out in the garden being treated by whatever sunshine there was to be had. But surely, he would find undamaged clothes to put on.

One of his footmen took his reins and he jogged inside.

Whatever he'd thought he would come upon in his house, it had not been pandemonium.

Servants ran back and forth under the direction of the butler. Mr. Jennings whipped round at his entrance. "My lord," he cried, "they are everywhere!"

"What?" he asked.

"The moths!"

His butler had cried out as if French soldiers had invaded the house. Marcus did not know what to make of it, Jennings was usually so regulated.

Cresswell appeared at the top of the stairs. "Everywhere!" his valet shouted. "They've come from that old case that was sent to you which I've since buried in the garden. Why would Lady Monroe inflict them upon you?"

"I do not think that case came from Lady Monroe," Marcus said.

"Then this is is sabotage!" Mr. Jennings cried. "You have a devious enemy, my lord. Just this morning, I found a telltale hole in the velvet of the drawing room sofa!" Mr. Jennings wiped his brow with a handkerchief. "They've made it downstairs, though we tried to hold them off."

So he supposed Radler had not, after all, exaggerated the moth problem. "I imagine Lord Radler decamped already?"

"At the first word of it, my lord," Cresswell said derisively.

"And Lord Kendrickson too," Jennings said dismissively. "They flew out of here like bats at sunset!"

Marcus sighed. "What are we to do about this?" he asked.

"I have called for a specialist, my lord," Jennings said. "I sent the word out to my network of acquaintances and got the word back that there is only one person who can be relied on to solve a problem of this magnitude. Mrs. Crumdek. She should be on her way even now."

"I see," Marcus said. "And what is Mrs. Crumdek to do about it?"

"I have no idea," Jennings said, looking at him quizzically. "If I did, I'd do it myself."

"Cresswell, do I have any coats left that I can actually wear?"

His valet seemed to be weighing his answer. "Sort of, my lord. I've patched up one of the coats that was not too badly damaged and wrapped it up in sheets with cedar chips to protect it from the devils."

"Very well," Marcus said, making his way up the stairs. "I will need a bath, and then I will wear that coat. Let us get on with it, I have somewhere to go and would like to get there as soon as possible."

Cresswell set off to arrange for bath water to be heated. Marcus hoped he did not drop dead of apoplexy over the moths. His valet's complexion was white as new-fallen snow. He supposed that for a valet, finding the clothes one was meant to be tending riddled with holes was a disaster of momentous proportions. Considering what most of Marcus' coats cost, he would not be far wrong.

"Also, my lord," Jennings said, "these two letters were dropped off by some fellow out of his livery. My instincts told me he was a footman by trade, but he was out of uniform and refused to say where he'd come from."

His butler handed them over and Marcus took them above stairs to read while he waited for his bath water.

And what letters they were. One was short and direct, wishing him to the devil, signed by a certain Mrs. W. The other was longer, had dispensed with his title, and hinted that the writer had sent the moths. Who were these people though?

Both letters had been delivered by the same footman out of livery. He did not know a Mrs. W. The second letter certainly emanated from the duke's household as it hinted it knew all about what had happened at the masque. How else would they know, if not told it by Lady Patience? Who in that house would dare such a missive and own sending moths into his house?

Marcus could not put it beyond reason that the duke might have sent the moths, as there really was no telling what that gentleman would get up to. But why? They had arrived well before the disastrous masque. Further, the letter did not sound like him. The handwriting suggested a woman, it was close and neat and felt like a woman's hand.

Marcus put them aside, as he was getting nowhere attempting to divine their authors. All he could gather from them is that while he imagined he'd had a steep hill to climb, it seemed he had a mountain to climb. Climb it he would, though. He had a quick bath to take and a misinformed lady to see. Somehow, he would convince her of the truth of things, and then if she were to see the truth of it, he supposed he did not care where the letters came from. Or the moths, assuming they could be got rid of.

A HALF HOUR later, Marcus leapt on his horse and set off for Grosvenor Square. He had never bathed or dressed so fast in his life. The water had not been topped off with hot to make it tolerable, but he could not wait. Poor Cresswell had dressed him with shaking hands, and it finally occurred to Marcus that the man might be expecting to be dismissed. Once he'd cleared that up, his valet instantly settled into a better frame of mind.

Marcus wore the coat Cresswell had "saved," and if one did not examine it too closely, one might not notice where his valet had made attempts to weave over the small holes near the bottom of it. It would require an expert weaver to repair his clothes, if any could be saved, but there was no time for that now.

When he arrived at the duke's house, he dismounted, but no footman or groom came to get his horse. It was exceedingly odd. How did one run a household without keeping somebody on the watch at a window to look out for visitors?

He ended up paying a boy to hold the reins, warning him of an unholy death if he tried to make off with his horse, and went to the doors and knocked.

Marcus had expected that the door would be opened at once. Whoever was meant to be keeping an eye out the window had likely dozed off. The knocking would rouse him.

Somehow, nobody came. It was unaccountable.

He knocked harder and finally heard some sound behind the door. It swung open, revealing an older fellow in an apron. Where was the butler? Where were the footmen?

The man bowed. "Can I help you, my lord?"

"I have come to see Lady Patience," he said.

The fellow shook his head and murmured, "No, no, no."

Marcus pushed his way into the house, as obviously something was very wrong here. The servants had disappeared and this person who did not seem as if he belonged to the household seemed to be the only individual about? Had the family been taken hostage? Was there some other disaster unfolding? "Excuse me, who are you? Where is the duke's butler?"

"Oh, aye."

"Oh aye, what? I demand to know who you are."

"Me name's Rider, which is funny I always think, as I don't have me own horse to ride. The rider who don't ride, as it were."

"Are you in the duke's employ?" Marcus asked, ignoring the man's speculations of the irony regarding his name.

The man nodded. "I'm the watcher. I wander round here and watch things, so nothing don't go amiss. Good job of it I do, too. Been years at it and nothin' has gone amiss."

Marcus was beginning to think that this man suffered from some sort of derangement. "What is going on here?" he asked.

Rider, as that was the name he claimed, looked round as if to ascertain what was going on. "Nothing goes on, my lord. That's me job—to see that nothing goes on."

"Where is the duke? I demand to know where the duke and his family are this instant."

"Where is the duke? How should I know? He don't confide in me. Be right funny if he did. When he's here, I ain't, and vice versa."

"I demand you tell me everything that you do know!" Really, Marcus wished to throttle the fellow.

"Aye, well I best sit down then. I'm a watcher, you see. Me old body is used to sitting."

"Well, then, sit down!"

Marcus did not know where the man planned to sit, but he was taken aback by the audacity of it when Mr. Rider let himself into the drawing room and sat heavily down in the duke's chair.

"It's a whale of a story," Rider said. "Seems like we ought to have tea, but it's such a palaver. Nothing more aggravatin' then waitin' for water to boil. I always said so. Seems like there ought to be a better way to do it. But what do I know? I'm just a poor working man."

"Just get to it," Marcus said between gritted teeth.

"Right you are. You see, good sir—"

"Lord," Marcus said.

"Oh, aye. I should'a known, what with the fine clothes that only been patched up a bit." The fellow's eye's drifted down to the bottom of Marcus' coat, examining it. Whatever else this man was, he had sharp eyes.

"Never mind that, go on. Get to the point," he said.

"The point, yes, everybody does like a point. Well now, the point is I weren't supposed to be here just now. I was to come in a month so I was staying with my sister just outside of Wembley. That's my habit when the duke's in Town. She, meaning my sister, likes my company and I help around her little place with the chickens and such when I'm not here watchin' for the duke, you understand. She's got five chickens at the moment, if I'm countin' them up. She's got a fine rooster what keeps the whole thing thrivin,' if you understand me. I like chicken, but then I reckon everybody does so nothin' special about it. Anyway, right out of the clear blue sky, a fellow from the duke's household comes barreling up in a carriage and says I'm wanted. Well, what was I to do? When the duke wants a fellow, that fellow has to go. So I say my goodbyes to Aggy, that's my sister, and I got in the carriage. No wait, Aggy packed me a piece of ham and an apple, for the journey and *then* I got in the carriage."

Marcus clenched and unclenched his fists. He wanted to kill this man. How had he just talked for so long and only managed to get himself inside a carriage at Wembley?

"Then I heard all about the situation while I was ridin' in the carriage. That's what they're all callin' it—the situation. I was ridin' with one of the duke's footmen and he had a story to tell about why I was wanted before my time."

Rider gazed out the window, as if reflecting on that remarkable conversation.

"Well? What story were you told?" Though Marcus asked, he could well guess the story about the 'situation' was the story of the ill-omened masque and his alleged part in it.

"Oh, aye. Turns out, one of the young ladies has suffered a tragedy of the heartbreak variety. Seems there is this rogue lord what made the whole family, even the duke, believe he was inclined toward the lady. His problem, they all thought, was he was of the foot draggin' variety of lords. 'Tis my understandin' that foot draggin' ain't unusual in those that has lots of funds. 'Course us workin' folks don't have time for foot draggin,' we'd starve if we tried it."

"I do not care what you have time for. Get to the point."

"Oh, aye, I'm honin' in on the point like an arrow to a bull-seye. Ya see, disaster struck at some kind of fancy party where they was all dressed in costumes. I hope you don't mind me sayin', but that's the sort of thing that makes us workin' folks think lords and ladies got too much time on their hands. Anyhow, he acts very badly and she collapses on the floor. What was said between 'em to cause it? That I don't know—working folk like me got no time to be bangin' about a place in a costume. What I did hear, is that the rogue ran away. *Ran*, mind. Shameful business."

"The lady collapsed?" Marcus asked. Radler had not said anything about Lady Patience collapsing. Had she fainted? What a picture that must have made! Radler running away and Lady Patience falling to the floor. This was worse than he thought.

"Oh aye, I understand the duke, her father, put it off as some kind of fainting disease, as rich ladies are prone to. Mind you, I never seen my sister faint in her life—we workin' folk don't have time for dropping on the ground at a moment's notice. Maybe we would if it were convenient, but it ain't. 'Course, I understand that high-flyin' ladies carry round vinegar for just such emergencies so I reckon they're well-prepared for it. Now, I understand the lady sees herself badly used, as does the duke. They've scrammed out of London and that footman told me it was just as well. He couldn't say what the duke would do if they stayed, but 'parently he's an excitable sort of fellow. That seems a dangerous situation—an excitable duke. Though I don't know him personally so I'm just goin' on hearsay and good luck passin' that by a judge—they don't like it."

Rider took that moment to pause and stare at a portrait on the wall. Then he laughed.

"What is funny in all this?" Marcus demanded.

"It's just that the rogue what broke the lady's heart ain't getting off as easy as he might hope."

"What does that mean?" Marcus asked. He had a very bad feeling about what that might mean. As far as the duke was concerned, his daughter had been treated abominably. Had he some plan of revenge in the works?

Rider leaned forward and laid his forefinger along the side of his nose. "It's the duke's housekeeper what's at the bottom of it, she's a bold sort. I can confirm the truth of it as I met the lady several times. Don't cross her, no, do not cross *her*! She arranged it so that rogue of a lord what broke the girl's heart gets overrun with case moths. She went into the attics to find 'em and she did find 'em and sent them on their way. Grimsby, that was the butler, even helped her do it. Why shouldn't he? He was leaving to open his own shop. At least, that's what the footman said. 'Parently, Lady Marchfield, that's the duke's sister, is mad as a hornet over it, though I can't claim to know why she cares about somebody else's butler. I don't even fathom why anybody needs a butler. A man should really question himself when he can't open his own door no more. Anyway, back to the point. Women can be inquirin' more than is right, in my experience, don't know if you've noticed that yerself. My sister Aggy is forever peering into her neighbor's business, even though I say, 'Aggy, leave them people alone.' For all that, we get on well enough. Me and me sister, that is."

Marcus would be very lucky if he were not guilty of a murder before he left this house. The man was positively enraging. "I presume, by that roundabout answer, that the duke and his household have set off for Yorkshire."

Rider shrugged. "I can't know it for certain, as they don't tell me where they go, but it seems to me they must have done. If I were a duke and I had a big estate to go to, that's where I'd go. I wonder how many chickens they have—more than five, I'll bet!"

Marcus could go no further with this irritating gentleman and assumed he'd got all the relevant information out of him that was to be had. The impression Radler had left behind him in his flight was ruinous. Lady Patience had been so struck that she'd collapsed. The housekeeper had sent the moths into his house, though he still could not account for why. The duke had taken his family out of London, most likely to Yorkshire.

Marcus was in no doubt that there was still plenty of *irrelevant* information Mr. Rider would like to offer up if he chose to linger. However, he already knew more about the fellow's sister and her chickens than he ever cared to know.

"When did they set off? What time?"

"I reckon it was coming on eight o'clock. Early for them, though gettin' late in the day for us working folks."

Marcus stared at the man. "You have mentioned 'us working

folks' several times now. I really do not see what could be so onerous about the position you currently maintain. Nobody is here to boss you about the place. You just sit here and watch things."

Mr. Rider nodded his head. "Aye, because I'm the watcher. The duke would hardly employ me if I weren't watching."

"By the by," Marcus said in a low and deadly voice, "*I am the rogue lord in question.*"

He'd thought this might embarrass the fellow. Instead, Mr. Rider leapt up from his chair and said, "You haven't brought moths into the duke's house?"

"If I have, I have only brought them back from whence they came!" Marcus shouted. He turned on his heel and strode out. He would leave London at first light and follow the duke and his household—all the way to Yorkshire if necessary.

He hoped it would not be necessary to allow that much time to pass. He would be on horseback and they would travel in a caravan of carriages. He should be able to catch them on the road. Then he would fix this disaster. This disaster that was far more serious than he'd thought when he'd received Radler's letter. His friend had relocated himself to Bedford Square, but considering Marcus' mood at the moment, America would be a safer place for him.

CHAPTER SIXTEEN

THE NICOLETS HAD arrived at The Pig and Pony the day prior with still some daylight to permit a stroll through the small town it was attached to. At a stationers, Patience bought a small diary. It was a lovely little thing, covered in lavender kid with gold embossing. Its looks were not why she'd bought it though.

There were so many feelings coursing through her. She began to realize that in all her life she'd never slowed down to examine her feelings, or to really feel them. She was forever rushing to the next thing. It had almost been as if a feeling would come upon her, and she would close the curtains on it, and it would be out of view.

This had been an advantageous quality when she'd been younger. If she fell and skinned her knee or was scolded over stealing away with Cook's biscuits, these small matters were shaken off. She'd been like a duck exiting a pond—one good shake and it was as if she'd never been wet at all. Unlike her twin, she did not linger over disappointments or sadness. Serenity might weep over a dead insect, but it might be accidently dead because Patience had carelessly stepped on it in her hurry forward.

What had happened with Lord Stanford could not be shaken off, though. The feelings of it sat in her mind with a resolute stubbornness. The curtains would not close. All that might have distracted her—her father's insistence that he must have brocabbage pie, Mrs. Right's survey of the kitchens and subsequent argument with the innkeeper's wife, Nelson making off with a joint of beef from another dining room, even the footmen singing off-key in the yard very late at night having once again drunk more wine and ale than they should have—would capture her attention for a moment, but fail to keep it. Her mind insisted on sinking back into sadness.

That night, she'd slept in the same bed with Serenity. They were not identical twins and they were night and day different, but there was a certain kinship and knowing between them. After all, they had traveled in very close quarters together for months before making an appearance in the world.

"I know you are very sad, Patience," Serenity had said softly, "though you do not like to show it."

"I do not even know *how* to show it," Patience said. "I have never been so afflicted. But it makes me think I ought to have learned how to sit quietly with my feelings before this moment. I never have, though, and have always teased you for it."

"Well now, I believe I feel my feelings a little too much," Serenity said. "I live in terror of my season. What if I cry at Almack's? You know the smallest thing can set me off."

"And no thing has ever really set me off, until now."

"You ought to cry, you know," Serenity said. "I find it sort of drains the feelings out of my body and then I regain my equanimity. I should burst if I could not cry to get them out."

Patience did not answer. She *would* cry, but she was doing everything possible to hold it in until she was in her own bedchamber in the Dales. As kind as Serenity was in this moment, she did not wish any of her sisters to see her cry. She already felt like a failure, she had no wish to add to it. She noticed she had an absolute abhorrence of appearing weak, which was a thing she'd not known about herself.

To think, she had marched into the season full of confidence. She had pointed at a gentleman, confident that he was for her. Somehow, she'd expected everybody and everything in the world to fall into place to accommodate her inclinations. She'd been so childish.

Now the morning had come after a fitful night. She rose early and took her little diary to the garden. There, she poured out all her thoughts and feelings.

She was rather surprised at how wide-ranging they were once she got going with it. Who knew one mind could think so many things at once?

In one line, she wished Lord Stanford's house would burn down with him in it. Hopefully, he would be shouting her name while he perished. On the next, she wished this was all a dream she would wake from to discover him at her doorstep. Then she wrote assurances to herself that her heart would mend. Then she circled back to writing out terrible ends to Lord Stanford. She finally stopped when she'd described an unfortunate impalement while taking a horse over a fence that included his moment of clarity that she was for him all along, seconds before dying.

It felt good to put it all down—the sadness, the fury, the hurt, the shame and embarrassment. There was something cathartic about it and she supposed it was how Serenity felt after she'd dried her eyes. It was so strange that she'd never considered there was an advantage to Serenity's wide-ranging emotions.

Patience closed the book and took in the morning air. The sun had risen despite her upset and would continue to do so. The world would go on, regardless of what she thought about it. She must, as her father would put it, tighten her horse's girth and ride on.

Upon noting a dead beetle on the stonework, she gently picked it up and hid it under a leaf to save Serenity from having to weep over it this morning.

Nelson came bounding out to the garden and Patience presumed Charlie or Thomas had let him out. Patience watched as he made a sentry's parade round the patch of greenery hemmed in by a short stone wall, sniffing at everything to assure himself that all was as it ought to be. He occasionally stopped, ears up, as if he listened for intruders. He wagged his tail all the way round, happy for the sunshine and to be doing the job he was born to do.

He really was a funny little dog—so oblivious to his deficiencies. Nelson had been badly used and come out of it missing a leg and the sight in one eye. Did it get him down? Not that she could see. He barreled forward, working with what he'd got.

That was what she must do. She had been damaged, but she was not dead. Soon enough, she would be home. The ponies would follow in some days and then she would take Penny on a wild ride across the moors. That would be the beginning of the restoration of Lady Patience Nicolet. Then she would return to London next season chastened. She would put a brave face on it and get on with the business of life.

The door to the garden swung open. The duke popped his head out. "There you are, you've missed all the fun in the breakfast room. I asked for another supposed Yorkshire staple— Grassington Hambac. Told the fellow it is bacon and ham put in a pestle and ground up until it is unrecognizable and then reshaped into a crown and fried. Guess what? They actually did it and it was not bad at all."

"Oh, Papa," Patience said laughing.

"Come inside, my girl. Have some breakfast and then we will be on our way."

Patience nodded and rose. Something about this morning felt momentous. It was as if she'd taken a giant step forward in understanding the world and understanding herself. She would give herself some grace to wallow in her feelings and then she would go forward.

After all, she must remember all the advantages she'd been blessed with. She was a duke's daughter; she'd grown up in comfort and had nary a want. She was not cold at night, she was never starved, her clothes were not worn out. She did not have to rise at dawn each morning and work her hands to the bone until the sun set again. She did not have to worry if necessary medicines could be afforded or whether her landlord would raise the rent. She was enveloped by six genial sisters. Mrs. Right was always there to stand in for her mother. Her father was indulgent and attempted to amuse her with Grassington Hambac.

For the first time in her life, Patience Nicolet had stepped outside herself and viewed her circumstances dispassionately. It began to feel as if she were rather spoiled to be going round like her life was over, simply because one thing had not gone her way. She'd been blessed backward and forward, and it was time she started acting like she knew it.

MARCUS HAD RIDDEN hard along the likeliest route the duke's carriages would have taken. With so many carriages in the duke's caravan, His Grace would stick to the better-maintained roads. There might be several shortcuts to be taken and they might be convenient to a rider on a horse, but the chances of getting stuck somewhere would be relatively high and help would be relatively far off. No, the duke would not risk it.

He stopped at The Lion and the Lamb, that being a very likely inn where a party of such size would stop on a journey to Yorkshire.

He dismounted and a groom took the reins. As was usual in such places, the innkeeper hurried out to the yard. Innkeepers were rather renowned for keeping an eye out and sizing up a gentleman before he'd even hit the ground. They always seemed to know who had deep pockets and who was only working to appear as if they did. He supposed they were so good at it because it was a necessity. There was no end of men going round England attempting to present themselves as rich as Croesus, though they had more debt in their pockets than money. Such a man might conveniently forget to pay his bill, slipping off when nobody was looking, or claim his "man" would be by later with the funds, though no "man" was in existence. All the while, they paid particular attention to their appearance to keep up the ruse.

Marcus did not know what exactly would tip off an innkeeper as to the real case of the thing, but presumed he had passed muster and been deemed a very welcome arrival. The innkeeper's wife had hurried out as well, throwing her apron to a serving girl and smoothing her skirts.

"My lord, welcome to our humble establishment," the innkeeper said, while his wife curtsied.

It seemed de rigeur for any innkeeper worth his salt to refer to his inn as humble. In fact, this particular inn was very large and appeared prosperous. Precisely the reason Marcus imagined the duke would stop here.

"I do not stay the night," Marcus said, ignoring their dropped expressions at that pronouncement. "I need a change of horse, a plate of food, and some information."

Marcus had been certain the idea of a meal, which he would be charged a stupid amount of coin for, would brighten their visages. And so it had.

"A plate! Yes, indeed, my lord. Just this way. Randy—take care with the lord's horse or I'll have your hide. This way, my lord."

He was led into a private dining room. This was not necessary, but it would assist the innkeeper in accounting for the stupid amount he would be charged for whatever was laying around in the kitchens that they threw on a plate.

"You'll want ale, I'm sure," the innkeeper said, "and an array of cold meats, rolls, a salad, the best of our cheeses, perhaps claret to top the whole thing off? Then we have our famed apple pie topped with cherry glaze."

"Fine, but for the pie," Marcus said. "When was the Duke of Pelham here? Was it last night? What time did his party set off?"

The innkeeper's wife was just coming in with the plates and silverware for his stupidly expensive meal. She froze in her tracks as if he'd inquired into the travel plans of the devil himself.

"The duke," she whispered to herself.

The innkeeper had gone rather pale. "The duke! The Duke of Pelham? Is he coming? Why? I was assured he would pass us by. His valet assured me that was the case. Why is he coming here?"

"So, he has not been here?" Marcus could hardly understand it. For one, an innkeeper would generally be delighted to see a duke and the large party he brought with him. For another, Marcus would have noted a caravan of that size had he passed it on the road. As it was, he'd not seen anything of that significance. Surely, the duke would not press on to the detriment of his horses.

"No, he has not been here. Not yet," the innkeeper said, twisting his hands together. "But you imply he is coming? Are you certain? Because we have been counting on him passing us by!"

The innkeeper's wife said, "We could lock the doors. Or say we are full. Do not let that duke set foot past our threshold, Freddie, or I am off to Oakham! Oakham, I tell you!"

Marcus could not imagine what had set these two people off. "Might I inquire why you seem to be terrorized by the idea that the Duke of Pelham might choose to stay at your inn?"

"Terrorized," the innkeeper's wife said, "now that's a very good word for it!"

"Mary," the innkeeper said to his wife, "go and see about the lord's victuals. I will handle this."

Mary sniffed. "I won't stand for it. I simply won't stand for it, my mother will welcome me with open arms in Oakham," she said, before marching herself out of the room.

"Well?" Marcus said, drumming his fingers on the table.

"I'll tell you, my lord, if you must know it. Mind you, it is not my habit to go round disparaging them that's above me. I do have a respect for the order of things. But that duke! Well, it's not to be borne, that's what it is."

"What exactly did he do when he was here last?" Marcus asked, beginning to be intrigued by what the duke could have possibly done to provoke such feelings in the man. In the usual case of things, an innkeeper would be happy to overlook quite a lot as long as he was paid. And really, how much trouble could one get into when stopping at an inn?

"Let's see," the innkeeper said, "it started with the bro-cabbage pie he insisted on. A Yorkshire staple, he called it. Well, nobody ever heard of it and the kitchen staff were doing their level best to discover what it was. We asked the duke to describe it, but he shouted that he was not a cook and did not know recipes. We even sent a boy on horseback, racing to The Pig and Pony two miles farther down the road to see if they knew what it was. They claimed they did, but wouldn't say. My cook began to speculate that it might be broccoli and cabbage but who would put that into a pie? Guess what it is?"

Marcus shrugged. "I have no idea."

"Neither does anybody else, because it does not exist. That duke made it up for his own amusement!"

That did sound like something the duke would do.

"But that was not the end of it. Oh if only *that* were the end of it. He's got a whole slew of daughters who are up to no good. One of them accused my waiter of looking shifty, and another claimed it was a very common thing for waiters to look shifty, and another one hid in a linen closet and they turned the whole place upside down looking for her, and the duke's footmen drank me out of house and home, only the cheapest wine mind you, which they then grossly deposited all over my innyard while singing songs in the middle of the night. Badly singing, I might add. Oh, and the entire time they were here, they set loose a dog so maimed and horrifying-looking that he frightened my other guests!"

That would have been Nelson.

"At the conclusion of this fiasco, I had a word with the duke's valet as they were leaving. A very pleading word, if I'm to be honest. Not usually my way, but it was an emergency! I down-right begged him to find the duke another inn—do not bring him back! My Mary said if he comes back, she's going to her mother in

Oakham until he's gone."

Marcus pressed his lips together, as Mary had already mentioned her imminent departure. "I see. I expect they are ahead of me, so it appears the valet was as good as his word. Do you have any notion of where else they might have stayed in these parts?"

The innkeeper shuffled his feet. "If I recall rightly, I might have suggested The Pig and Pony. Now, I had my reasons for it! The innkeeper there is a smarmy sort and always hinting that his inn is superior to mine. I say I have a humble establishment, as any right-thinking man would, and he says, 'Yes, you do.' Hah, we'll see how superior he feels when that duke is done with him! Also, I sent a boy there to inquire into brocabbage pie and they swore they knew all about it. Liars!"

"If you will hurry my meal and saddle a horse, I would be much obliged. I am determined to catch up to the duke."

"Oh, I see—you're to call him onto a green regarding some insult he's hurled at you. I only say, were you looking for such a place, have a look at the expanse next to Jenkin's farm a half mile north. That lawn has been used for such before. Just a month ago, one of the local wheelwrights engaged in fisticuffs with a fellow who tried to move in on his trade. Very entertaining, though I cannot say who positively won it."

"I have no intention of challenging the duke," Marcus said. He did not bother to point out that it was well known that the duke would never turn up for such a meeting as he did not prefer the early morning.

"I can't say why you chase after him, then. Seems to me that most sensible people are running away from that duke, not toward him."

"I believe you have expressed enough of your opinions regarding the Duke of Pelham. He may be… unusual, but he is a duke, after all."

"Yes, my lord, I have forgotten myself is all. The strain of it has got to me, what with my Mary threatening to set off for Oakham."

Though the innkeeper made a very great effort to look abashed, Marcus did not think he regretted a single thing he'd said. The man hurried out and, soon enough, Marcus' plates of food arrived. He made good use of the offerings and did not take too long a time doing it. He was on the duke's heels and must catch up to him without delay.

He set off from the inn under the glare of Mary, the innkeeper's wife, who ought to be looking more cheerful, as she would not be required to travel to her mother in Oakham.

The Pig and Pony, as had already been explained to him, was a mere two miles north. On a fresh horse, he made good time. As if it were some sort of repetition of his earlier stop, he dismounted, handed the reins to a groom, and watched an innkeeper stride out, followed by his wife straightening her cap.

"My lord! Welcome to the illustrious The Pig and Pony—an inn far superior to all others, especially superior to the one you would have sensibly passed by two miles ago."

Marcus did not respond to that highflying praise, but could see why the earlier innkeeper held an animosity toward the fellow. "I am attempting to catch up to the Duke of Pelham's party—have they stopped here?"

At the mention of the duke, the innkeeper staggered just a little. His wife turned and went back inside.

"Yes, I imagine he has," Marcus said drily.

"Never in my life…" the innkeeper trailed off.

"Let me guess—the duke asked your kitchens for something he made up in his mind, claiming it is a Yorkshire staple—"

"Grassington Hambac!"

"His daughters were troublesome—"

"One of them accused my waiter of looking shifty while another one was seen picking up a dead beetle and hiding it and another one disappeared and required an extensive search and another of them kept naming everything that went on as a 'usual case'!"

"And they brought along a very distinct looking dog—"

"Distinct? I should say he was distinct. That three-legged cur stole a joint from one of my regular guests. The beast is very fast on his feet for only having three of them. Then the duke said he would not pay for the joint because the dog does not have any funds of his own!"

"Though I suspect he did pay for it, in the end."

"Oh yes, in the end," the innkeeper said, "though most people would not wait until the end! And let us not forget that diabolical housekeeper!" the innkeeper said.

That might be the one point Marcus must agree on, as the duke's watchman had given her away as the author of the case moths. Considering what his household had suffered at the hands of Mrs. Right, she *was* diabolical.

"*She* marched right into the kitchens, bossing round everybody in her path. Threw things out that she deemed not up to snuff! My cook tried to turn in his notice."

"When did he leave?" Marcus asked.

"Oh no, he's still here. I talked him out of it by giving him the afternoon off."

"Not your cook, the duke. When did the duke leave?"

"Hours and hours ago," the innkeeper said, "though we are still recovering from it. I pulled aside the duke's valet and begged he make arrangements for the duke to stay elsewhere the next time they passed through. I recommended The Lion and the Lamb. It is only two miles south and while it is not as superior as my own establishment, it has the room for them. That valet had the nerve to tell me that could not be! That inn had already wished for the duke not to return and had sent him to me!"

"So I understand," Marcus said. He took the reins from the groom, mounted, and set off. He would like to catch up to Lady Patience before he was forced to deal with any more broken-down innkeepers.

CHAPTER SEVENTEEN

THE DAY HAD passed by uneventfully, if a bit bumpily, as days of travel often did. Patience could not manage writing in her diary in such a situation and contented herself with looking out the window.

Her father and Mrs. Right had seemed to deem the danger to her passed and they had gone back to their usual carriage arrangements. She rode with Winsome and Serenity, while Verity and Valor rode with Mrs. Right.

"You must settle the debate between us, Patience," Winsome said. "Is it better to be angry or sad?"

"I should think neither," Patience said, "though I experience both at the moment. At the same time, oddly."

"Did you really think Lord Stanford was your true love?" Serenity asked.

Patience could already see her sister's eyes getting a little brighter. Tears were surely on the way. "You are not to fret over it, Serenity. I have counseled myself to remember all the luck I've had in life. If I continue to remind myself, I cannot help but to be happy."

"Having a gentleman run away from you and then falling on the floor in front of a crowd of people does not sound very lucky," Winsome said.

"Oh, Winsome!" Serenity said. "Do have a heart."

"Never mind it," Patience said. "The trick is to think of all the things we have to look forward to. Our ponies will arrive, and we will take wild rides all over the neighborhood."

"We can jump Farmer Whimple's fences, as that always does put him out," Winsome said. "He shouts like the devil and calls us heathens."

"And Valor can tell the vicar that Papa dressed as him going up in flames for the masque," Patience added.

"And our aunt will only be able to send letters, instead of terrorizing us in person," Serenity said. "I do love my aunt, in my way, but she can be so frightening."

"And even now, we approach the inn where we found our dear Nelson," Winsome said.

They all gazed down at the sleeping dog. As was his habit, he was on his back with his legs in the air. Patience suspected that position was most comfortable for him due to his infirmities.

"I wonder if he will recognize the neighborhood," Serenity asked.

They had pulled into the innyard along with the rest of the duke's carriages. The innkeeper hurried out and then stopped in his tracks. "Your Grace! Gracious me, you are back. I did not expect that you… would be back. I was certain your valet gave us the sad news that you would stay… elsewhere."

"I do not know why Reynolds would have said so. Reynolds, why did you tell this good man we would not be back?"

Reynolds, always grave, said, "I was under the impression there would be renovations done and it might be uncomfortable."

"Ah, I see. Well here we are, and the place looks untouched. We come back unexpectedly soon, but here we are."

"I did not know… that is… we had no notice of your arrival. We have a rather large party here at the moment. The Marquess of Maidstone and his retinue are here. They take up most of my rooms."

The duke laughed and said, "Well I suppose you can move the retinue, can you not? Do see to it, my good man."

The innkeeper looked positively nonplussed.

Just then, a tall creature of a man dressed as the foppiest of the fops, wandered outdoors. "Did I hear a Your Grace has arrived?" he said lazily.

"Pelham," the duke said. "I suppose you are Maidstone? Do be so good as to move your retinue elsewhere."

"Move them? Elsewhere?" the marquess said.

"Yes, that's right. We require rooms."

The marquess' eyes drifted toward Patience and her sisters. "Well, if I am given the opportunity to accommodate such fine ladies, then I suppose I ought to do it."

"Excellent, I was certain you would," the duke said. "Move them all out and we'll move in and then I would hope to see you in my dining room."

As Patience was well aware that this inn only had one private dining room, she tried not to laugh at her father commandeering it and graciously offering the marquess a seat at his table.

"Ah yes, *your* dining room, of course. I would be delighted," the marquess said. He turned to the innkeeper. "Might you arrange for my servants, but for my valet, I must keep him near, to be relocated to The Blue Boar? Not the accommodations I would usually arrange for my people, but in this case…"

The innkeeper hurried off to make the arrangements. As he did so, Serenity struggled with Nelson to get him out of the carriage, though the dog was making a heroic bid to stay in it. Serenity finally won and set him on the ground. The marquess took in the sight and one eyebrow slightly raised.

"That is Nelson," Valor put in. "He is the best dog in the whole world, except when he is dragging Mrs. Wendover all over the house."

The marquess' eyes drifted toward Mrs. Right, in case she might be the lady being dragged all over the house by a three-legged dog.

As for Nelson himself, he kept himself very close to Serenity's skirts. He was usually so happy and outgoing, but Patience suspected he did recognize his old neighborhood and did not wish to be returned to the scene of his unhappiness.

"I pray for Mrs. Wendover's continued safety," the marquess said.

"Do not we all?" Valor said. "There have been times I was convinced she was gone forever, but then I'd find her hiding under the servants' table or behind a sofa."

"Gracious, the lady seems hard-pressed," the marquess said.

Valor nodded in full agreement.

There was something both interesting and off-putting about the marquess. There was a languidness to him that Patience could not like, as if he were bored with all the world. He also did not seem to look favorably upon Nelson which must be a mark against him. And then his clothes... really, it was well for a gentleman to have a care in his dress. However, it did not strike her as attractive when it appeared he must spend half the day on it.

The duke introduced his daughters, and they all made the obligatory curtsy. Then the marquess was made known to Mrs. Right and he was informed that the housekeeper would dine with them.

As others had been, the marquess seemed very surprised to hear it. But then, Mrs. Right narrowed her eyes at him and he claimed he was delighted.

Valor looked the marquess up and down, obviously taking in his shiny hessian boots and his wildly embroidered waistcoat of peacocks in a garden. "If you do not mind me asking," Valor said, "your pants look too tight. Do they hurt?"

The duke roared with laughter as the marquess gazed down at the little lady. "Do not answer that, Maidstone, it will only lead to more uncomfortable questions!"

Valor, seeming to comprehend that she ought not have asked such a question, said, "What I meant to say, my lord, is how are you finding the weather?"

Patience bit her lip. Whenever Valor suspected she'd taken a wrong turn, she backtracked to discussing the weather, as their short-lived governess, Miss Pynchon, had advised.

"The weather has been unusually fine, in my view," the marquess said. "But I detect some dark clouds on the horizon, just west of here. I would not be at all surprised if we see some heavy rain in an hour or so."

All the sisters nodded in approval over the marquess' answer. His kindness in answering Valor's question with thoughtfulness went a long way toward raising their opinion of him. Perhaps his clothes could be overlooked if he meant to be indulgent of a younger sister.

"Do allow me to escort you inside. I will see to it that the ladies are situated comfortably in their rooms as quickly as possible. Lady Patience?" the marquess asked, extending an arm.

Patience laid her hand on his offered arm, and they proceeded indoors. They were met with a stream of surly servants moving trunks out of the inn. The glares were rather marked, particularly toward the duke's servants. Patience could not blame them for it, as it must be aggravating in the extreme. They were causing a terrible inconvenience. She hoped The Blue Boar was comfortable for them. She would speak to her father about sending over funds for them to order whatever they wished while they were so inconvenienced. She was certain the duke would be happy to oblige and it might go some way to soothing sore feelings.

She was also certain it was not a remedy that would have occurred to her before this moment in her history. It was as if, now that she was determined to count her blessings, she was more awake to the world around her.

In rather short order, she and her sisters were led to their very recently vacated rooms. She would share a bed with Serenity again, but it was quite a commodious bed so neither of them minded. Verity and Winsome would share a bed, and then poor Mrs. Right would be left with Valor, probably to be kicked all night long.

"What did you think, Patience?" Serenity asked.

"Think of what?"

"Of the marquess, of course. We have unexpectedly encountered a gentleman of the *ton*. Did it give you the idea that perhaps next season you could look upon other gentlemen and become attached to one of them?"

"Not in the least, I'm afraid," Patience said. If anything, the marquess' fripperies simply reminded her of the handsome restraint Lord Stanford employed.

"I cannot say I feel anything for him either," Serenity said. "Though I was hard pressed not to laugh when Valor inquired into the tightness of his breeches."

Patience nodded. "I did think he was very kind to ignore it and give her a thoughtful answer on the weather." She paused and peered out the window. "I also think he was right about the weather. I think we have been lucky to reach an inn before the rain comes, it is looking very dark indeed."

As they both peered out the window, they could see that a storm of some significance was heading their way. In the distance, trees swayed in the wind and the horizon had taken on a gray and misty appearance.

"We shall be very cozy here, I think," Serenity said. "We will be very snug at dinner while a storm rages out of doors."

Patience nodded, but did not say that a storm raged inside her too while she worked to quiet it and let it pass. Rather, she took her diary to a corner of the room, sat in an overstuffed chair, and wrote out all the feelings that washed over her at the moment.

An hour passed by with Patience writing and Serenity reading, and then it was time to dress for dinner. As they were exceedingly seasoned travelers at this point in their history, it did not take more than an hour to accomplish it. It might have taken even less time, but Patience's hair always acted unruly when rain threatened. It seemed to double its volume and was difficult to tame.

They descended to the dining room, where they found the rest of the party gathered. It was a cheery room at the front of the inn with large bow windows overlooking the innyard. Patience supposed that during the day it would have an advantageous view of who was coming and going.

As everybody else had already seated themselves before their arrival, the duke at one end and the marquess at the other, there were only two chairs left. Serenity made a dash to the empty chair by Mrs. Right, leaving Patience to sit next to the marquess.

The wine came round and Patience was glad of it. She felt uneasy in some way. Perhaps it was the thunder crashing outside or the flashes of lightning that made, for a moment, night into day. She did not mind storms when she was safe in her own house in the Dales, she even enjoyed them, but there was something about being a traveler that made it feel a bit perilous. It would have been downright perilous had they been caught on the road. Heavy rain had a habit of creating holes in the road. Once the holes filled with water, the horses could not perceive them and might injure a leg. Particularly not with wind and rain whipping their faces.

As she had decided to count her blessings, she must be glad their own horses were stabled, warm, and dry.

Still, she felt uneasy about the weather. It sounded so violent. Their house in the Dales was of Yorkstone and it seemed as if nothing could hurt them while they were inside it. The inn's flimsy stucco walls could not be as sturdy.

At least they were indoors. And really, they must be safe enough. She'd never heard a story of an inn's roof blowing off or walls collapsing because of a rainstorm. She just must hope nobody had been caught on the roads before reaching shelter.

The marquess did his best to entertain her, and he did a fairly good job of it. He had no end of amusing anecdotes. It was particularly funny when he described a horse he'd been recently bamboozled into buying. It seemed the stallion was very good at a short burst of a gallop, which he'd seen and been impressed by. It was only later that he discovered the horse positively refused to do anything farther than that. He would simply stop and refuse to go on. The marquess had ended walking the beast home as he could not bear to beat a horse and did not think it would do any good anyway. The horse was now enjoying a life of leisure in one of his fields.

Patience felt herself relax and allowed herself to be amused by the marquess' tales of woe. She reminded herself that by the morning, the storm would have passed and they would set off, getting ever closer to the Dales now, and the air would be particularly fresh, everything having been washed clean by the rains. Perhaps she would herself feel as refreshed as the country-side. She was determined to appreciate it.

MARCUS HAD KNOWN perfectly well that he would not reach the next inn before becoming drenched. The lightning was another and far more worrisome consideration. He'd been forced to take shelter in somebody's barn on account of it. The horses who called it their primary residence gave hard glances to his own horse, viewing him as an interloper. Perhaps they'd even shot some hard glances at him too, when they watched him rub down his horse, water him and then feed him some of their precious oats. The oats were clearly the furthest stepping out of bounds. Even the friendliest and easygoing horse was possessive about his oats and Marcus ignored the snorts and stamps and even one kick at a stall door.

Finally, the lightning and thunder eased, and he could set off again. The rain still came down in sheets and his horse was not the least impressed with the situation, but he had no intention of spending the night in a barn. He supposed the other horses were glad to see the back of them.

He understood from a boy he'd encountered before the rain had begun that the next inn was five miles up the road. Though the rain was inconvenient, it was perhaps a blessing in disguise. Certainly, the duke would not press on farther when he'd seen a storm on the horizon. He was eccentric in the extreme and had driven mad half the innkeepers in England, but he did have a care for his family. He would not risk a broken wheel or getting stuck in mud or a horse going lame from a newly formed hole in the road.

Marcus would go forward carefully, giving his horse the time and latitude to judge the state of the road and act accordingly. It was aggravating in the extreme as he would like to gallop, but it would be careless to do so. He must just assure himself that if the duke stopped as Marcus guessed he would, his party would not go anywhere until morning.

She must be there. Lady Patience must be at the next inn. He would chase after her all the way to the Dales if necessary, he would chase her to America if that were required, but he prayed she would be there. The longer she was allowed to live with the idea that he'd run from her at the masque, the more hardened against him she would be. He could not allow so much time to pass that she'd turn away from him permanently.

It did occur to him that he'd rather thrown caution to the winds. It felt foreign, to be this devil-may-care person galloping after a lady. It felt like something Radler would do, and not himself. But Lady Monroe had been right—it was time to go after what he wanted, not what he was trying to avoid. A man could not live his life attempting to dodge any difficulties that might come up in the hopes of leading a staid life devoid of surprises. A man should not even wish for such a life.

He did not wish for such a life, as it had finally dawned on him that it would be no life at all. He wanted to be surprised and risk it all. He was certain it would come out well. Or if not certain, he was no longer held back by the risk of it.

As the wind whipped his face and the driving rain clouded his vision, he must just pray that Lady Patience had not altogether given up on him.

Finally, he saw the telltale lights of an inn ahead. No other structure was ever lit up as well and so close to the road, signaling to all travelers that rest and repose was soon within reach—it was a cheerful beacon that was meant to feel hard to pass by. A low roof ran along the front of the building, with oil lamps hanging in intervals.

Marcus swerved into the empty innyard, all the hostlers having taken shelter elsewhere. He supposed they would do, not expecting anybody to turn up in this weather. He leapt off his horse and tied him to a railing under the roof and out of the worst of the rain.

That's when he saw her.

The dining room of the inn was lit like blazes. The curtains had not been closed. There was Lady Patience. And somebody. Who was that fellow sitting next to her at the head of the table? Why should she be dining, and laughing no less, with some strange gentleman? Who was he? Where did he come from? What was he doing?

Was he a cousin? Was he a suitor?

A fit of jealousy overtook him. It was a very strange feeling indeed. He'd never been a victim of it and now he felt rather murderous. He'd never felt such an outrage. That man, whoever he was, must be made to depart this instant!

Throwing whatever bit of caution he had left into the howling winds of the storm, he threw the inn's doors open.

The innkeeper, just this moment becoming aware of his existence, hurried forward. "My lord! The storm, you are in a state. How have you been out in it? And we… goodness me… well we… we are full. There is not a bed to be had. Of course you are welcome to sleep in a chair, oh I really have nothing else to offer! It is terrible."

Marcus stared incredulously at the innkeeper. "I did not come here for a bed! Why should I concern myself about a bed at a moment such as this?"

Naturally, as soon as he said it, Marcus realized precisely how deranged that had sounded. A man staggers into an inn during a violent storm and claims he did not come for a bed. What else did one come to an inn for but a bed?

"No?" the innkeeper asked, beginning to look a bit wary of him.

"Certainly not. I have come to see the Duke of Pelham's party. This instant."

Marcus could not avoid noticing that the innkeeper was now looking rather frightened and surreptitiously glancing at the dining room doors. He supposed he must paint a rather alarming sight just now, considering his recent encounter with the weather. And as he'd claimed he had no use for a bed, he might even seem a bit of a madman.

"Now, my lord," the innkeeper said soothingly, "you *are* a lord, I think? Of course you are, you are a gentleman. Why don't I take you to our cozy little snug and fetch you something warming and then we'll see what ought to be done. As a gentleman."

The man was attempting to put him off. He was trying to soothe the madman with hints that he ought to remember he was a gentleman. But he would not be put off. "I already know what ought to be done," he said. He turned to the doors to the private dining room and shrugged the innkeeper off as if he were no more trouble than a fly.

"I will not have violence on the premises, my lord," the innkeeper called after him. "If you would fight the duke, you must take him elsewhere!"

Marcus threw the dining room doors open. "Lady Patience," he said. "There you are."

CHAPTER EIGHTEEN

PATIENCE FELT AS if everything in the world had stopped—time, the storm, her mind, and her heart. How was this? How was Lord Stanford standing soaked through from the rain in the middle of nowhere at an inn?

"Ah, it's Stanford," the duke said, sounding very jolly over it. "Can't say I'm surprised."

"Lord Stanford?" Patience choked out. Why was he here? Why, why, why?

"Why are *you* here?" Valor asked. "Didn't you get my letter?"

"Ho, Stanford," the marquess said, "I haven't seen you in an age, what's all this?"

"Yes," Winsome said, "What is all this?"

"This is very upsetting, whatever it is," Serenity said.

Verity sighed. "It's an all too common thing—Lord Stanford broke Patience's heart and now he's come to stomp on it."

"No, I haven't," Lord Stanford said.

"Good God man, what *have* you been up to?" the marquess said, laughing.

Patience wanted to hit the marquess over the head to stop him from talking. Lord Stanford needed to be talking.

"I would rather ask you what you are up to," Lord Stanford said to the marquess.

"He tells funny stories, and his pants are too tight," Valor said, in a bid to explain what the marquess was up to.

Lord Stanford did not respond to the explanation. "I've come," he said, his coat making the soft sounds of dripping water on the carpet, "to clear up some things. Lady Patience, when you approached me at the masque, it was not actually me."

"Told you," the duke said to Patience, "I said he was not in his right mind. He was spooked."

"I was not spooked. I was not there, Your Grace," Lord Stanford said. "I was attending Lady Monroe, an elderly relative in Kent, who required my assistance. Lord Radler wore my mask."

As that news settled over Patience, Lord Stanford went on. "Lord Radler was taken by surprise, acted the idiot, and ran away. Had I been there, I can assure you I would not have gone anywhere. Now, I fully realize that all of this is my fault, with the exception of Radler being an idiot. I have been foot dragging to no purpose and that stops now."

"Does it?" Patience whispered.

Valor said, "Well, now that I know more than I did, you could crumple up the letter from Mrs. Wendover. Which I wrote for her."

Lord Stanford nodded at Valor. "Lady Patience, I have treated you abominably. I have resisted following my own heart, but if you will have me, I would be eternally grateful. If you can forgive how I have conducted myself so far. That is, if you can somehow look past—"

Patience had leapt from her chair and pushed past the marquess, who had at that moment been unfortunately leaning back on only two of the legs of that chair. As he went down in a crash, Patience threw herself into Lord Stanford's arms.

Through her hair, which was fast coming undone, Lord Stanford said, "Your Grace, if I might have permission to escort Lady Patience to the snug to say a few private words?"

"Go on with you, took you long enough, after all."

Lord Stanford swept her up in his arms and carried her out of the room. In the corridor, the innkeeper rushed forward. "Lady Patience! My lord, put the lady down at once. I cannot have a kidnapping in my inn. Put her down, I say!"

"Stanford, do not you dare put me down," Patience said, laughing.

The innkeeper, hardly knowing what to do next, ran into the dining room. Patience presumed he went to tell the duke that one of his daughters was being carried off by a strange gentleman.

The snug, a small alcove in the back of the inn, was lit by just a few candles. Its primary piece of furniture was a gray velvet settee, which Lord Stanford promptly threw her on.

He was not long in following her there. He brushed her hair from her eyes and kissed them and then moved to her lips. He was so gentle, but strong too—exactly as she'd imagined him to be. No, better than she imagined him to be.

"I am sorry for Radler's behavior," he said quietly.

Patience giggled. "Do not be, I cannot imagine what else would have got you going in my direction."

"I was always going in your direction; I was only moving at a snail's pace. I have learned from my mistake, though."

"You were very gallant to come chasing after me," Patience said.

"I would have galloped all over England to catch up to you. It turns out, once I get going, I cannot be easily stopped."

Patience thought his words were very nice indeed. But she thought his lips were even nicer. She kissed him until he forgot all about what he meant to say. He was soaked through from the rain and soon enough she was soaked too, but who cared for that? She began to be very bold about tracing the outlines of his chest and kissing his neck and, as far as she could tell, it was very much approved of. He also became rather bold, and ran his hand up the side of her dress, which was thrilling in the extreme.

They were coming to know each other, very personally.

In situations such as these, it is always a complete guess as to how much time has passed. Time very gracefully bows out and takes itself elsewhere. There were moments when she detected the innkeeper nervously pacing just outside the snug. Sometimes he even loudly cleared his throat. Other moments, the dining room door would briefly open, and she would hear her family's chatter and laughter. She did not pay too much attention to any of it though. How could she when she had Stanford, *her* Stanford, right here before her, leaning against her, kissing her.

He'd wrestled himself out of his greatcoat and covered them with it, though Patience could see that only made them even more drenched than when they started. She appreciated the sentiment though; it was lovely to have somebody care for her person.

She'd known he was for her, and then she'd faltered. But she'd been right all along. A month ago, she might have flattered herself over her supposed keen understanding of the situation.

Now, though, she simply gave thanks to God for seeing her through so happily. She really was blessed.

He pulled away from her just a little and peeked under his great coat to survey her dress. "I know your father is liberal, but this might be pushing it far even for him. Though, I do find it rather delightful."

Patience glanced down and instantly perceived his meaning. Now that the front of her muslin dress had been thoroughly soaked through, it did not conceal much.

"We've got to do something about it and rejoin the others," Stanford said. "I would much rather stay here all night, but out of respect for your father…"

"I will go upstairs and get a shawl. I have a large India shawl that will cover me sufficiently if I wrap it properly." She kissed his forehead and disentangled herself.

Aside from the innkeeper looking as if he would fan himself if he had a fan, it was all done with little fuss. After returning looking more modest than she had done, including adding back some pins to her hair that had been irretrievably lost, she and her betrothed went into the dining room.

"I assume it is settled between you, eh?" the duke asked. "Otherwise, I will need to have a word with you, Stanford, about exactly what you've been doing in that snug."

"They look like they've been fighting, Papa," Valor said. "Their hair is all messed up."

"It is well-settled between us, Papa," Patience said, laughing. "With no fighting whatsoever."

The duke nodded. Since that gentleman was ever willing to make everybody comfortable except those for whom he cared little for their discomfort, he promptly moved the marquess out of his seat so that Stanford might take his place. A waiter brought over a chair and the marquess found himself squeezed in between Valor and Verity. The marquess was questioned ruthlessly about his clothes on the one side and advised of various usual cases on the other side. Fop though he might be, it was to his credit that he managed to keep a smile on his face for most of it.

Though she and Stanford were in a room full of people, Patience turned her chair toward him, and he turned his chair toward her, and they went forward as if they were the only two people there.

"Tell me of how you came to chase after me," Patience said. "You see, when I was told you had departed the town, I imagined you were heartsick over Lady Alice."

Stanford wrinkled his brow. "Lady Alice? Why should you think so?"

"Because of the fan," Patience said. "Why did you buy her a fan? Did she hint she needed one?"

"I did not buy her a fan. I returned the fan she left behind after the duke's dinner. Your footman seemed overly alarmed about it and I was going to be in her neighborhood, so I said I'd take it to her."

Patience sat back. "Gracious, when she said she was obliged to you and it had become a favorite…"

"I think I see. After the misunderstanding about the fan, you spoke to Radler, who ridiculously ran away from you. Then you thought I left Town when I was in fact already gone and you thought—"

"Yes, I did think."

"I had to attend Lady Monroe as I began receiving alarming things that I was certain she was sending—a clock, a note to hurry up, a bottle of molasses, other things."

"Oh dear, my Papa sent the clock and the molasses. He does like to jest when it suits him, and he thought you might take it as a hint to go a bit faster."

"Yes, I guessed as much eventually, and of course he was right. And then, when I was convinced that Lady Monroe was not in any particular danger, I received Radler's letter. I decamped to Town and went to your house, but you were already gone. I had a rather enraging conversation with your father's caretaker to shake out of him where you'd gone."

Patience nodded. "I could not bear it, the idea that I could have been so wrong in my feelings."

"You were never wrong, and I should have known the rightness of it the very first time I saw you flying by atop your Dales pony."

"You know the rightness of it now, though?"

"I know it through and through."

"When we first danced, when you hesitated to put your name on my card and went on about *people* suggesting you be introduced to Lady Alice—was that because your home life as a child was not happy? You thought someone like her would suit you best?"

Stanford laughed. "You have put me on the back foot, again. Please do not remind me about *people*. I knew it sounded ridiculous as soon as I said it. But yes, that was the reason."

"I think we will get on very well. I am not a shouter. Are you a shouter?"

"Never."

"There now, it will be all right. If we have a disagreement or argument, it will be very quiet."

Stanford laughed over the idea. "I intend to disagree with you very little. As for practicalities, I will speak to your father on the morrow. My hope is that we can return to London and get the marriage contracts out of the way and wed as soon as possible."

"I adore your impatience," Patience said. Then she paused. "I should probably tell you that the burden of all this misunderstanding is not to rest solely on your shoulders. I have a very great fault—I am a terrible toe-tapper."

"Yes, I know. That's why you approached Radler. You thought to throttle me into action and reveal my inclinations."

"I had to know; I could not wait longer. Though, I am determined to correct the habit."

"Do not go too far in the correcting, I rather like it and have found it instructive."

Patience smiled. "I suppose when we are married, we will go to your house in Town?"

For some reason, Stanford looked a bit concerned to be asked that question. Perhaps they would not go there? Perhaps they would set off for his family seat at once?

"There is a small problem with my house in Town. Somebody, who I have been informed was your housekeeper, sent a case infested with moths to me. I thought it was from Lady Monroe, and I foolishly left it in my dressing room and now it seems my entire house is invaded by them."

Patience's gaze drifted to Mrs. Right, who was just now having a fine time entertaining the duke. "She has been like a mother to me, and well, when she thinks somebody has hurt one of her girls, she… can be forceful."

"But what did she think? I received the case long before the masque."

"I imagine it must have been the fan we all thought you bought for Lady Alice."

"Oh, I see. Then I will not hold it against her, though I will not say the same for my butler and valet. In any case, a certain Mrs. Crumdek has been called in on the case. Apparently, she is the only person living who can manage it."

"I have an idea," Patience said. "Why go back to London

when we are so close to the Dales? You cannot even go to your own house. Your solicitor could make the journey and Papa's man is in York."

"I would be agreeable as I would very much like to see the house that has produced Lady Patience Nicolet, but I could not impose on the duke in such a manner. As well, though perhaps I should not care about such things, it would appear unseemly for me to stay in your house before we are married. If it were a house party and I was one of many, perhaps…"

"If you will not stay in the house, there is a gardener's cottage that is not being used at the moment. Our current gardener maintains a small farm nearby. I've been inside the cottage—it's not large but it's comfortable."

"I would sleep in a tent if your father were enthusiastic about the idea. Really, I think he's been very indulgent of me so far. I would not like to push him past his indulgence."

Patience leaned forward and whispered, "Let me tell you something about my Papa—he is the kindest man living. To his daughters, at least. If it makes me happy, he will not mind it."

"Then we will see," Stanford said. "By the by, your hair looks utterly charming in its rather mussed state."

And so they went on, Patience confident that they would proceed to Yorkshire and Stanford making a list of everything he found charming regarding her person.

MARCUS HAD SET off on a wild goose chase to catch up to Lady Patience, explain the mix-up with Radler, express his inclinations, and propose a marriage. Somehow, he'd accomplished it all.

He'd slept in the snug, which had been a rather damp and cold situation. Therefore, he did not sleep long. He was up with the dawn and found some almost dry clothes in his panniers to change into. As his valet was not with him, he could not say that he presented a particularly dashing figure, but it was all he could manage.

His Grace had descended early, and Marcus suspected it was ungodly early as far as the duke was concerned. He would have known, though, that Marcus would be eager to make arrangements.

They made those arrangements in all efficiency, and they would leave the solicitors to do the rest. The duke claimed he generally made a fuss and caused delays at such a juncture, mostly for his own amusement. Mr. Stratton's father had nearly been driven mad over his ludicrous demands, but he would not amuse himself this time. His daughter had already experienced enough drama and suspense for the moment.

"Well now," the duke said, "I understand we're to continue on to the Dales and you're to take the gardener's cottage until the wedding."

"Only if it suits you, Your Grace."

"Fine by me, I have no wish to turn round with this circus when we are so close to home. Send word to your man in London, we'll put him up somewhere. He won't mind the butler's quarters? They are commodious and they are gloriously empty."

"You really do not ever wish for a butler, then?" Marcus asked out of curiosity.

"Why should I? Mrs. Right runs my house smoothly and everybody seems happy with it. Why should I upset the apple cart with some stiff fellow who will be pursing lips and raising eyebrows every other minute?"

Marcus nodded. He really did not understand how one got on without a butler, but as seemed to be usual, the duke went his own way with things.

Fortunately, his solicitor was a good-humored fellow. He suspected good humor would be very much required in his dealings with the duke.

The rest of the day passed very pleasantly. The marquess was urged to set off so that might free up his room for Marcus, which he did after the duke hinted he would not be invited into *the duke's* dining room that night. He left with Valor advising him to think seriously about his tailor and urging him to do better.

Marcus and Patience claimed that they both needed something or other from the village shops and walked off together. Anybody who paid attention might have noticed that Marcus carried a wicker hamper for this shopping that was so urgent.

As it was, they needed nothing at all and used the excuse for a picnic in the countryside where anybody looking might have been shocked by the goings on. Patience was never shy to begin with and Marcus had thrown off the shackles of caution.

He'd not thrown off the shackles of his lady's reputation, however, so he used all his self-control to avoid taking things irredeemably far. His betrothed had not helped him in that effort, but he had prevailed and she'd said she adored his care for her.

That evening, he got a full dose of the Nicolets. It had been a jolly party with nary a lag in the conversation.

Winsome told him she was surprised he'd come through for Patience, as she'd already decided that if he ever needed anything from her, she would not help him. Now she would have to revise her opinion and carefully consider any of his future requests.

Marcus was not certain what he ever would have needed from her, but thanked her all the same.

Valor informed him that she'd had a stern talk with Mrs. Wendover over the letter that had been sent. As that stuffed rabbit had spent much time being dragged around by both Valor and Nelson, it did in fact look dejected.

Serenity dabbed at her eyes and waved her handkerchief at him, which he supposed meant she had given up whatever resentment of him she'd had.

Verity claimed she had all along supposed everything would come right, as she understood it was usual in these cases. Winsome called her a liar. In retaliation, Verity told Marcus not to bother asking Winsome for any favors, as he would not get any.

The housekeeper, that diabolical Mrs. Right, had even seen fit to vaguely say to nobody in particular, "One does make small mistakes from time to time. One would not be human if one did not. It's best to simply view it as just water under the bridge."

Marcus refrained from pointing out that infesting his house with case moths was hardly a *small* mistake. He found it very convenient that she named it water under the bridge, as if it were something that just happened on its own and could not be accounted for. However, he did not wish to get on the wrong side of the lady, as he'd been informed that he would be permitted to ride in Lady Patience's carriage, with only Mrs. Right acting as duenna.

He really did not wish for that plan to change. One, because he wished to ride with Lady Patience. And two, because he did not wish to find himself in close quarters and being questioned by her sisters all the way to Yorkshire.

CHAPTER NINETEEN

THE DAY OF their departure for the Dales had dawned, and as was beginning to feel usual, the innkeeper could hardly hide his glee over shortly being rid of the duke and his party. The man even went so far as to help the footmen load the trunks into the luggage carriage. It was probably well he did so, as the footmen both looked exceedingly under the weather and not capable of much. Marcus had overheard the duke's valet warn them that if they dared vomit in one of the duke's carriages, they would find themselves walking back to the Dales.

The journey to the duke's estate had been one he would forever remember. Despite the housekeeper deliberately infesting his house with case moths over a perceived slight, she was rather liberal with her supervision of her charge. The lady either slept, or pretended to sleep, most of the way there.

Eventually, they left civilization behind and traveled the well-worn tracks of the moors. It was such an expansive countryside, with rises that provided views for miles and miles. Not like his own neighborhood of flat ground hemmed in by old trees and broken up by plowed fields. It was also such an isolated country-side. It struck Marcus that if he had been so isolated with his own parents, he would have felt trapped, he would have gone mad.

But here was a happy, jolly family who liked nothing better than their own company. There were foibles galore regarding the sisters, but they seemed to pay little mind to them. Each were permitted to be just as they were.

It was a model he intended to adopt. After all, why should society's rules be so rigid? Why was everyone expected to act just the same, despite differences in temperament? He'd never questioned it, but he questioned it now.

"There," Patience said, "just at the top of that hill. There is our house."

Marcus leaned out the window. It was a colossus of a house made of local Yorkstone and sitting atop a rise like a sentry overseeing its sparse neighborhood. There were cottages peppered round the property for those in the duke's employ.

The village was half a mile off. It was small, just a few lanes of houses, a few shops, and a church. There could not be a more remote place in England. Of course, it did explain the duke's unique way of going on. He had no close neighbors who pursed lips or frowned or shook their head to guide him on the ways of society. Nobody had been able to convince him that society's rules must be followed. Rather, he did just what he liked with nobody but an ineffectual vicar to counsel him.

"Ah, it is so good to be home," Patience said.

Marcus smiled. Those particular words had never been uttered by him, but they would be in the future. Very soon, home *would* be a welcome place.

What an idea.

MRS. RIGHT COULD not be more pleased. She had returned to her real home, the Dales, sans Lady Marchfield's latest attempt at a butler. She hoped Mr. Grimsby was making out well with his haberdashery and she hoped Lady Marchfield was still steaming over it. She never knew how, exactly, she would rid the house of a butler, each case requiring its own strategy. But rid the house she did. It was rather a challenge she had begun to enjoy, and this year had ended, as had the other years, in a job well done.

If she had anything at all to regret, it might be sending the case moths into Lord Stanford's house. But what was a poor housekeeper with no real power in the world, a poor woman, to do when one of her own was injured? What else could one do but lash out in a fury and attempt to ruin the perpetrator's life?

In any case, it had been a mistake, but that was all water under the bridge now. Fortunately, he did not seem to be absolutely certain who had sent that damning letter that had come along with Valor's letter. She hoped to keep it that way now that he was to wed her Patience.

Lord Stanford had been installed into the gardener's cottage and everything done there to make him comfortable. The sheets and blankets had been changed to the finer ones from the house, as had the pillows. His small kitchen had been well stocked with things he could prepare for himself—tea, coffee, breads and biscuits from the duke's kitchens, plentiful bottles of wine and a variety of fruits and cheeses. Despite being well-supplied, he never spent much time there. He would rise and arrive in time for breakfast, and then spend the day with Patience, and then dine with them at night.

The vicar, as was to be expected, approached the duke about the seemliness of the situation. Lord Stanford and Patience had even been spotted in the village, holding hands. One of his elderly women of the congregation had even claimed that Lord Stanford was seen kissing Lady Patience on the cheek, though her eyesight was very bad so that was not definitely confirmed.

Fortunately, Valor had been eavesdropping as was her habit. She marched into the library to tell the vicar that her papa had dressed as him going up in flames from the devil for a masque and it was very funny. *If* the devil was coming for him, it was probably because of all the screaming murdered ladies on the moors. Though, she did not have personal conversations with the devil, that was just what Mrs. Wendover thought.

The duke had laughed uproariously and did not correct the

idea. The vicar staggered out of the house and back to his vicarage.

Really, at some point the man must notice that every time he brought a problem to the duke he ended staggering out of the house. She did not know why he went on with it.

She supposed the vicar was very like Lady Marchfield—on a sinking ship and refusing to get on a life raft like any sensible person would do.

Mrs. Right sighed in contentment. She must conclude that the season had gone very well indeed. Now, she was back to her roots and the staff had settled comfortably under her lax management, doing just enough but not too much. All was right with the world.

PATIENCE WAS DELIGHTED with her new circumstances. What a glorious month in the Dales it had been. Patience and Stanford had been together for almost all hours of the day. If they were not walking the countryside or riding over the moors, they were hiding away in one of the duke's endless and rarely used public rooms.

They *did* have to hide, too, as Valor was always intent on finding them. It seemed she would never run out of embarrassing questions to pose to her betrothed. Occasionally, Valor seemed to notice she'd gone too far and would inquire into Stanford's views about the weather.

When they were all together with the family, they might play Fact or Fib or just enjoy each other's company. She noticed at those times that Stanford was very observant of all that went on. He admitted to her that he had no frame of reference regarding a genial household and was keen to take it all in.

During one of those nights in the drawing room, Stanford inquired if his lady-love might indulge them all and play the crwth. Naturally, he could not understand why the request sent the entire family into paroxysms of laughter. At least, not until Patience explained that she did not own one, could not play one, could not play any instrument at all, and had made the whole thing up. Neither she nor her father could have imagined that Lady Jenner would have owned that item. Fortunately, the duke thought of pretending he had injured Patience's hand so that she could not play. Now the only thing to do was either to never go to Lady Jenner's house lest the lady bring out the crwth, or always go with a bandaged hand.

Her fiancé took the news of his future wife having no musical talent whatsoever with surprising equanimity. As it happened, his mother had played the pianoforte and used that instrument to shout out her moods. All in the house would know there was trouble on the horizon when she took to violently banging on the keys. He had not liked it.

Stanford also ended up getting on famously with the duke. Both gentlemen agreed that it was a sensible thing to bring the port and brandy into the drawing room, rather than sit in the dining room after the ladies had departed. Stanford said that though the duke was forever crossing the lines society had set up, the crossing was often anchored in good sense. If one stopped to really examine it. At least, most of it.

For a few days, there had been talk of a wedding in London, St. George's being the place it was most favorably done. That did not hold though. Stanford wrote to the archbishop to allow them to dispense with the banns, really only because the duke had riled so many people over the years that one never knew if an injured party might wish to stir up some trouble for him. They would marry in the duke's local church with little fanfare.

The vicar, as was entirely expected, had been rather shaken over the responsibility. He was given a few weeks to settle into the idea though, as invitations to the blessed event had gone out to the most important people in their lives and those people would need time to make arrangements to travel to the Dales.

It was not to be thought that Lady Monroe could make such a trip, but she kindly sent a whole box of Lord Monroe's things as a wedding present. They were promptly donated to the church so that somebody might make use of them.

As for Lady Marchfield, Patience had been torn. She thought she ought to invite the lady, and she also thought she did not wish for cold water thrown on her happiness. In the end, she did invite her aunt, despite her father gamely listing dozens of reasons why she should not.

Felicity would necessarily miss the wedding, as her baby was far too young to travel that far. Mr. Stratton had experienced some sort of mental collapse when it was suggested they leave the baby with a nursemaid. He was a doting father who carried round his infant girl as if she were made of porcelain and might break at any moment. Felicity was adoring of it, especially since she said her little miss was a rather sturdy baby.

Grace and Dashlend did come though, with their young son in tow. It was well that the duke was an indulgent grandfather not overly concerned with his possessions, considering how many of them were broken by the little terror. Never was there a toddler who swiped at things far more than he picked them up. Never was there a toddler who seemed delighted to get into the cold ash of any fireplace he could get to before somebody caught up to him. It did not help that Nelson had made a game of running ahead of the boy and only giving it up when he tripped, fell, and sent up a whopping scream over it that could only be soothed by biscuits.

Lord Kendrickson came with Lady Alice on his arm, the new bride and groom both looking pleased as Punch with one another. Patience had a long and confidential conversation with Lady Alice regarding the mistake about the fan. Both of them agreed that no fan in England had ever caused so much trouble. After the air was cleared between them, their friendship blossomed.

Lord Radler fairly tiptoed into the house, rather surprised

he'd been invited at all, considering his unhelpful participation in the courtship. He was not quite certain if he'd been forgiven or whether he was being lured to the house for a proper pounding. He was instantly reassured that, while he *was* an idiot of epic proportions, he was entirely forgiven. Though, Marcus did point out that had things not ended well, he probably *would* have given his friend a proper pounding.

Lord Jeffries, Marcus' father's elderly cousin, was duly invited but a flare-up of gout prevented him from making the trip. He did send along a letter though, to be given to his staff and used as an admission into his house in Wales if it was wanted.

At the wedding in their small village church, Valor acted as flower girl, as she claimed she had dreamed of it her whole life though this was the first anybody had heard of it. She proudly walked down the aisle clutching white roses and taking in admiring glances. She'd dragged Mrs. Wendover along for the occasion as she said the lady could not bear to be left behind at such a moment.

Nelson apparently could not bear to be left behind either. Finding himself quite alone in the house, he'd visited every room, determined to display his dissatisfaction with the situation. He pulled a plate of chops off the cook's counters and ate them, leaving the bones and broken crockery behind as a comment. He had a rather violent argument with one of the duke's books, the torn pages indicating who had won and who had lost. He dragged blankets off beds and chewed up a few pillows. As a final rebuke, he pulled a pair of curtains down in the drawing room and relieved himself on them. Then he made his escape upon finding a window cracked open. He pushed on it and leapt out, heading toward the village as fast as his three legs could carry him.

Fortunately for him, the window was on the ground floor, else he might have found himself down another leg, or worse. He crashed into the ceremony and tipped over a standing pot of flowers. Finally, he took his proper place in the wedding party.

The vicar was clearly irate about a dog in his church, but as the duke was laughing over it and the bride did not seem to mind, there was not much he could do.

The wedding breakfast was a jolly affair. Much wine and champagne was poured and the people in the village came to the duke's door and sang a wedding song of their own making. It was rather dreadful, having been put together hastily and raucously referring to the joys Lord Stanford would soon enjoy. One might expect a father to be rather irate about such a hint, but the duke pretended he did not hear that part of it. He invited them all in and poured them wine himself.

Lady Marchfield was, not surprisingly, not very approving of bringing the people of the village into the house and not at all willing to pretend she did not hear their outrageous song. However, Lord Marchfield worked hard and kept her views under wraps as much as possible.

It did eventually become impossible for her lord to mask Lady Marchfield's views, as the villagers took full advantage of the duke's generosity and drank down half his wine cellar. That sort of situation will always very reliably lead to an array of vulgarities as men were freed from whatever manners they might usually employ or whatever respect they might hold for rank.

Lady Marchfield was shocked to her shoes to be pinched in a nether region by a very scruffy individual who perhaps was not as acquainted with soap and water as he should have been. She stalked up the stairs after that same individual asked her if she wanted to be escorted to his barn for a confidential tryst. He claimed they could slip out the servants' entrance with her lord none the wiser. It is to be supposed that it was just as well that Lord Marchfield was none the wiser regarding that proposition. He was easygoing and liberal, but that likely would have been a step too far. By the time he was informed of it the following day, the scruffy individual had long taken himself off to the moors with his sheep herd.

None of that was at all disturbing to Patience and Stanford, as they had made an early escape to the gardener's cottage. Stanford had made arrangements beforehand, and Patience arrived to find a bright fire burning to fend off the chill of the moors, bottles of champagne, and platters of such edibles as would sustain them until morning.

She found herself not the least interested in food though. Patience locked the door, threw the curtains closed, and threw off her wedding dress, the buttons coming loose and skittering across the stone floor.

While Stanford might have been very good regarding self-control over the many weeks of severe temptation, this was rather too much. He picked her up and carried her into the lone small bedchamber. They fell into bed and did not get out of it for some hours.

Stanford found his bride far more enthusiastic than he had been led to believe a bride of elevated station generally was. It seemed his future happiness was not to be contained only in the drawing room.

As for Patience, she'd been well prepared for what was to come after the wedding, as both Grace and Felicity had given her rather graphic and detailed descriptions. Felicity had even drawn pictures and filled in any gaps she might not know, her knowledge mostly coming from observing farm animals. Her impatience overrode any shyness or worry over it. As both Grace and Felicity had pointed out that relations between man and woman were interesting in the beginning and then improved markedly as one went on, she did not give Stanford very much rest that first night.

He was delighted to oblige.

As the dawn broke, they drank champagne and watched the mist over the moors play its usual game of slipping away imperceptibly until it seemed impossible it had ever been there at all.

Patience brushed his hair to the side, admiring of its rich sable tones, and situated herself in the crook of his arm. His lovely strong arm.

"I have an idea for a wedding trip," Stanford said. "We might leave directly from here, though it will be a journey."

"That's all right," Patience said, "I'll follow you anywhere."

"Only if you like it, I will not take you anywhere you do not wish to go. Lord Jeffries, a relation, has a house a few miles outside of Holyhead in Wales. He tells me it is not large, but it overlooks the sea and is devoid of close neighbors. He says the staff retreat to their own houses by the late afternoon, but for a watchman who can be sent away. Jeffries says one can be free to swim in the sea without worry of onlookers."

"Oh, I see! Without clothes, you mean."

"I believe that is what Jeffries meant by it."

"We must go then," Patience said, all enthusiasm for the idea. "How often does a lady get the opportunity to swim naked in the sea?"

Stanford laughed. "Not often, I'd imagine."

"It will be lovely. I have heard if one goes to Brighton, one must enter an unwieldy bathing machine. It sounds like an unnecessary palaver just to get wet. We do not do so here, we just swim in our underthings while Mrs. Right keeps a lookout for anybody coming along. But naked, well that would really be something."

"Then we are off to Wales. Jeffries says we can stay as long as we like."

They set off the very next day, leaving their wedding guests to be entertained for a week by the duke. At least, they were entertained except for Lady Marchfield. That lady had several conferences with the vicar to commiserate with one another regarding the deplorable habits of the duke. Unfortunately, they did not come to any firm conclusions about what to do about it. Lady Marchfield had all but given up on her brother and had decided she would not even bother to attempt another placement of a butler in his London house.

The vicar, perhaps looking out for a relation or perhaps spotting an opportunity to confound the duke, urged the lady to persevere in it. He recommended a cousin who'd been meant for the clergy but had failed to secure a living. Mr. Cremble had, out of necessity, turned to a position in service. Though he had not made a career in the church, he was as pious a man as ever was. The viscount he served had died and the new viscount was profligate in his ways and had given his pious cousin notice of his dismissal due to certain frowns that had been noticed.

Lady Marchfield found herself very cheered by the thought of a pious butler. After all, anybody daring to attempt to run the duke's household with a semblance of regularity would do well to call upon Godly assistance.

MARCUS AND PATIENCE spent three days traveling to their destination. Fortunately, they traveled in a direction the duke had never taken, so they did not encounter any resentful and bitter innkeepers. They may have encountered two shocked innkeepers, though, as they rose exceedingly late, and it was no mystery to anybody what caused it.

Toward the end of the third day, they made their way to Clyd Cartref, or Cosy Home, as Lord Jeffries had named it. It turned out that the good gentleman had sent a letter to his steward, alerting him that there was the remote possibility that Lord Stanford and his bride might descend upon them.

As the Welsh never like to be caught out short on the hosting front, they had prepared extensively. This had the further benefit of supplying themselves with all sorts of good things to eat and drink should the lord not turn up after all.

The house was the most charming thing Patience had ever come upon. One story, made of whitewashed rubble stone topped by a heavy thatch roof, it sat atop a dune overlooking a flat sandy beach and the sea. Stanford had written ahead that they would be arriving and they were greeted by the steward, the cook, and a maid of all work.

They were led inside the house to a large room that seemed to be used for near everything. There was a stone fireplace, already burning brightly against the setting sun, a sofa in front of it, a bookcase well-stocked, and a few chairs round a dining table. A bow window looked out upon the sea and a short corridor led to the only bedchamber.

The dining table had been set with a hearty stew, Welsh cakes, and Glamorgan sausages, a pitcher of ale, several bottles of wine, and a bottle of whiskey.

The staff having done their duty and the watchman delighted to be sent away, Patience and Marcus listened to their chatter down the lane until it faded away and the only sounds were of the waves gently breaking out of doors.

While it was not their first night together, it was somehow different. The cottage was so removed from any other person on earth that it felt different. Patience could not put her finger on it until Stanford said, "This is it, is it not? This is our family."

Patience had nodded. "For now, anyway. I am well aware that I must deliver you an heir. My chief wifely duty to carry on the line."

Stanford had pulled her close. "Actually, we will be fine either way—let the title go to my idiot cousin if that is what fate has in store. If we are blessed, that is well too. The point is, here we are, just now and just here, a complete family."

Patience, of course, understood that her lord's feelings were deep-rooted and reflected his own early family life. She said, "Are you worried that you might be as your father was? You will not be, of that I am sure."

Stanford let out a little breath, as if that particular point was one he needed to hear from someone else. "No, I suppose not." He laughed and said, "I do wonder though if I can reach the heights of indulgence your father has achieved."

"I will show you how it's done. We will be the most ridiculously indulgent mother and father who ever were, and our children will adore us for it. Now, they might come out strange and toe-tap and claim to play the crwth, but we will love them all the same."

AND SO, PATIENCE'S prediction did come to pass. It was not all a smooth road to get there though. When Stanford was informed that his bride was with child, he did behave as if she were the first and only lady to fall prey to that condition. He was positively convinced that her chances of dying were exceedingly high. He blamed himself and Patience had a time of it trying to convince him that she had played her own part and all would be well.

As he *was* convinced that she would probably die, it made for a rather uncomfortable journey toward motherhood. Any time Patience even rose from a chair or did anything else deemed dangerous, Stanford had her by the arm. There were times when she woke in the night and found him wide awake and staring at her.

An army of midwives and physicians were sternly interviewed by the lord, though really, he knew so little about what was required. He finally settled on three midwives and four physicians, but he ended with only one of each since he insisted those people move into the house a full month before any expected arrivals of the baby variety.

On the momentous day, Patience was not clear on who was in more distress. She, from the physical pain, or her lord, wildly shouting in the corridor.

Still, all such moments do have an end. This particular end brought into the world a baby girl with an entirely silly tuft of brown hair atop her head. She was named Lily and promptly wrapped her father round her fingers as soon as she could get them working properly. Lily was followed by two boys and it might be thought, as boys were such forceful little personalities, that even though Lily was the eldest she must be bossed about by her brothers. That was not at all the case.

Lily, being a rather shrewd young lady, was very observant. She took those observations and used them to her advantage. Should one of her brothers misbehave, Lily would sigh and say, "Gracious, must I go to father and tell him you are creating a troublesome family life? Must I weep and tell him how upset I am?"

Everybody connected to him knew Lord Stanford wished for peace in his household and the boys were promptly put back in line. Those two young gentlemen, Marcus and Charles, were in their late teens before their sister's manipulations finally dawned on them and by then it was rather too late to do anything about it.

They were not too terribly put out, as they had experienced a rather jolly time of it in the house. Their mother looked upon them all as if they were geniuses and the best children living. Their father followed their mother's opinions on anything to do with family and so they grew up feeling very much admired. Other households in the neighborhood who held rather more strict views on children were perplexed over how these indulged children were not spoiled and selfish. They very naturally missed the fact that children will watch how their parents move through the world and act accordingly.

As for Stanford himself, he'd begun with an inordinate amount of caution and had developed the habit of slowly and methodically weighing options. He did not entirely give up his inclination to turn over a question far longer than anybody else in the world before coming to a decision. However, he did realize it drove his wife positively mad.

Therefore, he took on the habit of posing a question to Patience only after he'd given it due consideration. He might examine the question of purchasing a new carriage for months. Once he'd decided to go forward, he might say, "What do you think of purchasing a new carriage?" Patience would say, "Lovely idea." He'd say, "Consider it done." Patience liked to think she'd been a good influence on him as it seemed he did not foot-drag half so long as he used to.

But then, was that not what a good marriage was? Was it not making those little adjustments that made one's partner more comfortable? Whether they were true or not seemed beside the point.

Before all that was to be, Patience and Stanford spent a full month in Wales. Their routine was rather glorious. The staff turned up in the morning. They prepared breakfast and then, before setting off in the early afternoon, made a dinner to leave behind. Patience and Stanford walked the beach and, if it was a fine day and the staff were gone, stripped down and ran into the sea. There was a small area that was hemmed in by rocks and filled by a high tide that Patience called the bathing tub. The water was clear and still and warmed in the sun. They spent many an afternoon lazing in it.

One day, they were walking the beach and were visited by a lovely little brown terrier. She was a female and her low belly hinted that she'd brought puppies into the world sometime recently. Her owner could be spotted far down the beach chasing after the naughty thing. As Patience gave the dog a good pet, the boy finally did catch up to his dog.

"Magda," the boy said scoldingly.

The dog, now having been introduced as Magda, wagged her tail as if to say her running off was all in good fun.

The boy tipped his cap and said, "I'm sorry she's come to bother ya. She likes to shirk her responsibilities though I told her over and over, you've got young ones to look out for."

"She is not a bother at all, she's lovely," Patience said.

The boy seemed to take her measure. "As it happens, I still got three pups lookin' for a place to call home. It's a mighty task, as near everybody round here already has one of Magda's pups. You wouldn't care to have one? Or two?"

Patience looked toward her husband. He laughed and said, "It cannot be worse than Nelson, I suppose."

"We will take one, then," Patience said. "Two might lead to a lot of trouble, but I am certain we can manage one little dog between us."

The boy tipped his cap and said, "I'll run home and back as fast as I can. Come on, Magda, you scoundrel."

The boy set off and, as he had promised, he did not delay in returning. By that time, Patience and Stanford were back in the cottage with a tea tray. He had a pup in either hand and said, "I brought the two best so you can choose between them."

Patience thought the boy a cunning little person. He would have thought she'd set eyes on them, be unable to choose, and take both. And he was right.

They were now the proud owners of two Welsh terriers and of course if one knows anything about terriers, it is that one is ambitious and two are terrifying in their energy and zest for life. Carwyn and Cecil, as those were the names the boy had given them in honor of his two grandfathers, would prove to be quite the handful on the journey home. It seemed they deemed the inside of the carriage as if it were the outdoors and there was not one day they did not descend from that vehicle covered in paw prints.

After a month of walking and reading and bathing in the sea, and of course other things, Stanford received a letter from his butler. It seemed Mrs. Crumdek had been successful in waging war against the case moths. There had been ramifications to her treatments, as some of the furniture and all of the linens had been thrown out and the house smelled like a cedar forest. They would return to London to rectify things and then close up the house and ready it for the next season.

The next would find Serenity stepping into the light and taking her turn in society. Stanford had already been warned that they would need to be on hand. All manner of things could, and would, cause Serenity to weep. The extended family would need to surround Serenity and act as a soothing and calming influence.

Whether a certain Roland Garner, the Marquess of Thorpe, was prepared to take on a lady who might sink to the ground and lament over a dead bee in the garden was yet to be seen. But perhaps that stiff and reserved marquess had his own problems in the weeping department.

The End.

About the Author

By the time I was eleven, my Irish Nana and I had formed a book club of sorts. On a timetable only known to herself, Nana would grab her blackthorn walking stick and steam down to the local Woolworth's. There, she would buy the latest Barbara Cartland romance, hurry home to read it accompanied by viciously strong wine, (Wild Irish Rose, if you're wondering) and then pass the book on to me. Though I was not particularly interested in real boys yet, I was *very* interested in the gentlemen in those stories— daring, bold, and often enraging and unaccountable. After my Barbara Cartland phase, I went on to Georgette Heyer, Jane Austen and so many other gifted authors blessed with the ability to bring the Georgian and Regency eras to life.

I would like nothing more than to time travel back to the Regency (and time travel back to my twenties as long as we're going somewhere) to take my chances at a ball. Who would take the first? Who would escort me into supper? What sort of meaningful looks would be exchanged? I would hope, having made the trip, to encounter a gentleman who would give me a very hard time. He ought to be vexatious in the extreme, and *worth* every vexation, to make the journey worthwhile.

I most likely won't be able to work out the time travel gambit, so I will content myself with writing stories of adventure and romance in my beloved time period. There are lives to be created, marvelous gowns to wear, jewels to don, instant attractions that inevitably come with a difficulty, and hearts to break before putting them back together again. In traditional Regency fashion, my stories are clean—the action happens in a drawing room, rather than a bedroom.

As I muse over what will happen next to my H and h, and

wish I were there with them, I will occasionally remind myself that it's also nice to have a microwave, Netflix, cheese popcorn, and steaming hot showers.

Come see me on Facebook! @KateArcherAuthor